WHEREVER YOU GO

Books by Tracie Peterson

*with Judith Miller **with Kimberley Woodhouse

For a complete list of Tracie's books, visit her website
www.traciepeterson.com

WHEREVER YOU GO

TRACIE
PETERSON

BETHANYHOUSE

a division of Baker Publishing Group
Minneapolis, Minnesota

© 2019 by Peterson Ink, Inc.

Published by Bethany House Publishers
11400 Hampshire Avenue South
Bloomington, Minnesota 55438
www.bethanyhouse.com

Bethany House Publishers is a division of
Baker Publishing Group, Grand Rapids, Michigan

Printed in the United States of America

Library of Congress Cataloging-in-Publication Data
Names: Peterson, Tracie, author.
Title: Wherever you go / Tracie Peterson.
Description: Bloomington, Minnesota : Bethany House, a division of Baker
    Publishing Group, [2019] | Series: Brookstone brides ; 2
Identifiers: LCCN 2018048930 | ISBN 9780764219030 (trade paper) | ISBN
    9780764233371 (cloth) | ISBN 9780764233388 (large print) | ISBN
    9781493418589 (e-book)
Subjects: | GSAFD: Christian fiction.
Classification: LCC PS3566.E7717 W55 2019 | DDC 813/.54—dc23
LC record available at https://lccn.loc.gov/2018048930

Scripture quotations are from the King James Version of the Bible.

Cover design by Jennifer Parker
Cover photography by Mike Habermann Photography, LLC

19 20 21 22 23 24 25   7 6 5 4 3 2 1

To John Peterson, once again, for your
great information on firearms.
Thanks to Julie Cook Kimble for her help in
researching weapons and old west shows.

———◆◇✕◇◆———

"Come one, come all to the Brookstone Wild West Extravaganza—the only wild west show to give you all-female performers of extraordinary bravery and beauty! Women whose talent and proficiency will amaze and delight people of every age!"

———◆◇✕◇◆———

❖⫶ ONE ⫸❖

Mary Reichert posed for the newspaper photographer as she'd done hundreds of times before. As the Brookstone Wild West Extravaganza's top trick and sharpshooter, she had earned a reputation for being second only to Annie Oakley.

"Smile, Miss Reichert," the photographer called from behind his tripod. "This one is for the paper."

Mary beamed a smile and held her Smith & Wesson hammerless .38 revolver at an angle to show off the elaborate etching on the nickel plating. The photographer took the picture, then motioned for the winner of the day's shooting competition to join Mary. He was hardly more than a boy. He wore a suit of brown tweed two sizes too small but was fiercely proud of having beat all the other competitors to shoot in one final round against Mary.

The competition was the idea of the show's owner, Oliver Brookstone, and his assistant, Jason Adler, whose father had a financial interest in the show. Prior to each show, the promoters and town officials set up a competition between locals.

7

Participants would shoot both a rifle and pistol of their own choosing until the top man or woman was chosen. This person would then be called down from the audience to compete against Mary during the Brookstone show.

"What is your name?" the photographer asked the young man.

He tugged at his collar and cleared his throat. "Boyd. Boyd Butler."

"All right then, Mr. Butler, I want you to stand next to Miss Reichert and hold up your pistol toward her. Now, Miss Reichert, you hold your pistol toward him."

Mary nodded and shifted into the desired pose.

The man focused his camera and then raised his head to address Mary. "I wonder if we might push your hat back just a bit. I'm getting a shadow."

"Of course." She gave the custom red Stetson a slight nudge. It was one of ten that had been specially made for her by the John B. Stetson Company.

The photographer eyed the scene again and nodded. "That's good. Now, instead of a smile, I think a serious expression would be fitting—show a little competition."

They did as instructed, and he completed the picture just as Oliver Brookstone appeared. Oliver was resplendent in his master of ceremonies costume—a bright red coat and black pants. His vest was gold and his bow tie black, and atop his head he wore a black top hat.

"My dear Mary, it's time to take your place. The show is about to start." He turned and hurried back toward the arena.

Mary could tell from the sound of commotion that the audience was growing more and more excited. She looked at the young man beside her. "Well, Mr. Butler, are you ready for your big moment?"

He gulped and nodded. She wondered if he would freeze up altogether once they were in front of the large crowd.

Mary took pity on him. She slipped her revolver into her holster and reached out to pat his arm. "Don't be nervous. Just pretend nobody is there. It'll just be you and me having a friendly shooting competition."

He flushed. "Yes, ma'am."

She might have laughed at his wide-eyed look of fear, but she knew he was just a boy trying hard to be a man. Laughing at him would only make matters worse.

Music sounded from the arena, and Mary knew that was their cue. Oliver was about to start the show. In years gone by, there was always a big parade of all the performers, but this year the attention and excitement behind the shooting competition made it necessary to start with that. Should the competitor beat Mary, there would be a big to-do, with a trophy presentation and purse given to the winner. So far, however, no one had bested Brookstone's top shooter, and no one really expected that anyone would.

When Oliver cued Mary and Mr. Butler to join him in the center of the arena, she saw the young man freeze in place. She looped her arm through his. "Come on." She all but dragged him out in front of the cheering audience.

"Topekans," Mr. Brookstone announced through his megaphone, "I give you the talented and beautiful Mary Reichert and your own Boyd Butler. Boyd is the winner of your community shooting competition. Let's give them a hand!"

Cheers went up all around. Mary smiled and waved with her free arm. She nudged Boyd. "Wave. They're cheering for you."

He nodded and lifted his arm. She wondered if he'd even make it as far as the actual competition before fainting dead away.

"Boyd will attempt to best Miss Mary in a little contest we've put together," Oliver continued. "It's nothing arduous, folks—we wanted to keep everything fair and square. We're going to toss glass balls in the air, and Mary and Boyd will take turns shooting. The first to miss is the loser, and the other will be our winner."

The audience clapped all the louder, and some began to chant Boyd's name. It further unnerved the young man, and he glanced at Mary.

"Try not to think about them. Just remember you won the competition fair and square against the others. Now you just need to best me." She winked and immediately realized it was the wrong thing to do. Poor Boyd. He looked like he might be sick at any moment.

Mary couldn't give him a second thought, however. The contest began, and for a moment she thought he might actually be able to go the distance. As the balls were slung high into the air, Boyd met the challenge. Mary didn't think he'd best her, but he might at least make the competition interesting. But on the sixth ball, his concentration was broken by a sudden rousing cheer. The ball flew into the air and he fired . . . and missed. Across the audience, an exasperated cry echoed.

"Well, folks," Oliver Brookstone called out, "that's just the way it goes. Let's give Boyd Butler a big hand for being the finest shooter in Topeka and for being able to go a few rounds with our Miss Mary Reichert."

The audience burst into cheers and applause. Mary waved, then took Boyd's hand and raised it in the air. After the clapping began to die down, Oliver presented Boyd with a certificate and a consolation prize: two free tickets to the next Brookstone performance in Topeka.

Mary was glad when the competition concluded and the routine of the show began. She joined the parade on horseback with the other performers. So far the show had enjoyed great success and a very busy year. If she hadn't been so preoccupied with the loss of her brother, August, she would have been the happiest of any of them. Unfortunately, August's untimely death the year before continued to haunt her. Especially knowing he was murdered and no one was being made to pay for it.

She lined up with the other performers and waited for Ella Fleming to Roman ride a two-horse team into position. Standing atop the bare backs of the matched geldings, Ella waved to the crowd, her long blond curls fluttering behind her. A second and third team came behind her, but it was Ella who held Mary's attention.

August had been killed on Ella's family's farm, and Ella had overheard her father and former fiancé admit to the deed. Mary had wanted nothing more than to see justice done and those two men forced to admit their guilt. But instead, nothing had happened to them. Nothing at all. They had reported that August had been trampled to death by two wild colts, and the sheriff and doctor who'd investigated the matter agreed. Not that anyone would dare to say otherwise. By the men's own admission, there wasn't a person in the town or surrounding counties who would ever make a stand against them. Both men held the local populace in their debt, and those who didn't owe them feared them and would never dream of speaking out against George Fleming or Jefferson Spiby.

The injustice of it ate at Mary day and night. She wanted her brother's killers to confess and take their punishment. She wanted someone to put aside their fear or devotion to the two men and see them jailed or, better yet, hanged for their offense. She tried to pray for peace of heart and mind, but it wasn't to be had. She didn't think God was even listening. Her grandmother had once told her that God heard every prayer, but if that were true, then why wasn't He answering?

Everyone exited the arena except the Roman riders. Their performance was first. Ella would be busy for the next twenty minutes.

"Are you all right, Mary?" Lizzy Brookstone rode up alongside her. She looked concerned.

Mary dismounted and handed her horse off to one of the wranglers. "I'm just brooding over August."

Lizzy gave a sympathetic nod. "I suppose being so close to your grandparents' farm brings all of that back."

"It does." Mary had quit the Brookstone show prior to last year's season and had been living near Topeka with her grandparents in order to prepare for her wedding to neighboring farmer Owen Douglas. When news of her brother's death had come, they had been devastated—shocked beyond reason. Now, being back in the area only reminded her of how bad it had felt to lose him. How she had still found no way to gain justice for his murder. Since arriving in town, Mary hadn't been able to put it from her mind.

"Are your grandparents here today?" Lizzy asked.

"They said they planned to be." Mary shrugged. "Kate too. She said she had to speak to me about something."

"Mary?" a feminine voice called.

Mary turned to find her sister. "Kate! I was just telling Lizzy that you planned to be here."

From atop her dappled buckskin, Lizzy waved. "Nice to see you again, Kate. That dress is beautiful. Pink definitely suits you."

Kate smiled and touched the lace at her throat. "I bought it with the last of my teaching money."

"The last?" Mary asked, looking her sister up and down. "Why the last? Did you quit?"

"As a matter of fact, I did. That was part of what I came to tell you."

"But I thought you loved teaching."

Kate looked at her gloved hands. "I do, but the school prefers their teachers to be unmarried." She glanced up as if waiting for the full effect of her words to settle on her sister.

Mary knew Kate had been interested in Owen Douglas, and

when Mary jilted him to rejoin the wild west show, Kate had asked if she might seek him out. Mary had given her blessing. She and Owen had been childhood friends, and everyone had supposed they would marry. But while Mary had loved Owen as a brother, she could never work that love into something more marital. Owen had understood. Neither had ever fallen in love with the other.

"Owen and I were married a few weeks ago," Kate blurted. "I wanted to have you at the wedding, but I knew you were tied up with the show. I know I should at least have written to let you know, but things happened so fast, and before I knew it . . ." She let the words fade into silence.

Mary couldn't hide her surprise. For a moment, words wouldn't even come. It was Lizzy who reached down from her horse to extend a hand of congratulations.

"I'm so happy for you, Kate."

"Thank you, Lizzy." Kate only glanced at Lizzy before turning back to Mary. "I'm so sorry if this is a bit much for you."

Mary shook her head. "It's all right. I'm just surprised." She tried to force her thoughts into order. "Of course I'm delighted. You and Owen are well suited for each other, and I know you'll be happy together." She embraced her sister. "I wish I could have been there."

As they pulled apart, Kate reached out to touch Mary's cheek. "Are you truly all right with this? I know you said you were back in October, but we didn't talk about it after that."

"I thought you might write and tell me how you were progressing, but honestly, it's all right." Mary pressed Kate's hand with her own. Her little sister and only living sibling was married. "Is Owen here?"

Kate nodded. "He's keeping our seats with Oma and Opa. He thought you might appreciate not having to face everyone at once."

"That was thoughtful." The reality of it all began to sink in. Mary was happy for her sister, but at the same time, almost felt as if she'd been wronged. That was silly, of course. If Owen and Kate had found true love, and she had no reason to think they hadn't, then she was glad they had married. Still, the thought of having to face them all was more than she wanted to contend with right now. Especially since she still had to perform, and her concentration was of the utmost importance.

"Look, I need to get ready for my act." Mary looked over her shoulder at Lizzy. "I can't remember—are we here overnight or leaving right away?"

"Neither. Our train is out at midnight. If you'd like, there's plenty of time to go out to the farm and visit your family."

"I was thinking maybe we could just go to dinner. I'd be happy to pay," Mary said, turning back to her sister. "A celebration dinner to congratulate the newlyweds."

Kate smiled. "I know I'd like that, and I'm sure the others would too, but you know Opa will never let you pay for it."

Mary smiled. "Well, just tell him I insist. I'll see you after the performances."

Kate leaned forward and kissed Mary's cheek. "I'm so glad you're happy for us." She hurried from the staging area and back to the arena.

"Are you really all right?" Lizzy asked.

"I'm fine. Really. Shocked, but fine." Mary watched Kate disappear back into the stands. "I teased her about taking our wedding date so the plans we'd made wouldn't have to be undone." She drew a deep breath. "I'm honestly happy for them. Owen needed a wife. Since his folks died and he had the farm all to himself . . . well, he needed someone."

Lizzy tugged at a loose button on her sleeve. "Still, it can be hard to have it actually happen this way, what with your sister marrying him."

Mary shrugged. "I've always seen Owen as a brother, so maybe it's exactly as it should be. Now he's really my brother. At least, my brother-in-law."

"So long as you're going to be all right. You'd best hurry. You'll be on in five minutes. I need to find Agnes and ask her to secure this button."

"I saw her and Brigette heading to the dressing room earlier."

"Then that is where I must go, and you must dazzle the audience with your greatness."

Mary looked at the clock and nodded. "Indeed. The show must go on."

⤛ TWO ⤜

C hristopher Williams didn't know when he'd enjoyed anything as much as this all-female wild west show. He'd seen
Buffalo Bill Cody's show and even traveled for a time with
him in 1898 so the magazine could run a serial on him and
the performers, but this show had them beat for charm. The
ladies were just as lovely as Brookstone promised and ten times
as talented as Chris had expected. He was especially taken by
the female sharpshooter, Mary Reichert. Watching her shoot
in the contest with the local man had been a fun diversion, but
observing her talented main act had left him wanting to write an
article, if not a series of articles, on her. Perhaps on the entire
troupe. Of course, he'd have to talk his editor into the idea,
since that wasn't the reason he was in town.

Due to his editor's interest in spiritualism, Chris had come
to Topeka in order to do a story on the Bethel Bible College
and Pastor Charles Parham. This story had been planned since
the previous New Year's Eve incident that had made public
the supposed miracle of speaking in tongues. From what he'd
learned, there'd been a watch night service to usher in the
New Year and pray for wisdom and guidance. A woman named

Agnes Ozman had asked to be prayed for and afterward began to speak in Chinese. Although from what Chris had been able to learn, no one knew for certain it was Chinese. However, they did attest that for three days Agnes could not speak any English but could only write in Chinese characters. Chris had done his best to interview anyone who had witnessed the actual affair. He had hoped to speak to Agnes herself, but Miss Ozman, who wanted to be a missionary to the Chinese, was said to be in Omaha doing the Lord's work. He found the entire matter rather absurd.

Still, he would write up the story using the best of his information and let his editor do with it what he would. Thankfully, one of Agnes's best friends had a nice photograph of her that they were willing to give him. That, along with photographs he'd arranged to be taken of the former school—and ones he'd obtained of the pastor involved—should suffice for the magazine article. He'd leave it up to the readership to decide if a true miracle of God had taken place.

As the wild west show concluded, Chris was already formulating the story idea he would pitch to his editor. This would be a series of articles. Stories that would stimulate the heart of Americans both male and female. His magazine, *My America*, looked for unusual bits of Americana interest, and nothing could do that as well as the Brookstone Wild West Extravaganza. Of this, Chris was certain. His magazine readers would love learning about the all-female wild west show, and he personally wanted to learn more about the lovely Miss Reichert. She was incredible, and he'd met many an incredible woman.

Chris made his way through the streaming lines of people and then cut away to slip back into the realm of the performers. The corridors were littered with crates that had contained props and targets for Mary Reichert's sharpshooting and that of her counterpart, Alice.

He reached down and lifted a small glass orb from the crates. It was delicate—like one of his grandmother's beautiful knick-knacks. Mary and the lovely young woman who shot solely on horseback using a bow and arrows had used the orbs for proving their shooting prowess. He put the ball gently back in the crate, then headed toward a gathering of people.

"Excuse me. I'm a journalist looking for Miss Reichert."

The older woman in the group introduced herself. "I'm Agnes, the seamstress and costume designer. What do you want with Mary?" Her tone was protective.

"As I mentioned, I'm a journalist, and I'd like to interview Miss Reichert for *My America* magazine."

Agnes considered him for a moment, then gave a nod. "Her dressing room is down that hall on the left. Second door."

"Thank you." He tipped his hat to the group. Making his way down the hall, Chris reached an open dressing room door. Inside, Mary sat surrounded by two men and two women, no doubt admirers.

"I wonder, Miss Reichert, if I could have a word," he called to her. "I'm a journalist and would like to interview you for *My America* magazine." He extended her a card with his magazine's information.

Mary glanced at the card. The people around her parted to allow him access. The old man who stood at her right looked protective as well. "I would be happy to speak with you, Mister . . ." She paused. "What is your name?"

"I'm sorry. It's there on the card, but I should have stated it straightaway. I'm Christopher Williams, but most folks call me Chris."

She smiled. That was a good sign. He offered her one in return.

"These are my grandparents, Oscar and Hannah Reichert," she said. "As well as my sister, Katerina, and her husband, Mr. Owen Douglas."

"Mr. and Mrs. Reichert, it's a pleasure to meet you." Christopher extended his hand to the old man. "I'm sure you must be very proud of your granddaughter."

"Ja, ve're very proud," the old man replied, giving Chris a firm grasp. He was stocky in build, and a crown of snowy hair topped his head. His thick accent left little doubt that he was of German descent. "Our Mary is quite a talent."

"I agree." Chris then offered his hand to Mr. Douglas. "Mr. Douglas. Mrs. Douglas. I'm pleased to meet you as well."

The formalities had gone without a hitch, and Chris began to relax. Mary furthered his sense of accomplishment as she turned to her family.

"Go ahead to the supper club without me. Order me a thick steak, medium rare, and I'll join you after I finish speaking with Mr. Williams." She pulled a piece of paste jewelry from her upswept hair. For much of her act she'd been dressed in western style, but for her final performance, she had changed into a refined, tasteful look, wearing a beautiful evening gown and costume jewelry. She looked as if she were ready for a night on the town.

Chris couldn't look away from her. She captivated him like no one he'd ever met. She seemed not even to notice his interest, but when Chris was able to look away, he found Mr. Douglas watching him.

"If you're certain," Mr. Reichert said. "But ve can vait."

"No. Go ahead. I need to get changed anyway. I'll give Mr. Williams his interview and join you in no more than thirty minutes. Certainly by eight o'clock." She kissed her grandmother's cheek and then her sister's before the foursome agreed to go. Then she cocked her head to one side and offered Chris a smile. "Now, what would you like to know?"

He found himself momentarily flustered—something that hadn't happened for a long time. At twenty-five, he was usually quite certain of himself. Mary, however, had a way of setting him off balance.

"I . . . ah . . ." He frowned. "I'm sorry. I guess I'm a little starstruck."

She laughed, and he was even more charmed. She took his arm. "Why don't you come with me? I'm sure I can give you enough information to please your readers and be on my way in fifteen minutes."

Chris said nothing. He didn't dare. Otherwise he might have really made a fool of himself by declaring that he didn't want just fifteen minutes with her. He wanted a whole lot more.

<hr />

"And then he asked me about the show in general," Mary said as she finished off a large piece of chocolate cake. The private supper club had the best desserts in town, and their chocolate cake could not be beat. The moist cake was layered with milk chocolate mousse and covered in a thick dark chocolate icing, then topped with dollops of whipped cream. It was rich and decadent and entirely too sweet, but Mary loved it.

"I go pay for our supper," Opa said, getting to his feet. "I'll tell dem to bring our carriage around."

"No, Opa. I want to pay for our dinner." Mary stood. "You get the carriage and help Oma. This is my treat, and I won't hear otherwise." She picked up her little purse and smiled. "I can never repay all you've done for me, but this is something that makes me feel better. So you see, you must allow me to do it."

"Ja, you must allow her to," Oma said, patting Opa's arm.

The old man yielded but grumbled as he helped Mary's grandmother to her feet. Mary took that moment to slip away and pay the bill. She hoped that by the time she finished, the others would already be loaded in the carriage and ready to go. Her time with Kate and Owen had been harder than she'd anticipated.

Not because she was in love with Owen, but because she envied their happiness. They had each other, and she had no one.

Still dressed in her finery from her last act, Mary noted the approving looks she received from the men around her. She had often been noted in the newspapers as a "handsome" woman and knew she could probably have her pick of suitors, but so far no one had appealed to her. Perhaps she was one of those strong women destined to go through life alone.

"Mary?"

She turned to find Owen waiting for her.

"Here is your change, ma'am," the supper club manager said. He counted out seven dollars, and Mary handed him back two. "Please give this to our waiter. He was generous with his time and service."

The manager smiled. "Of course. I'm glad to hear it."

She put the five dollars back in her purse, then walked toward Owen. "I thought you'd be with the others."

"I wanted a moment alone. I told them I would make sure you didn't get mobbed by fans." He smiled. "I just wanted to be certain that you aren't upset over me and Kate getting married."

Mary chuckled. "Oh, Owen, I'm delighted. I always thought of you as a brother, and now you truly are. That day last year when we parted company, Kate lost no time in declaring her feelings for you. I think she's been sweet on you for a very long time, and how wonderful that you two could finally be together."

"She's amazing." Owen's entire face lit up.

"So you truly love her?"

He frowned for a moment, then nodded. "With all my heart. I never fully understood what you meant about us not being right for each other. I cared so much about you and your family that it seemed wrong that we not marry. But then, when I found myself in Kate's company . . . everything changed. I suddenly realized that what you'd been saying was true. If we had married, I know you and I could have forced our way to happiness, but happiness with Kate takes no effort at all."

"That's all I wanted to hear, Owen."

"I will endeavor to be a good husband to her, but also a good brother to you, Mary. After all, you were wise enough to see the truth and do something about it."

She felt a warmth of happiness spread over her. She might be alone, but Owen and Kate were right to be together, and she could find joy in that truth. "I pray you'll both be happy, Owen. It's also such a comfort to me to know you're there for Oma and Opa. I feel I am free to continue seeking justice for August, since you are there keeping watch over my grandparents and sister."

He frowned. "Seeking justice for him? How are you doing that? From what I read in your letters, the men you believe responsible have denied any involvement and have impeccable reputations in their community."

"I don't care. The devil himself has friends and appears as an angel of light when it serves his purposes. I intend to find a way to make them pay."

"It sounds awfully dangerous. If those men truly murdered your brother, what's to keep them from killing you?" Owen's concerned expression touched her.

"My brother was unaware of there being any danger, whereas I know what those men are capable of doing. It's just like clearing out a pit of rattlers. I'll go armed with foreknowledge and a good gun." She smiled. "You know me, Owen. I can take care of myself."

He nodded. "I suppose I do. At least I always knew you didn't need me to take care of you."

"But Kate does. Kate has always needed looking after, and now she has you. I couldn't be happier, Owen. I hope you two are blessed with a great many children and happiness that stretches across the years."

They made their way out to the carriage. The evening air was heavy and humid, but the night sky was clear. When Mary saw her family in the carriage, she felt a mix of joy and loneliness. She loved them all so dearly, but she didn't belong. Opa and Oma had each other, and Kate and Owen were together. August had always been the one who understood Mary best, and now he was gone. She was alone.

Owen helped her into the carriage, and she wedged herself into the seat beside her grandmother. Oma took her hand and gave it a squeeze. "I have missed you, but I know you're doing vat you love."

Mary nodded and fought back tears. "I've missed you too, Oma."

"Vill you come home in the vinter?" Opa asked as he put the team in motion.

Going home after the show concluded in the fall hadn't even occurred to Mary. "I'm sure to come for a visit, if nothing else." It was the best she could offer. She wasn't sure the farm would ever feel like home again.

⊰≈ THREE ≈⊱

Chris looked around at the train car office. Oliver Brookstone kept a much more refined office than Buffalo Bill Cody. Chris wondered if his niece had a hand in that. He'd heard that Elizabeth Brookstone had taken her father's place in helping her uncle run the show.

"Tell us what you have in mind, Mr. Williams," Jason Adler said with a smile. "We are always happy to accommodate the press."

"I would like to do a series of stories for the magazine, *My America*. Are you familiar with it?"

Jason shook his head, but Oliver Brookstone gave an enthusiastic nod. "I often enjoy your magazine, Mr. Williams. I appreciate stories of unusual people and activities."

"Then as you probably also know, our magazine is devoted to sharing the various events and people who are of an unusual nature, but who clearly make America a great place to live."

"Indeed?" Jason's eyes narrowed slightly. "Yet, if I'm not mistaken, I detect an essence of my homeland in your speaking manner."

"It's true," Chris said, smiling. "I was born in America but raised by my grandmother in England from the age of six. I returned to America after my education at Oxford, and so find my accent rather comingled."

"Oxford, you say." Jason gave a smug smile. "I'm a Cambridge man, myself."

Chris heard the tone of superiority but chose to ignore it. The rivalry between the schools was well known. "As I was saying, I believe our magazine would be interested in featuring a series of articles on the show. I can't help but believe this would be a wonderful way to promote your troupe in America."

"And it might be equally to our advantage in England," Jason said, looking to Brookstone. "With our upcoming trip to England later this summer, Mr. Williams could accompany us and perhaps act as our publication liaison."

"I didn't realize you were headed to England. I'd be happy to act as such an agent," Chris replied. "I'd also be happy to introduce you to newspaper friends there. I'm sure there would be widespread interest. After all, the queen, God rest her soul, loved the wild west shows."

"I am quite gratified by the idea," Brookstone said, rubbing his hands together. "I see this as a wonderful opportunity. Ah, here she is." He rose, and the other men also got to their feet.

"Wes said you needed to see me," the young woman announced as she entered the office. She crossed the small space and gave Brookstone a kiss on his cheek.

"Lizzy, this is Mr. Williams. Mr. Williams, my niece, Elizabeth Brookstone."

Chris extended his hand. "I'm pleased to meet you, Miss Brookstone. I understand you have taken your father's place in helping to run this show."

"Call me Lizzy." She shook his hand and then took a seat at the table. "And no, I didn't actually take my father's place. I'm not a true partner. I just like to help my uncle put on the best show we can deliver." She looked at her uncle as he claimed the seat beside her. "Now, how can I help?"

Brookstone gave her arm a pat. "I'll let our friend explain."

Lizzy fixed Chris with a curious gaze. He smiled at the pretty brunette. She was confident, and he liked that about her. He took the chair opposite her. "First, I must say that I am quite impressed with your abilities. I was captivated as I watched your performance in Topeka."

Lizzy laughed. "Well, that is the point of my act, Mr. Williams. I'm glad you enjoyed yourself."

"I did, but please call me Chris. I was also taken with the sharpshooting. I interviewed Annie Oakley for an article several years ago, so I find myself particularly drawn to such acts."

"I can't blame you, Chris," Lizzy replied, seeming to try the name on for size. "Mary and Alice are wonderful."

"I met Mary Reichert. We spoke briefly after the show, and I was able to do a short interview with her. You see, I'm a writer for *My America* magazine. I'm hoping once we get to Kansas City, I'll have a telegram awaiting me from my editor in New York approving my idea. As I mentioned to your uncle and Mr. Adler, I want to do a series of stories about the show. I believe readers will want to know all about the Brookstone Wild West Extravaganza and its all-female performers."

"That is exciting." Lizzy raised her eyebrows and cocked her head as she turned to look at Jason. "What say you and Uncle Oliver?"

"We agree. It's a marvelous idea, and I believe readers both in America and England will find the articles interesting," Jason declared.

"I thought maybe you could introduce Christopher to the others," Brookstone said. "Since he has a particular fondness for sharpshooting and has already met Mary, you could start there."

"I need Lizzy's assistance on several tasks related to our England trip," Jason interjected before Lizzy could reply. "I wonder if, since Mr. Williams has already made the acquaintance of Mary, perhaps she would be a better choice to show him around."

"That would be a grand idea," Brookstone replied. "Lizzy can take you to Mary. I'm sure she'd be more than happy to help in this matter."

Lizzy nodded and got to her feet. Chris rose and extended his hand to Oliver Brookstone. "Thank you, Mr. Brookstone. I appreciate your confidence in me."

The Kansas City performances went without any trouble or complications, and they made their way to St. Louis. The city welcomed them with a parade that showered confetti like rain. In St. Louis, Mary's shooting contest proved to be even easier than the one in Topeka. The older man who won the St. Louis title was enamored with her and far more attentive to sweet-talking than shooting. He only managed to shoot two of the globes before missing the third.

Mary waited to perform her final tricks while Alice commanded the audience's attention with her last act. A row of ten flaming hoops had been arranged for her to shoot through while at a full gallop. Alice loosed a series of arrows from one end and then the other, and each time not only hit her mark, but hit the bull's-eye. The crowd rose to give her a standing ovation. Alice gave them a wave with her bow as she slowed her mount and exited from view.

Meanwhile, Mary had set up a series of targets and would seek a volunteer from the audience to finish her performance. She would complete what Oliver called her "deadeye" tricks, which were the ones that always received the biggest applause. After all, they endangered the life of a human being.

"And now comes our chance to involve a member of the audience," Oliver announced. "We need a brave soul—one who has no fear of Mary shooting directly at him or her."

For a moment the audience went silent, then one by one, several men raised their hands.

"Mary, darling, please come out here and make a choice."

That was Mary's cue. She had donned a different costume for her final act. Rather than wear her standard red Stetson and split skirt with an embroidered western-style blouse, Jason Adler had convinced her to dress up for her final act. He thought it would further the amazement of the audience to see a beautiful young woman decked out in jewels and silks making crack shots like a buffalo hunter of old.

Tonight she wore a fashionable gown of blue silk. The dress had a tightly fitted waist to show off her slim figure and puffed sleeves banded just above the elbow, trimmed in ivory lace. Lizzy had helped her fashion her dark brown hair into curls piled high upon her head. In the middle of this, they had secured a costume broach that flashed whenever the light hit it just right. Judging by the deafening applause she received, the look was successful.

Taking her time, Mary sauntered to where Oliver stood with his megaphone in hand.

He took her gloved hand and kissed it as he bowed. Then he turned to the audience and roared, "Isn't she the most beautiful sharpshooter in the world?" The noise level threatened to bring down the roof. Satisfied that the audience was stirred to a frenzy, Oliver quieted them again. "Now, Miss Mary—who will be the lucky man to partner with you in tonight's final shooting act?"

Mary scanned the crowd. There were hundreds of men with their hands raised. Some waved madly, while others stood not moving a muscle. She was about to choose a rather burly-looking older man when she caught sight of Christopher Williams. She'd already spent a good part of the morning with him and found he rather intrigued her. She liked that he was educated and yet still fascinated by the show.

She leaned in close to Oliver. "I'm going to choose Mr. Williams. After all, he wants to experience this show firsthand."

Oliver chuckled. "It's up to you."

Mary nodded and made her way over to Chris, who sat with his hand in the air. She reached out and took his hand. A sigh of disappointment swept across the audience, but Mary was used to this.

She and Chris made their way to the area where she was set to perform her tricks. "I hope you realize you're putting your life in my hands," she said with a smile.

"I have a feeling the risk is minimal," Chris replied with a wink.

She tried not to show the effect he had on her with that simple action. If she wasn't careful, she'd end up making a mistake, and then Chris might be injured.

Oliver explained the trick she was about to perform. Mary went through several exaggerated motions of placing Chris in just the right position. For one trick she had him hold a small chicken feather out in front of him. She then shot the feather in half.

The next trick offered a little more risk. Mary had him hold a small candle between his teeth and stand sideways. She then had Oliver light the candle. Silence blanketed the stands. Mary took her mark and aimed her .38. She fired and easily extinguished the flame. The audience cheered and clapped wildly. Chris ran the back of his hand across his forehead to show the audience the pressure he was under. Mary couldn't help but smile at his theatrics.

For her final trick, she placed Chris a foot in front of a thick curtain and then set an apple atop his head. Rather than use the .38, she opted for her Stevens Crackshot .22 rifle. She also picked up a mirror and walked farther away than she had for the other tricks.

With a trained eye, Mary considered the target for a moment, then motioned to Oliver. She pretended to whisper something in his ear, and Oliver pulled back, putting a gloved hand to his mouth. As the audience became caught up in the moment, he replaced the hand with his megaphone.

"She says the target is too big!"

At first there were murmurs, then *ah*s and finally applause as the apple was replaced with a large strawberry. Mary smiled as the look of confidence left Christopher's face and was replaced with worry. The way his brows knit together gave her a momentary feeling of guilt.

Pushing that aside, Mary took her mark and raised her rifle with one arm. By now, most everyone had forgotten the mirror she'd taken from the table. She pretended to sight the target for a moment, then whirled on her heel and put her back to Chris. She turned the gun around and rested it on her right shoulder.

"Ladies and gentlemen, we must have absolute silence," Oliver announced. "This trick is deadly at best, and with the new difficulties Miss Reichert has put upon herself, we must insist on doing everything possible to aid her."

You could have heard a pin drop. Mary raised the mirror with her left hand and found her target. Chris looked a little unnerved by this latest development, but he stood in complete trust, at her mercy.

She aimed and pressed the trigger with her thumb. The rifle fired, and the strawberry blew to pieces. She lowered the rifle and turned. The audience, although momentarily stunned, began to cheer and call her name. It was the perfect ending to her act.

Walking back toward Chris, who stood stock-still despite

the pieces of strawberry in his hair, Mary grinned. "You were a very brave participant, but I fear you'll need to wash your hair."

"It was my . . . well, not exactly my pleasure, but it was an interesting experience." He reached up to feel the top of his head. "You sure all of that is just strawberry? No blood?"

Mary laughed and turned him toward the audience as Oliver called out for the crowd to herald his bravery. Chris took a bow, and Mary sent him back to his seat.

All in all, it was a satisfactory evening. Still, she couldn't help but chuckle as she made her way from the arena. It would be interesting to hear what he had to say about the act once they were alone.

But to her disappointment, Mary saw nothing of Chris when the show ended. The local newspaper reporters came to question the performers and get statements from Oliver, but Chris was nowhere to be found. Hopefully she hadn't frightened him off the story. Jason Adler had already spoken to her about the importance of the magazine covering the wild west show.

When the interviews concluded, Mary gathered her things. First, she saw to her rifle and pistol. No one else was ever allowed to handle her firearms. She placed them in their custom-made carrying cases. Once they were on their way to the next city, she would clean them, but for now she just wanted to ensure their safety. Next, she worked with Alice to finish packing the props. With Jason's focus on saving the show money, the performers found themselves responsible for many things that had once been done for them.

"Ladies, I need your costumes as soon as you can get back to the train and change," Agnes said, her niece Brigette at her side. "We need to get to the laundry first thing."

"Not a problem, Aggie," Mary replied before Alice could. "We're nearly done."

"I'll manage it all from here, girls," Phillip DeShazer said, coming from behind Mary to hoist up a crate. Phillip, Wesley DeShazer's brother, had come along with the show to help wherever needed. Most of the time he worked with the animals, but when it came to heavy work, he and Alice's husband, Carson, were in charge.

"Thanks, Phillip. I'll see you on the train," Mary said, picking up her firearm cases. She turned to speak to Agnes, but the seamstress and her niece were already on the move toward where Gertie was trying to manage her horse.

It was raining as Mary stepped outside. She paused under the awning to see where the performers' carriage might be. Lizzy was talking with Jason in the doorway of one of the stock buildings across the way. Not ten feet to Mary's right, Wesley DeShazer stood watching them from the shadows.

"You look put out," she said, joining him. "Surely you don't think you have anything to worry about with Adler."

Wes gave her only a momentary glance. "He irritates me. Lizzy told him she has an understanding with me, but he doesn't care. He's insistent that he can woo her and win her over."

"Perhaps you should put a ring on her finger and make your feelings more . . . visible."

"It wouldn't stop a man like Adler."

Mary looked at the couple. Jason moved even closer to Lizzy and leaned his face close to hers as if to share a secret. Wes started to move, but Mary put her arm out to hold him back.

"You don't want to make a scene, Wes. Lizzy can handle Adler. You know very well that she's completely devoted to you. She has been for most of her life."

Wes drew in a deep breath and let it go. He looked down at Mary and nodded. "I'd best go find Phillip and help with loading up."

"He's inside, getting our props."

"At least he's sober."

Mary had heard that Wes was having trouble keeping his brother from sneaking out to get a drink during the tour. She didn't want to dwell on that, however. "He certainly seems to enjoy Ella's company."

Phillip had spent the winter at the Brookstone ranch in Montana following Ella Fleming around whenever he wasn't busy breaking horses. He was quite smitten, and since Ella had run away from home, she was a permanent resident at the ranch. It afforded them many chances to see each other.

"He doesn't have the sense the good Lord gave him," Wes replied. "I honestly don't know what's going to happen to him. He's no good for anything or anyone until he stops drinking completely."

Mary could hear the pain in his voice. "He has to figure things out for himself. You can't be his savior."

"I know." Wes finally seemed to relax and forget about Lizzy and Jason. "Nor do I want to be. He was gone from my life for a long time. Left after our pa died. Ma worried something terrible, and I admit I did too. I figured he'd show up at the funeral when our ma died, but he didn't, and now that he's back . . . well, I don't want to lose him again. I figure the next time he disappears, he might get himself killed." Wes stiffened. "Sorry. I know what with August, that was probably an unfeeling thing to say."

"It's all right, Wes. I miss August more than I can begin to say. I keep feeling like there ought to be something I can do to get justice for him. I keep praying, but God hasn't done anything about it."

Wes shook his head. "I know it can't be easy for you. Especially with Ella around to remind you of it. I admire you for being her friend though. It's clear she had nothing to do with it."

"She has become a dear friend. I wish she'd told us what she knew sooner, but I can understand that she was afraid of her father and that monster, Spiby." Mary sighed and gave a shrug.

"I guess you and I need to find a way to rest in the Lord and let Him see to our problems, but it sure isn't easy."

Wes glanced at Adler, who now stood alone. "Nope. It sure isn't."

Mary left him there and made her way to the carriage that would transport the performers back to the train station where the Brookstone cars waited on the siding. She wished she could find peace of heart where her brother was concerned, but the outrage of his murder wouldn't allow it.

Even after supper, when most of the troupe had retired for the night, Mary couldn't settle her mind. She decided a long walk might help her sleep. Dressing in her split skirt and work blouse, Mary considered the dangers that might await her in the large city. She put on an oversized men's coat and then slipped her five-shot pistol into the right-side pocket. With her gun at hand, there was nothing Mary feared. She'd been dealing with attackers since she was a little girl. Most of those had been snakes and other varmints, but now and then a man had tried to strong-arm her. It was his last mistake where she was concerned. She'd never had to shoot to kill, but she had wounded a couple of men in her life. Jefferson Spiby, her brother's killer, was one of them. When he nearly choked the life out of Ella, Mary had found it necessary to shoot. She'd wanted nothing more than to kill him, but her conscience had won out, and she'd winged him instead.

"I wish I'd put that bullet in his head," she muttered as the gravel beneath her feet crunched.

"Where you headed, Mary?" Chris appeared from the shadows between train cars.

"I needed a walk. What are you doing, skulking around in the dark?"

"I was just plotting my article." He shrugged. "I do some of my best thinking this way. How about I walk with you? St. Louis isn't the kind of place for a lady to be out walking alone at this hour."

Mary smiled and patted her pocket. "I'm not quite alone. But I'm always happy for the company of a friend."

"And you consider me a friend? I'm honored."

She heard the pleasure in his voice and shrugged. "I see no reason we should not be friends. Especially since you'll be with the troupe for the rest of the year."

"True enough, but I find friendship can be difficult to cultivate. I haven't many friends."

"My oma says you must be one to get one." She smiled. "So perhaps this is a good place to start. I can get to know you better as we walk."

"What would you like to know?"

"I heard Jason Adler say that you grew up in London, but you were born here in America."

"That's true enough." They started across the tracks toward the depot. "I moved to London when I was six years old. I have few memories of life in America prior to that. I returned to America just last year and started to work for the magazine earlier this year."

"And what did you do in between?"

"In between what?" he asked.

"Between coming back to America and starting to work for the magazine. Surely you must have had another job." He fell silent for a moment and Mary wondered at his hesitation. "Did I pry too deep?"

Chris shook his head. "No. I was, ah, trying to figure out how best to say this."

"Just say it. You don't need to worry about phrasing it in any particular way. I'm pretty down to earth, and you don't have to impress me."

"Well, that's the problem. I didn't want to sound as if I were trying to impress you. You see, I received an inheritance, and when I returned to America, I used some of that money to spend a year traveling and getting to know my homeland again."

"I think that's marvelous." Mary nearly lost her footing in the gravel and was glad Chris took her arm. "Thank you. I'm afraid I wasn't thinking when I slipped on these shoes. I should have gone for my boots."

"It's not a problem."

As they neared the depot building, Oliver Brookstone and Jason Adler came through the door. They were surprised to see Mary and Chris.

"What are you two up to?" Oliver asked.

"Just needed a little air," Mary answered.

"Well, the train is going to be hitched at eleven thirty, and we're leaving soon after that." Oliver took out his pocket watch and held it toward the lamplight. "That's in just one hour."

"Don't worry. We won't be gone that long, Mr. Brookstone," Chris said before Mary could reply.

"Now, son, I told you to call me Oliver. We don't stand on formalities around here. We're a family, and since you're going to be traveling with us for the season, you are family as well."

Chris nodded. "I like the sound of that, Oliver."

The older man nodded and replaced his watch. "Good. Then I'll expect you two back well before we're ready to leave."

"You can count on it," Mary declared. She waited until the two men had gone before looking at Chris. "Unless, of course, we run into trouble."

The handsome man at her side grinned. "Mary Reichert, I have a feeling that wherever you go, trouble just naturally follows."

"I could say the same about you, Mr. Williams. There's an air to your nature that suggests you can handle yourself in just about any situation."

"I won't pretend I can't." He shrugged and looked ahead. "I don't go looking for trouble as some men do to prove their abilities. However, I am always looking for a story. Especially when that story allows me to put trouble in its place or disprove its power."

Mary cocked her head and studied him. He was handsome in the sort of way Michelangelo might have fashioned a statue. She thought back to one she'd seen at an art museum in New York. She couldn't recall the name of the artist or the statue, but it definitely reminded her of Chris. Both he and the statue had a square cut to the jaw, a shapely nose, and finely arched brows. Where the statue had hair of white marble, Chris had sandy blond hair with just a bit of wave. It curled around his ears, peeking out from under his hat.

"Do I pass inspection?" he asked, not turning to look at her.

"I suppose."

He chuckled. "Well, at least you're honest."

"Always," Mary replied. "I've never seen the purpose of dishonesty. It never works to one's advantage, and it certainly has very little value in the long run."

"So you never lie or hide the truth?" He turned to look at her, his gaze intense.

Mary didn't look away. "No. It's never suited my purpose as much as just speaking the truth—or demanding it, if I found it necessary."

"Still, there must be times when you don't want someone to know everything about you or a situation."

Mary considered that a moment. "When that happens, I simply tell the person questioning me that I'd rather not talk about it. Otherwise, Mr. Williams, you'll find I'm pretty much an open book. What you see is what you get. If you are offended by that . . . well, I suppose you'll just have to be offended."

"Did I say I was offended?" He looked at her with a raised

brow. "Frankly, I find it refreshing. In my experience, most people deal in secrets and pretense. They say one thing but mean another, or play games with emotions and then get angry when you refuse to play along."

Mary knew the same to be true. "I think you'll be happy to know that with the people in this show, there's very little of that. Pretense may be part of the entertainment, but we haven't got time for it where relationships are concerned. Far too often we are reliant upon each other for our very lives. That tends to take the desire for pretense out of the picture."

"Still, your entire livelihood is based on a sort of pretense. You convince the audience that the danger is much greater than it truly is."

Mary stopped and put her hands on her hips. "Oh really. Did you think I was firing blanks at you? I've made mistakes and wounded people before. Do you think it's pretense when Ella stands atop the back of a galloping horse or jumps a team over an obstacle? How about when Lizzy is hanging upside down between the legs of her horse? The danger is there, Mr. Williams." She smiled. "If it weren't, our jobs would be of little interest to us."

He laughed. "Do you mind if I quote you on that?"

"You mean for your article? By all means. As I said, I'm very open about my feelings and the things that matter to me."

Chris smiled. "I think I'll enjoy getting to learn exactly what those things are."

⤙＝ FOUR ＝⤚

Safety is of the utmost importance." Mary looked at Chris and held up her pistol. "You must always treat a gun as if it's loaded, even if you are one-hundred-percent certain it's not."

For weeks they'd been traveling together, and after he confessed he knew very little about guns, Mary had insisted he have at least a working knowledge. Since Jason had arranged for the show to have a two-day rest at this beautiful Indiana farm, Mary thought it the perfect opportunity.

"Target shooting is great entertainment and I love what I do, but guns were designed with one main purpose, and that is to kill . . . or at the very least, present the threat of death. They are wonderful tools in the right hands, but always—*always*—they must be regarded as dangerous." She began loading the revolver.

"Of course, guns can do nothing by themselves. My grandfather made that point very clear to me when I was a little girl. He had a rifle mounted over the fireplace. It belonged to his father and, before that, to his grandfather back in Germany. It was a precious keepsake to him, but it was fully functional, and he kept it loaded. He told me to keep watch over it and come get him if it ever tried to get down from its perch and shoot something." She smiled. "Of course, it never did any such thing, and my grandfather used that as an object lesson. Guns can't do anything by themselves. They require the action of someone else."

"I get what you're trying to say." Chris frowned. "I've known a lot of people who should never have had access to guns. I guess that's why I never wanted to learn anything about them. Of course, growing up in London in the heart of city life, there was never any reason to. In fact, in this day and age of readily accessible food, I'm not sure I see a purpose for firearms at all. Unless you're a soldier or a law official."

Mary smiled. "For as long as I can remember, we had guns. Father and Opa told us what they were and took us out to demonstrate their power. We were told never to touch them unless an adult was with us to instruct. When I was eight, I told my father I wanted to learn how to shoot, and that was that."

Chris seemed shocked. "He let a child shoot?"

"A great many children in America learn to shoot. Especially if they live in rural or rugged landscapes. And despite what you believe, there are still quite a few people who hunt for their meat sources. Even in Kansas we shot rabbits and squirrels for meals. Sometimes even deer. We rarely ever had beef. It was too expensive. But I remember you inherited from your family, so I presume they had plenty of money to purchase what they needed. Still, didn't your father have a gun and hunt?"

His surprised expression changed to a frown, and Chris looked away. "Yeah. He had a gun. My three brothers did too. And before you ask, yes, we relied on hunting as well, but that was here in America. Rural America."

"I didn't know you had brothers." Mary lowered her revolver. "This is the first time I've heard you mention them. Where are they now?"

"Dead. Everyone is dead." His words were barely audible.

Mary couldn't help but think of August. "I'm sorry. That must be very hard on you. I know it has been on me."

He looked at her, his expression void of emotion. "I thought most of your family was still alive."

"My father and mother are both dead. My brother too. But we're losing our focus." She didn't want to talk about death and dying. "Let's get back to our lesson. Growing up in a rural area, as you did, and having a houseful of boys, as it sounds like you had, I'm surprised you didn't learn something of guns."

He frowned. "I learned they're dangerous—deadly. But I left that place when I was just six. I never had a chance to learn to shoot."

"Well, I believe everyone should have a working knowledge of firearms. You never know when you might need to use one."

His mood seemed to darken. "And would you shoot someone if that need arose?"

Mary could see he was upset by the conversation, but she wasn't sure at this point how to do anything other than answer his question. "I would weigh the situation carefully. I would never shoot another person unless it was a last resort. I don't take life lightly."

"Well, I'm glad to hear that."

"It seems I'm always answering your questions, so how about answering some of mine?" Mary gazed up at him. "Why did you end up in London at the age of six?"

This question didn't appear to bother him, at least. "My mother died. My father couldn't handle raising a young child."

"So you and your brothers were packed off to London?"

"My brothers were grown. I'm the youngest of the family, and the next in line was already eighteen when our mother died. I was sent to live with my grandmother, and I'm glad for it."

Mary considered this for a moment. "Still, it seems unreasonable. To lose your mother and then your father and brothers.

They must have known it would be hard on you to lose everything you'd ever known."

"What I'd known wasn't worth keeping." He turned the questions back to her. "What happened to your parents?"

Mary hadn't thought of her folks in some time. "My father died in one of Buffalo Bill's shows. He and Lizzy's father, Mark Brookstone, were performing. There was an accident, and both were hurt. My father broke his neck and died. My mother had died several years before that giving birth to my sister Katerina. You met Katerina back in Topeka."

"Yes, I remember. Mrs. Douglas."

Mary nodded. "Yes. Mrs. Douglas." She paused as August came to mind. "But when I said that death has been hard on me, I was talking about my older brother. He died last year. He was murdered."

"Murdered?"

She hadn't intended to talk about August's death, but it all came pouring out without warning. "The Brookstones had arranged to purchase two mares from Fleming Farm in Kentucky."

"Fleming? Isn't that Ella's last name?"

"Yes. It was her father's farm. The two families had become friends over the years, so when they went to get the mares, the Flemings insisted that the Brookstones spend the night at the farm. They also allowed all the show's animals to be pastured at the farm. It was something they'd done before.

"My brother was the head wrangler for the show, so it was only natural that he be there with the horses. Somewhere along the way he saw something he wasn't supposed to see. George Fleming, Ella's father, and Ella's fiancé, Jefferson Spiby, killed him."

"Killed him?"

Mary shook her head and picked up her gun again. "They said he was trampled to death by two wild colts, but my brother was too smart to let something like that happen. My brother never met a horse he couldn't handle. He wouldn't have climbed into a pen with those colts in the first place because they weren't his to deal with. He would have respected that fact first and foremost. But even if he had, he would have known how to keep himself from being killed."

"Accidents do happen," Chris offered.

She could hear the skepticism in his voice. He didn't believe her. Few did. "Ella overheard her father and fiancé talking—Spiby admitted he had killed August." She knew she sounded harsh. It was a nightmare to relive the memory. She quickly unloaded the revolver. "I don't feel like giving a shooting lesson today." She put the .38 back into its case and closed the lid.

"I'm so sorry, Mary. I didn't mean to offend you."

Hugging the case to her chest, Mary met his gaze. She didn't try to hide the tears that came. "I wouldn't even know that much if not for Ella. She's the one who overheard them."

"Did the two men go to prison?"

"No. Nor will they, as I hear it. They own everyone and everything for a hundred miles around—probably more. Ella said that half the state is terrified of her father and Jefferson Spiby, and the other half believes they can do no wrong. They've bought off all the authorities and judges, so no one is going to challenge them."

"Has it not even been investigated?"

Mary looked down at the ground. "No. Not really. Ella ran away the very night August was killed. Spiby is a terrible man, and she was desperate to break her engagement. Lizzy helped her escape. Ella came back with us to Montana and decided to join the show. After several months, her father and fiancé found her and showed up at the ranch to demand she return with them to Kentucky. Ella refused. She told them what she knew, but it didn't matter. Her father told her no one would believe her word against his. Her fiancé tried to force her to accept that fact, but Ella would have no part of it. When they were alone—or he thought they were—Spiby tried to strangle her. I think he thought he could scare her into acceptance. Either that or he decided that if he couldn't have her, no one would." Mary looked up. "To keep him from killing her . . . I shot him."

"You killed a man?"

Chris looked at her with such disbelief that Mary knew she had to continue. "It was just a flesh wound. I barely scratched his arm, but it told him I meant business. I wanted to do more." She squared her shoulders. "Does that shock you?"

"Not really. I can understand the desire to have justice—to see wrongs righted. What happened after that?"

The heat from the summer sun was relieved by a gentle breeze, but even so, Mary found the temperature unbearable. She contemplated whether to continue, then decided Chris might be of use to her situation. He might have some legal connections or wisdom that would help her find justice for August.

"We sent for the law and told the sheriff what happened. He took Ella's father and Mr. Spiby back to town and said he would check into it, but of course, nothing happened to them. I'm sure the sheriff made his inquiries and received a stellar report back from the sheriff in Fleming's home county. I wish there were something I could do. Short of killing them both myself, I would do just about anything. Sometimes I even consider that."

If her statement surprised Chris, he didn't show it. Instead he reached out and squeezed her arm. "I'd hate for you to do that. I've come to enjoy our time together."

Mary swallowed the lump in her throat and lost the fight with her emotions. Tears streamed down her cheeks. "I just hate that his death will go unpunished. It's not right. Those men didn't even accidentally kill him. They planned it and did it on purpose. And nobody cares."

Chris squeezed her arm again. His voice was low and soothing. "I care."

A tingle ran down to her fingers, but she didn't acknowledge the effect of his touch. She wasn't looking for a romance. She wanted to see justice done. That had to be her focus.

"Ella never said what August might have seen?" Chris handed her his handkerchief.

Mary dabbed her eyes. "No. She led a very sheltered life on the farm. At times she was a virtual prisoner, in fact. I believe her when she says she doesn't know."

"I know some people who might be able to help us get information," he said, dropping his hold on her arm.

Mary shook her head and handed back his handkerchief, noting his monogrammed initials, *C-W*. The material was of the finest quality, no doubt costing a pretty penny. "What could they do, even if they learned the truth? If no one is willing to come up against Fleming and Spiby, it's not going to matter."

Chris shrugged and tucked the cloth back in his pocket. "You don't know that. At least we can try."

"But how?" Mary couldn't allow herself to believe there might be a way. It hurt too much to hope.

"I could get my editor to put one of my fellow journalists on the job. He could go there on the pretense of doing a story on the horse farm. My editor has been wanting to do a spread on the Kentucky Derby. If we focus the issue on the horses and the race, there would be a good reason to visit some of the local horse farms. With the right man doing the job, he might be able to learn the truth."

"But that truth got my brother killed. I don't know if I could live with myself if this idea meant the death of another man."

"There's always a risk in reporting," Chris said with a hint of a smile. "I've run into my fair share of dangers. Like being shot at in a wild west show, for instance."

Mary couldn't help but smile despite her tears. "The biggest danger you faced then was having your hair permanently stained by strawberry juice."

Chris chuckled. "You try standing there and having someone you barely know take shots at you. I thought my knees might give out from fear."

"You wouldn't have been the first man to faint." Mary wiped the tears from her face. Chris had a way of making her feel better. Did he realize that? "Thank you for lightening my spirits."

The breeze ruffled his sandy blond hair, but rather than be annoyed, he just added to the wind's effort by running his hand through the mass and giving it a shake. "Sometimes it feels good to release our worries," he said, sobering. "I've learned that lesson over the years, and it's served me well. We do what we can to right the wrongs of the world, but sometimes we have to admit defeat and give it over to . . ."

"God?" She remembered something Lizzy had once said. "A friend told me that some reckonings will only come with judgment day. Although I must say, I don't have the strength of faith that she has. I am trying, however."

"Then there's another thing we have in common. I've never really understood what God was all about or what I was supposed to do with Him. I doubt I ever will. When I was in Topeka, I was writing about some religious school and a woman who supposedly was touched by God and spoke Chinese."

"I remember hearing about that from my grandparents. They're calling it a Holy Ghost encounter."

"Yes, well, it seems the school has folded and the woman who spoke Chinese has gone to Nebraska. I'm unclear on whether she's there to speak to the Chinese or if she's on some other mission, but it all seems rather silly to me. I told my editor the story was a bore. That's probably why he was so delighted to hear about the show."

"And has he enjoyed the first installments you've sent?"

"He has. He believes the readers will be exhilarated by the beautiful sharpshooter and her abilities. Much more so than an old woman who suddenly starts speaking Chinese." He looked up at the sky and tugged on his collar. "Say, it's gotten awfully warm. Why don't we go back to the house and have something cold to drink?"

"I was just about to suggest the same."

Mary didn't wait for him but started for the farmhouse. Chris easily caught up as she tucked her gun case under her arm. They walked in silence for several minutes, but then Mary couldn't help but pose the question on her mind.

"If you are so skeptical about God and what He can and can't do, why did you agree to take on the story?"

Chris stuffed his hands in his trouser pockets and shrugged. "I don't know. I guess everybody would like to believe in an all-powerful God who can do miracles. I was intrigued, and my curiosity got the better of me. But I wasn't surprised to find things as I did. I would have been surprised to find them otherwise."

Mary felt no condemnation for his doubt or lack of faith. She struggled herself, especially since August's death. Lizzy said such things should bring a person closer to God, but Mary felt the chasm had only widened. How could she trust God when He'd allowed her brother to die so violently? He could have saved her brother—prevented his death. If God truly loved August, then why hadn't He kept him from harm?

Ella trembled as she sat atop her horse, waiting for her turn to perform. The county fairgrounds near Cincinnati were just a few miles from the river that divided Ohio from Kentucky. Beyond that, not even seventy miles, her father and Jefferson Spiby were probably conspiring against her. The closer the show had come to Kentucky, the more that thought had been on her mind. They might even be in the audience right now . . . this very minute.

She knew better than to believe Jefferson would just forget about her. Especially since she'd accused him of murder, but even more because she'd denied him something he wanted: marriage. Jefferson was notorious for getting what he wanted—especially where women were concerned. She remembered hushed conversations where matronly women had tried to convince her mother of Jefferson's unworthiness, even going so far as to tell her of his mistresses. When Mother had tried to talk to Father about it, he had told her that men had needs and she should stay out of such scandalous conversations.

The buckskin shook his head as the roar of the crowd came down from the grandstand. She was using Lizzy's horse Thoreau, and he was anxious to be performing.

"Easy there, boy." Ella patted his neck. "We'll be out there soon enough."

Moments later, Oliver Brookstone announced Ella, and she urged the horse into a gallop and went into a series of spins and layovers for her first pass. Next, she got a little riskier with a roll back that put her upside down. From there she flipped over until her feet hovered over the ground, then pulled back up and onto the horse. She repeated the move on the other side of the horse as well, then maneuvered into a half-fender drag that left her hanging precariously. The audience cheered loudly and continued to clap as she lined up for another pass.

For another few minutes, she continued to thrill the attendees with twists and turns, spins and vaults. They loved the performance, and she loved performing. Ella felt as if she'd always been meant for this life. She straightened in the saddle and returned to her starting position with Thoreau. After giving her mount a pat of approval, Ella waved to the crowd as the applause died down.

"Ella Fleming, I love you!"

Ella felt her blood go cold. The voice sounded so similar to Jefferson's that she was certain he must be close by. She lost her concentration, and her entire body trembled.

Oh, Lord, help me.

It was time to go into another run, but the next trick required delicate maneuvering, and Ella wasn't at all sure she was up to it. Could Jefferson really have come there to harass her? Ella found herself panting for breath. She fought the urge to run and instead decided to change up her tricks and do one that left her feeling more secure and less at risk.

"Come on, Thoreau," she barely whispered and signaled the horse into action.

Turning to the left, she brought the stirrup up between her legs and hooked it over the horn and across her thigh. Next, she crossed her legs, grabbed a handful of mane, and slid into a sort of sitting position on the side of the horse. Her leg was completely secured in the leather strap, so she let go and laid her body back and upside down off the left side of the horse. Then, to make the trick look even more impressive, she stretched out her arms and put her right leg in the air.

Holding the pose for the rest of the run, Ella tried desperately to reclaim her confidence. Thankfully, she only had one more run, and then Lizzy would take over.

Even if it is Jefferson out there in the grandstand, he can't hurt you. The Brookstone team would never allow him to cause you harm.

She came back up into a sitting position and readied for her final run. She knew Lizzy and the others would notice the change in her tricks, but they would also know that she would have a reason. As Lizzy had once said, *"Sometimes you have to go with your instinct, Ella. If it doesn't feel right—don't do it."*

The worst of the moment was behind her now, and Ella felt

she could manage her planned ending. She brought Thoreau back around and maneuvered the straps and belts for her final trick—a back drag and then forward roll into a shoulder stand.

Then, in a flash, everything was complete, and Ella was exiting while Oliver urged the crowd in their applause and praised Ella for all she'd accomplished in such a short time. When she got to where Phillip was waiting to take charge of Thoreau, Ella burst into tears.

She tried to get hold of herself as she slid off the gelding's back, but her emotions were more than she could control.

"Ella? Are you all right? Did you hurt yourself?" Phillip asked as she slumped against Thoreau's side.

She didn't expect Phillip to put his arm around her and jumped at his touch.

"I'm sorry. I just can't bear to see you cry."

Ella wiped at her face. "It's nothing. I just got spooked."

"You can always talk to me about it." His voice was soft and sweet.

Looking up into his chocolate-brown eyes, Ella could see that his concern was genuine. "It's just . . . we're so close to the border of Kentucky and not that far from my father's farm. I suppose I'm anxious that he'll try something."

Phillip frowned. "He can try, but we won't let anything happen to you, darling.'"

His term of endearment left Ella shaken. She had come to care for Phillip, maybe more than she cared for any of the others. Her tears came anew, but she didn't try to hide them. "Thank you, Phillip. You've been such a good friend, and I feel so much better just knowing that you're looking out for me."

He touched her cheek. With his thumb, he wiped away the tears. "You're safe with me. I'll always look after you."

"Is everything all right?" Wes DeShazer asked as he joined them.

Phillip stepped away, still holding the reins of Ella's mount. "She just got a little shook up. Afraid maybe her pa might be looking for her, since we're just a short way from her home."

Ella looked at Wes, and he offered her a smile. "You're safe, Ella, but just to be sure, I'll have Phillip stay with you until you go out with the others to take a bow. Then stick with Lizzy, and I'll be nearby."

"Yes. Thank you. I'll do that." The fear faded. God was answering her prayers through the compassionate gestures of others. She drew a deep breath. "I'm ready to remount."

"Let me help," Phillip said.

"You don't have to do that. I may be small, but I can manage quite well."

He laughed. "Don't I know it. But I just want to help."

Phillip cupped his hand, and Ella stepped into his hold while reaching for the horn. Phillip easily hoisted her upward as she pulled herself onto the saddle. She smiled down at the dark-eyed young man. "Thank you. I feel so much better."

A lazy grin spread across his face. "Being near you always makes me feel better."

⟡═ FIVE ═⟡

Life on the rails going from town to town with the Brookstone show was one of the most pleasurable things Chris had ever done in his life. He and his grandmother had traveled extensively through Europe—most of that by train. But this was different. While travel with his grandmother had been luxurious and educational, travel with Mr. Brookstone's troupe was fun. He couldn't remember when he'd laughed more or had true camaraderie with people who accepted him for just being himself—without expecting something of him or condemning him for the acts of others.

Of course, Oliver Brookstone was exhilarated by the additional publicity they would receive once the magazine articles were published. Chris had explained to him that it would be months before they appeared in the magazine, however. The editor was planning to release them at the beginning of the next year and run them for twelve months in the 1902 editions. It would benefit next year's show rather than this year's.

Sitting in the men's train car and enjoying the conversation of those men who were still awake, Chris felt a sense of family that he'd never known. Especially not with other men.

"I figure it this way," Phillip DeShazer declared. "If you still want to pick up that herd of wild horses when we get back to Montana, I can have them broken for you in less than six weeks, and you can still make a profit in this calendar year."

Oliver Brookstone gave a yawn and nodded. "I think we'll plan on that, then. I know Rebecca said the calves were coming along great and will be ready to sell in the fall, but I figure it won't hurt to have a little extra. We do have repairs to make and other things to purchase. Lizzy was reminding me just last week how much her mother has always wanted a porch."

Wes nodded and put down the book he'd been reading. "She reminded me too. She's pretty set on getting it built." He smiled, as he always seemed to do when talking about the woman he loved. "I think she'll enjoy it as much as her mother."

"Then we'll make that our priority," Oliver declared.

Jason Adler shrugged. "Maybe she just wants to set things in order at the ranch so she can feel free to make other choices."

Chris knew there was a rivalry between Adler and Wesley for Lizzy's affections. He thought Adler rather silly in his pursuit, as it was clear Lizzy and Wes were completely gone over each other.

Wes narrowed his eyes as he considered Adler. "I think since she plans this to be her last year with the show, Lizzy would like to see the ranch put to order so she can start a family there."

Adler shrugged again. "Perhaps, but there's a chance she'd be just as happy to go elsewhere while knowing that her mother is happily provided for."

"Lizzy will be happy wherever Wes is," Phillip said, getting to his feet. "Porch or no porch. I'm gonna call it a night. We've got a lot to do first thing in the morning."

"I think you're right," Oliver said. "I'm going to check a couple of things and then retire as well. We'll pull into Washington, D.C., around three in the morning, and Jason tells me a committee there has already planned us an incredible breakfast, complete with speeches and then a bevy of other things. Then, the next day, we'll help the town celebrate Independence Day with our performance. I'll see you boys in the morning."

"Good night, Oliver," Wes said.

Chris watched Phillip head down the narrow hall. He climbed up into the top berth in one of the compartments and pulled the curtain while Oliver went to the end of the car and entered his private room. Wes had told Chris that at one time they'd had more private cars, including a family car, but Adler had limited the number to save money. Instead of the eight cars the show had used for numerous years, they now got by with five, and those had been renovated to be as efficient as possible. The staff had been lessened too, along with the number of performers. Adler said it was the only way for the show to operate more efficiently. As far as Chris knew, each of the performances had been sold out, so he couldn't imagine the show was still struggling to make ends meet.

Suppressing a yawn, Chris took out his notebook and pencil and jotted a few notes. He wanted to make sure he recorded all the details so that when he sat down to actually compose the next installment for his editor, he'd have everything at his fingertips.

He glanced around the room. This car was mostly bunks for the men, with a small area for sitting and Oliver Brookstone's private bedroom at the very end. Hooked onto this car was the Brookstone commons car, and behind that, the women's car. The commons car had a bathroom for the men to use, while the women had their own facilities in their car in the place of a private bedroom like Oliver's.

Chris remembered Mary mentioning the wonderful gatherings they had in the commons car each evening after the show. She said there was always a feast, and they would discuss all that had gone right and wrong with the performance.

"Wes, Mary mentioned that the show used to travel with a cook and have all their meals here on the train. Is that right?"

Before Wes could answer, Adler spoke up. "They did indeed. Mrs. Brookstone, Lizzy's mother, acted as cook and created some amazing meals."

"I believe he was speaking to me," Wes countered, his tone clearly irritated.

Adler cocked his head. "Yes, but you weren't with the troupe last year. I thought perhaps Mr. Williams would appreciate a firsthand account."

"But it's my understanding that Wesley was with the troupe when it was first formed," Chris said, not caring much for the way Adler constantly tried to diminish Wes's presence.

"Perhaps he was," Adler replied, "but a lot has changed since then. Mrs. Brookstone's decision to quit the show made it necessary to rethink how we feed the workers. I made arrangements with the local venues and included one main meal in most of the contracts. For other meals, we have arrangements with various vendors, depending on the city. For free tickets to our events, we were often able to get free meals. It's worked out nicely."

"I think everybody misses getting together after the performances to eat and discuss the show back here on the train," Wes said, looking hard at Adler. "In fact, I know some of them were just telling you that the other day."

"There's always a sacrifice to be made," Adler said, shrugging.

"Do you think the wild west shows will continue to be popular in the years to come?" Chris asked no one in particular.

Quiet until now, Wes's right-hand man, Carson Hopkins, spoke up. "I doubt it. What with automobiles and aeroplanes becoming popular, horses and shooting probably won't hold the attention of the public for much longer. Alice and I were just talking about what we'd do when Brookstone decides to call it quits."

"Even if the popularity fades here in America," Adler assured them, "in England and Europe we will still find an audience."

"Maybe so," Wes said, frowning, "but nobody wants to live in England and Europe. At least not in this troupe."

"That's true," Carson replied. He got up and stretched. "I'm turning in. I promised Alice I wouldn't be late." He crossed to the door that led to the commons car. He and his wife, Alice, were the only other people to have a private room. At least somewhat private. Jason and Oliver had put a bed in the costuming room for them, but little more. At least they were able to live as husband and wife.

"I'll bid you gentlemen good-night, as well . . . but don't be surprised if you're wrong about the interest others might have in living in England and Europe. I've been speaking to some of the performers, and they seem excited by the prospects," Adler said. He didn't wait for their response but went to the opposite end of the car where his lower bunk awaited.

Since the others had long since retired, this just left Chris and Wes. Wes opened a window while Chris closed his notebook and smiled. "You really shouldn't let him goad you. He's looking for a way to get rid of you." The rush of cool air was slightly smoky but welcome.

"Don't I know it." Wes shook his head and slumped back in his chair. "I've never met anyone like him. Most men I know respect the situation when a man and woman are interested in each other, but not Adler." He didn't bother to lower his voice.

"I've known men like him. I suppose he thinks his money entitles him." Chris's voice was hushed. "They don't respect man . . . or God."

Wes looked at him thoughtfully. "What about you? What are your thoughts on God?"

Chris considered the question. "I suppose I'm still trying to figure Him out. I didn't grow up with much in the way of religious training. I attended church services with my grand-mother, but it was all stuffiness and ceremony. Nothing like that quaint little church we visited last Sunday."

Wes smiled. "Oliver likes to keep everyone attending services when it's convenient to do so. Sometimes he's even led us in a bit of a Bible study. Although . . ." Wes paused, and his face seemed to sadden. "He hasn't done a lot of that since losing his brother."

"That was just last year, right?" Chris waited until Wesley nodded. "I suppose it really changed things for everyone."

"It did in some ways, but you need to understand that the Brookstone family built their lives on a foundation of faith in Jesus Christ."

"And how exactly did they do that?" Chris found himself intrigued.

"I can't say exactly how it all started. I do know their father and stepmother believed in God. Mark and Oliver were just little when their mother passed away, but their father kept up their religious training. Mark told me they were in church every time the doors were open." Wes chuckled. "Church was where their father met their stepmother, and the boys adored her. By the time they moved west, they had added five daughters to the family—although not all of them moved to Montana. Mark and Oliver did, even though they were full grown. In fact, Mark was already married to Rebecca and they had Lizzy. I started to work for Mr. Brookstone—their father—the year after they set up ranching in Montana. He insisted we all attend church on Sunday. He'd rotate the staff, and a couple of men would stay at the ranch and manage things while the rest of us drove the distance to Miles City and church."

"So they maintained this foundation you talked about by going to church?"

"Partly. But it was more than that. Every morning before breakfast, we had devotions. The family had them in the house, and the hands had them in the bunkhouse or out on the range, if you were riding herd. Mr. Brookstone would tell us what to read in the Bible each week, and let me tell you—he expected you to read it and be ready to discuss." Again, Wesley chuckled. "Nobody wanted to get caught not having kept up on their Bible reading."

Chris laughed. "Sounds tedious. Did everyone really abide by that?"

Wes sobered and nodded. "They did. And if they didn't, they usually left."

"They got fired?"

"No. Mr. Brookstone would never have fired them over that. But I think some of them wished they'd been fired. Mr. Brookstone would make it his business to corner them and discuss the Bible with them until they were either seeing things his way or they left to avoid having to deal with him."

"You know, I think I would have made it a challenge to the old man and stuck around."

"A few saw it that way." Wes grinned. "I remember when one kid joined on and decided he was going to be defiant. When Mr. Brookstone questioned him about what he'd read, the kid would tell him he didn't see any purpose in reading the Bible. He didn't believe in God. They used to go 'round and 'round."

"What happened?"

"Brookstone challenged him. Told him if he'd read the Bible and discuss it with him over a thirty-day period, Brookstone would pay him a bonus."

"And did he?"

"Yup. Surprised us all. Even more of a surprise, the kid had a change of heart. Last I heard, he was a preacher down in Cheyenne."

Chris laughed. "That's quite a change. I just don't know what

I think about all that. See, when I met up with you folks in Topeka, I was there to research a story about a group of people who believed the Holy Ghost had come to them. By the time I got there, the Bible school had closed and the preacher was being called a fraud."

"So do you believe that's the end of it?" Wes asked.

"I don't know what to think. To tell you honestly, I'd never even heard about the Holy Ghost. Well, except for people blessing you or closing prayers in the name of the Father, Son, and Holy Ghost."

"The Holy Ghost is God's Spirit that dwells inside us. He gives us comfort and counsel. Jesus promised the Holy Ghost to believers when He knew He'd be going back to heaven. It's through the Holy Ghost or Holy Spirit that we feel God's presence with us."

"And you believe that?" Chris asked, trying to imagine the depth of it all. "Ghosts? You believe in ghosts and spirits coming to get inside us and make us do things?"

Wes gave an indulgent smile. "I believe the influence of God's Spirit is the only way we ever come to the truth—to accepting Jesus as Savior. Otherwise, we've no more reason to believe the Bible than we would believe a book of Greek mythology."

"But the Greeks believed their mythology. A lot of people out there believe the Bible is the Christian's mythology."

"That's their choice," Wes said. He gave a big yawn. "God's given us all a choice." He got up and yawned again. "Personally, I know I'd be lost without my faith. My mother told me about Jesus dying for my sins when I was just a boy. She told me how without that sacrifice, I was hopelessly separated from God."

"And killing a man made you closer?"

"The Son of God dying as a sacrifice for sin, once for all— that gave me a means of reconciling with God. So I prayed with my mother, told God I knew I was a rotten fella and I wanted Jesus to be my Savior."

"And that made you good enough to be with God—to have the Holy Ghost come in you and tell you what to do?"

Wes rubbed his face. "There's nothing good about me without Jesus. Jesus is the only reason I have access to the Father. And the Holy Ghost doesn't dictate to me. He guides and encourages me. When I consider going astray"—Wes lowered his voice to a whisper—"say, to punch a certain fella in the mouth, it's the Holy Ghost that calms me and helps me rethink the situation."

The train jerked and rocked as it passed a rough spot on the tracks. Wes took hold of the back of the chair.

"I think it's time to turn in, but if you want, we can take this up again tomorrow. I'd be happy to share some of the things I've studied in the Bible. When we have free time, of course."

Chris rose and extended his hand. "Thanks. I'd like that. I appreciate that you don't look down on me because I don't think like you do."

"Jesus didn't call me to look down on you or anyone. The Bible tells me to be ready to give you an answer for the hope that I have." Wes smiled. "I just think I can give you a better one after I get a good night's sleep."

Chris lay awake most of the night. It wasn't the things Wes had said that kept him awake, however. It was returning to the area near where he was born that had made him uneasy. Most of the time he could forget the first six years of his life, but tonight those memories hung around his neck like a noose.

Having grown up in a rural town just outside of Washington, D.C., Chris was looked down on and bullied by others. There had never been enough money, and his three brothers were so much older that Chris hardly knew them. It was just as well he'd stayed clear of them. They were known for their fighting and mean spirits. His father was too. He had a violent temper, and the entire town knew it. Chris's mother often sported a black eye or bruised cheek. Those were just the injuries that showed, however. Chris knew that beneath the long sleeves and high collars she wore, there were other marks. Deeper still, her spirit had been completely destroyed.

Chris had always been a sensitive child. It was that same sensitivity to people and their feelings that made him a good reporter. He'd learned early on to watch people for signs of their feelings, because actions were sure to follow. His mother had taught him this, along with reading and writing. Well before he was old enough for school, Mother had encouraged him to pursue an education even if his father saw no value in it. She had also told him about God's love, but Chris found it hard to believe in or desire a relationship with God. Especially when his mother was hiding him away from his drunken father.

Rolling onto his back, Chris folded his hands beneath his head. Already his stomach ached at the thought of running into someone who might remember him or his family. Chris was the spitting image of his father and brothers. His piercing blue eyes, strong jaw, and high forehead were all Williams traits. His grandmother had even remarked that Chris was the young man she imagined his father might have been, had he gotten an education and learned to control his temper.

He sighed and closed his eyes. The last thing he wanted was an encounter with people who knew him or his family. He'd been so careful to disassociate himself from his father and brothers. At one time he'd even considered changing his name, but given *Williams* was so common, he'd kept it, hoping to blend in. His grandmother had done a good job keeping his name out of the papers, but there was always the chance someone would recognize him and remember. If anyone knew about the past and chose to confront him, he'd either have to admit the connection or lie. And if he lied and the truth was found out, then what?

When word got back to his editor, what would he say? Would Chris even have a job? With his luck, his editor would want to do a story about it for the magazine.

"Well, that's never happening," Chris muttered. It was this thought that made up his mind. While they were in D.C., he would be ill and stay in bed. He knew the summer temperatures inside the train car would be unbearable, but they'd be far more bearable than an encounter with anyone who knew his family.

⟶⟵ SIX ⟶⟵

Wes had fully intended to speak to Chris the next day at breakfast, but the journalist had awakened feeling ill and decided to stay in bed. Jason had arranged all manner of events for the show, from participation in one of several Fourth of July parades, to speaking to a group of older veterans, to a tea with the Daughters of the American Revolution. He always kept Lizzy close at his side, as if he thought he could claim her for his own. By the time the troupe returned after a political banquet, everyone was exhausted, and Wes found Chris asleep.

The Fourth of July dawned humid and hot. Chris felt no better, and Oliver offered to send for a doctor. Chris refused, telling them it was just the heat and perhaps something he'd eaten. Oliver promised to send ice and something to drink.

Wes felt sorry for Chris and did what he could to cool down the train car by opening windows and doors. Unfortunately, that allowed mosquitoes and flies in, but Wes figured it was easier to deal with those than the sweltering temperature.

The heat put everyone in a bad mood, and by the time the troupe performed for the city that afternoon, everyone was completely spent and out of sorts. Wes tried to keep everything in perspective and prayed more than once for patience to deal with unexpected situations.

Jason Adler managed to keep Lizzy busy that day, just as he had the day before. It was clear what kind of game he was playing, but Wes had no idea how to counter it. He remembered Mary's comment about making their engagement official. Was that what it would take to get Adler to back off?

By the time they were ready to load up the train, Wes hadn't seen Lizzy for several hours. In his frustration and growing anger, he'd turned to loading equipment instead of confronting Adler. He knew Lizzy loved him and had made it clear to Adler that she had no interest in his romantic notions, but it angered him all the same. There was a code among cowboys that you didn't mess with another man's girl. Apparently in Adler's social circle the rules were different.

"Wes, Oliver told me to finish up here so you could join him and watch the fireworks," Carson said, walking arm in arm with Alice. "They're waiting for you down by the monument to George Washington."

Wes wiped his brow. "Don't you two want to stay with the others?"

Carson grinned and slipped his arm around Alice's waist. "We'll be just fine. Besides, looks like you've managed to deal with most of the equipment."

"Yeah, I took care of it first thing. I needed to keep occupied. How was the trip to the White House, Alice?"

She smiled. "It was amazing and beautiful. I'd love to have me a big house like that."

Carson snorted. "You'll need a richer husband for that to happen."

"In that case, I'll settle for our train car. Just as long as you're in it." She gave him a look of adoration.

Their romance brought Lizzy to mind again. "Is Lizzy with

the others, or has Adler managed to whisk her off to some sup-posed bit of publicity?" Wes knew his tone left little doubt as to his feelings, but he didn't care.

"She's down there too," Alice replied. "But I wouldn't put anything past Jason Adler."

"Neither would I."

"Why don't you just marry her?" Carson surprised him by asking. "Adler would have to leave a married woman alone."

Wes shook his head. "Knowing Adler, it probably wouldn't matter. But, to answer your question, I intend to propose to-night." He hadn't realized until that moment that he'd made up his mind, but now that the words were out of his mouth, Wes knew it was the right thing to do.

"You do?" Alice bounced on her toes. "That's wonderful! Oh, I'm so happy for you both."

"Well, she still has to say yes." Wes didn't really think she'd refuse him, but Adler's interference had caused him to second-guess himself.

"She'll say yes. She loves and adores you, just as I do Carson."

"What do you want me to do while you're gone?" Carson asked.

"The horses are still in the pen. I hated to load them until it was absolutely necessary. It's just so hot. I thought the evening would cool off more. Of course, I don't think they'll enjoy the fireworks, so I suppose you might as well get them onboard."

"We'll see to it, boss."

"Just go find Lizzy," Alice said, smiling. "Pop that question you should have asked long before now."

Wes nodded. "I think I will. I just need to change my shirt and get the ring."

He left the happy couple and made his way into the men's train car. At the foot of his bunk, Wes found his trunk. Inside, his clean clothes were neatly packed and waiting. Thank goodness for Agnes and Brigette. Those two worked hard, maybe harder than any of the rest of the crew. He pulled off his dirty work shirt and put on one of his nicer shirts. He never cared much for dressing up but knew that the other men would be wearing their best.

He put on his tie and grabbed his Sunday coat. The idea of wearing a coat made him almost rethink his plan, but Lizzy was worth it. Besides, it wouldn't be for long and the evening would cool off eventually. With that taken care of, Wes pulled a small shaving kit from his trunk, then sat on the edge of his bed. Opening the box, he spied the ring he'd purchased months ago in Miles City. It wasn't anything fancy. Just a small ruby on a gold band. He hoped Lizzy would like it. It was very similar to the ring his father had given Wes's mother when he proposed.

He slipped the ring into his pocket, then returned the shaving kit to the trunk and closed the lid. As he passed Chris's bunk, he noticed the journalist was awake.

"Are you feeling any better?"

Chris nodded. "Oliver's sent a variety of things throughout the day, and I'm feeling much improved. I think after tonight I might be back up and running."

"I'm glad to hear it. Now, if you don't mind . . . I'm off to propose to Lizzy." Wes couldn't help but grin.

"That's wonderful news. I'd tell you good luck, but you won't need it," Chris replied, smiling. "It's obvious she's in love with you. Hopefully I can get you two to pose for a photograph. That way I can write up something about the romantic Fourth of July proposal in the nation's capital for the magazine."

Wes nodded. "Maybe later, when we're both feeling surer of ourselves." Chris chuckled, and Wes smiled. "Well, here I go."

Wes left the train and walked toward the center of the city. Band music was playing somewhere on the grassy parkway that stretched from the Capitol to the White House and a little beyond. There were people everywhere. Some had come to picnic and others to simply stroll. All were dressed in their finery, and Wes was glad he'd chosen to put on his good clothes. He made his way down the National Mall to where most of the Brookstone troupe had gathered by the Washington Monument.

"Wes, I was beginning to think you wouldn't come," Oliver said, giving him a pat on the back.

"I wasn't sure I'd find you in this mass of people. Makes me long for Montana." Wes glanced around for Lizzy. When he caught sight of her, he smiled. She was so beautiful.

Lizzy was talking to Ella but immediately seemed to sense Wesley's gaze. She looked up, found him, and gave a wave before saying something to Ella. She quickly left the younger woman's side and made her way to Wes, offering him a big smile as well as a tall glass of iced lemonade. "I've missed you."

Wes took the drink and nodded. "I've missed you too." He noted her outfit. She wore a beautiful rose-colored gown trimmed in lace and a large straw hat done up with ribbons and flowers. "I see you dressed up too."

Lizzy glanced down at her gown. "Jason said everyone would be dressed up, and I didn't want to stick out."

"You'll always stick out, Lizzy. You're the prettiest one here, and that color suits you." Even in the lamplight, Wes could see her blush. "I have something I want to talk to you about." A beautiful white star burst in the sky above them, much to the approval of those gathered to watch.

She raised her face. "Is something wrong? Are the horses all right?"

"Everything's fine, including the horses." He lowered his voice. "This is something more private . . . about us."

Several of the others, including Oliver, looked at Wes, clearly interested to know what he had to say. Adler edged closer with a look that suggested he knew what Wes was up to. Maybe it was best to propose in front of everyone—Adler included.

Before he could change his mind, Wes handed Oliver his drink and then dropped to one knee. Lizzy's brown eyes went wide, and when he held up the small ring, they filled with tears.

"I've been meaning to ask you this for a while now." He grinned. "Elizabeth Brookstone, will you be my wife?"

"Of course!" She squealed in delight as a huge firework exploded overhead.

Wes got to his feet and slipped the ring on her hand. All around them, the troupe was cheering and offering congratulations, but Wes only had eyes for Lizzy. He pulled her close and felt her wrap her arms around his neck. He pressed his lips to her ear. "I love you, Lizzy."

"It took you long enough to figure that out," she murmured.

"It did, and for that I ask your forgiveness."

He kissed her then and forgot about everything and everyone else. She was his entire world and always would be.

———◆◆◆———

Jason sat in the box office and finalized the ticket count and money they'd made that evening. Just the few changes he'd implemented to the show had doubled their income and put the show in the black again. His father would be pleased. Father had been pushing him to settle into a business, but nothing had really appealed to him. Jason's college education gave him great insight into legal matters as well as mathematics, but while he enjoyed both, he didn't feel drawn to either one. In fact, these days the only thing he felt drawn to was Lizzy Brookstone.

As he put the money and receipts in a money bag, Jason remembered the proposal Wesley DeShazer had made to her just two days before. He knew they were in love, but he figured it would be easy enough to woo Lizzy away from the cowboy. After all, Wes couldn't do half the things for her that he could.

"She did say yes," he muttered to himself. He didn't let it bother him, however. People got engaged and unengaged in the blink of an eye. In fact, women in his social circles were considered dull if they hadn't been engaged on at least a dozen occasions by the time they actually wed. No, he just had to figure out a way to separate them. He needed time alone with Lizzy. Time to show her a better life—a life only he could give her.

The trip to England would help. He would have at least seven days as they crossed the ocean where Lizzy wouldn't be preoccupied with work. He could take time to walk and talk with her and help her see how much they had in common. Then, once they were in England, the schedule was such that he would have plenty of time with her. The troupe was staying on his father's country estate, and that alone would afford him easy access to Lizzy.

But with Wesley DeShazer there, it would be difficult to get Lizzy to himself. There had to be a way to keep DeShazer from making the trip. It was just that simple. But how? What could he come up with that would keep Wes on the opposite side of the Atlantic?

He was still searching for a solution when Chris Williams walked into the box office. He spoke momentarily to the ticket sales people before making his way to where Jason was working.

"I thought you were watching the show and ordering photographers around," Jason said, barely looking up.

Williams ignored his tone and took a chair. "I've managed all of that and then some," he replied in a nonchalant manner. "Thought I'd come see what you were up to."

"Readying the receipts and money. We leave right after the show."

"Yes, I know. New York bound, and soon we'll be on the Atlantic and headed to England."

"Home for us both, I suppose." Jason tied off the money bag.

"I'm not sure where home is these days. I sold my grand-mother's house, so it's not like I have a place to go to in London."

"I mentioned you in a letter to my father. He knew your grand-mother. Said she was quite a remarkable woman."

"She was," Williams said with a thoughtful smile. "She was highly thought of by all in her society."

"And a very elevated society it was. Despite being an American."

Williams chuckled. "Well, she was fond of America and En-gland in kind. She said she might have been born an American, but London courted her like a suitor and won her over. That was why she remained there even after her husband died."

"Ah yes, John Lamb. He was, I believe, your grandmother's second husband."

Williams nodded. "He was. He went to England to work with Charles Adams, the U.S. minister to the Court of St. James's, and naturally my grandmother went with him."

Jason leaned back in his chair. "I did a little research into you when you asked to do the story on the wild west show."

"Well then, you probably know everything you need to know about me." Williams got to his feet. "And I can say in return that I've also done my research on you. Your family has a fascinating background. Mother was an American whose family made their fortune in some . . . interesting ways."

Jason fixed his expression so as not to let on that the jour-nalist's comment bothered him. His mother's family was both admired and feared as a powerful family. Their business deal-ings were sometimes questionable and had garnered more than a little attention in the 1890s, around the time of the nation's big financial troubles. It was also known that they held a great deal of power among the dockworkers and teamsters, but as far as Jason could see, there was nothing wrong with that.

Williams continued. "Your father was the fourth son of a poverty-stricken earl. Despite not being able to get the title passed down to him, your father's choice of brides brought money back to the family and reestablished the earldom. I'm sure your uncle was quite grateful, given he inherited the bulk of the estate. I can't imagine it being easy for your father to see all of his hard work handed over to his brother, but it did spare the family from ruin, and that alone had to be of value to him socially. I'd really love to do a story on it sometime, but for the moment the focus of my work is America." He smiled. "Now, if you'll excuse me, I should probably make certain those photographers are getting the proper pictures of the closing ceremonies."

Jason stared after the journalist in fury. He didn't know that much about Williams or his background. Little had been said about the woman who'd raised him or why, and that alone suggested something was being hidden. Still, the fact that Williams had gone to the trouble to dig into Jason's family was worrisome. Would he cause problems?

Shaking his head, Jason forced himself to calm down. He had nothing to fear. As Williams had already stated, Jason's family history was easily known. He rather liked that his mother's father had been feared far and wide as a city boss. Grandfather had run things his own way and ignored laws and other people when they became obstacles. Jason found that was an example he could embrace. Perhaps his mother's family could even help him accomplish what he wanted where Lizzy was concerned. A few telegrams here and there, and he'd have all the help he needed.

One of the box office employees cleared his throat. Jason turned to see what the man wanted.

"We've closed the box office and wondered how much longer you would be."

"I'm finished." Jason felt a moment of irritation but gathered his things. "Where's the nearest telegraph office?"

"Not but a block away, sir. I can take you there, if you like," one of the older clerks replied.

"Yes. Thank you."

He considered what needed to be done. He wanted to wire ahead to New York and let his mother's sister know he'd be in town. That would result in a family gathering—a dinner, no doubt—where he could rub elbows with his uncles and cousins. His father had warned him about getting into any obligation with that side of the family, but Jason figured it couldn't hurt this once. He wasn't sure what kind of solution would help him most, however. If he had thugs beat Wesley to a pulp, leaving him unable to travel, then Lizzy might change her mind and remain behind. If he arranged for Wes to be taken—to just disappear for a time—then Lizzy would no doubt insist on staying to look for him. No, it would have to be something that wouldn't upset plans for the show.

As they made their way to the telegraph office, a thought suddenly came to mind. Jason had the perfect solution for getting Wesley out of his hair. The ranch in Montana was being managed by Mrs. Brookstone, Lizzy's mother. Wes had been the foreman until Oliver asked him to work with the show this year. If Mrs. Brookstone requested Wes's return to the ranch for some sort of crisis, then the troupe could be safely on its way to England before Wes could get to Montana and realize it was a hoax.

"I could give him the telegram just before we leave," he muttered to himself. Even if DeShazer telegraphed back to Montana, someone would have to take the message from Miles City to the ranch, and then if Mrs. Brookstone sent a reply, it would have to be taken back to Miles City. That would buy Jason hours, if not days.

But what would happen once the situation was realized? Jason knew Lizzy would never appreciate him doing such a thing, but he felt confident of his ability to woo her. He was certain that without the interference of DeShazer and Lizzy's uncle, he could have Lizzy to himself most of the time. Once they were in England, Father could keep Oliver Brookstone busy, so it was just a matter of ridding himself of DeShazer.

Jason was certain they could have nearly a month, if not more, to themselves before DeShazer could rejoin the troupe in England—if he rejoined them. It would take a week to get back to the ranch and then another to get back to New York. Add the Atlantic crossing to that, and Jason felt confident the time would be enough to win Lizzy's heart. DeShazer might not even be able to rejoin the show abroad if Jason failed to leave him a ticket to sail.

The idea was taking shape, and Jason was nearly beside himself with delight. Of course, it was possible DeShazer would learn the truth sooner than expected and make a hasty path to rejoin the show. If that happened, Jason would simply deal with DeShazer when he showed up in England. He'd admit his desperation to win Lizzy, and on the slim chance he failed, he would take their condemnation and admit defeat. At least for the time being.

But there was one overhanging cloud.

His father.

Jason would still have to deal with the old man. Father expected him to choose a business in London and settle down. He expected Jason to marry and marry well. It was doubtful he'd see Elizabeth Brookstone as an acceptable choice, given his ambitions for royal favor and political power. And then, of course, there was the issue of money. Jason was expected to marry into wealth even greater than that of his family. His father had visions of him one day becoming a member of parliament. An American rancher's daughter would hold little appeal. Even once Jason convinced Lizzy to marry him, he would still have to fight his father for approval.

He gave a heavy sigh. He loved Lizzy enough to endure anything. To wage war if necessary. And why not? Men had gone to war over women before. History was full of such stories. Jason smiled. Wasn't there some saying about love being strong enough to conquer any obstacle? If not, then there should be.

Chris wondered how much Adler knew or how far he'd go to know every detail of Chris's life. He didn't like Adler. Not at all. He knew the Englishman was devious and determined, and just the way he had brought up the topic of Chris's grandmother had made it seem like a threat.

This was the reason Chris was cautious about getting too close to anyone. He'd been careful beyond reason, in fact, when it came to relationships. Yet here he was, traveling with the Brookstone troupe. Not just for a few days or weeks, but for months. And in such close quarters that he couldn't help getting into intimate talks with one or more of the crew. Already he'd grown closer to Mary, and then there were the late-night conversations he'd had with Wes. It was just a matter of time before Wes asked questions Chris didn't want to answer.

"And I was fool enough to find comfort in it," he muttered, shaking his head.

"I hope you're feeling better."

He stopped at the sound of Mary's voice and turned. She stood there smiling, dressed in her beautiful finery for the final act of her show.

He nodded. "It was nothing. Just summer malaise, I'm sure." His words were clipped.

"Is something wrong?"

Chris couldn't hide his annoyance. "Just that people don't seem to understand minding their own business."

He left without any further explanation. He didn't like the way things were going. On one hand, he'd made some good friends among the Brookstone folks, but on the other hand, he was starting to have feelings for Mary that could only lead to heartache. Maybe it would be best to go to his editor once they were in New York City and tell him to put someone else on the story. After all, if Adler decided to dig into Chris's past, the story would come out for all to know, and then Brookstone would no doubt want him to leave anyway.

He thought of Mary's hurt expression. He'd have to try to explain. But how? Mary believed in total honesty—no pretense or deception.

Chris sighed. "And my whole life is pretense and deception."

⊹⊱ SEVEN ⊰⊹

The rocking motion of the train made Mary sleepy, but Oliver had insisted on the troupe meeting once the train pulled out of the station in Philadelphia and headed for New York City.

"As you know, our next show will be the last before heading to England," Oliver announced. "Jason has seen to it that news of our great successes and sold-out venues has preceded us to London, so we anticipate that our shows there will be well attended. We will be headquartered at Jason's family home outside of London. We have created a fair amount of time for you to enjoy sightseeing and other pleasures, but Jason has also arranged for a variety of lectures and smaller shows for individual groups. Otherwise, we will perform regularly, most evenings for six weeks in London at the Earls Court Exhibition Centre.

"When we finish there and return to New York, we will head straightaway to Buffalo for the Pan-American Exposition, which is going on even now. As Jason and I work to create a memorable final act for 1901, we were wondering if we might ask a favor of Wes and Lizzy."

Lizzy looked to Wes, who sat protectively at her side. He shrugged. "I suppose that depends on the favor."

Oliver smiled. "Well, given the spirit of things and your new engagement, I wondered if we could prevail upon you to stage the engagement at the conclusion of Lizzy's act."

Wes frowned and shook his head. "Our engagement isn't for theatrics."

"I'm surprised you'd even suggest such a thing, Uncle Oliver." Lizzy looked perplexed. "It doesn't sound like you, so I'm assuming this was Jason's idea."

Jason held up his hands. "Yes, I suppose it originated with me in the sense that I reminded Oliver of how important you are to the show, and since you're planning this to be your final year, it might be nice to give your fans something special. After all, you are the most popular of all the performers, although each and every one of them is important." He nodded to the others and continued. "We thought this might be a perfect way to announce that you're leaving the Brookstone show to settle down with the man you love."

Lizzy eased back in her chair. "I see. Well, when you put it that way, it doesn't seem so unreasonable." She looked at Wes. "What do you think? I mean, we're already engaged, but it might be a nice way to make the announcement to the world."

"I don't see a need to playact at our engagement. Oliver could just announce it and tell the audience it's your final performance."

"Yes, he could do that, Wesley, but we thought it might be nice to advertise that there will be a special surprise for the audience at the end of the show. We just wanted to promote the positives, even have Lizzy announce that Ella will take her place and encourage everyone to support Ella in next year's performances. It's more to support the overall good of the show," Jason said, looking from Wes to Lizzy and back again. "Of course, if you're not certain about the engagement . . ."

"Ha! You wish." Wes shook his head. "Oliver, if it's something you feel will benefit you and Lizzy is agreeable to it, I suppose I can bear up under it."

"As long as you're willing to consider it," Oliver said, "we can discuss it when we're sailing and have plenty of time to decide the details."

Mary glanced toward where Chris sat taking notes. She wondered how he was feeling and what was going on with him. He had seemed so distant since being sick in Washington. She had tried to see him then, and he had sent her away, telling her he might be contagious and he didn't want to risk her getting sick. But it seemed to Mary that it was something else entirely. His whole demeanor had changed. He seemed so much quieter . . . lost within himself. She could relate to that. She too found herself lost in her thoughts of August and how he'd died. How there was no justice for him and probably never would be.

"Chris, will you be visiting your editor while we're in New York?" Oliver asked.

Chris stopped writing and nodded. "Yes. In fact, I believe it would be good if you joined us for a meeting, Oliver. I believe you and Mr. Maddox would benefit by getting to know each other. I won't stay on the train for our two nights in New York. I have my own apartment and need to repack for our trip abroad, but I will arrange the meeting and get back to you on a time."

"Certainly. I'd be delighted," Oliver said.

The meeting went on for another twenty minutes before Oliver finally dismissed everyone. He and Jason left immediately for the men's car, while most of the women headed to their own car. Wes and Lizzy remained for a few more minutes, speaking softly and sharing a good-night kiss, while Chris finished writing in his notebook.

Once Lizzy and Wes parted company, that left Mary and Chris alone, just as she'd hoped. Her feelings for him were growing. She cared about him but told herself it was just friendship.

Nothing more. And as his friend, she wanted to do whatever she could to offer her support if something were wrong.

"Chris, I wonder if we might talk a minute."

He looked up and glanced around the room, seeming to realize for the first time that the others had gone. He closed his notebook. "What about?"

He sounded all business, and it irritated Mary. "About you. About what's wrong."

"Nothing's wrong. What are you talking about?"

"Prior to our arrival in Washington, you were pleasant company. You were open and talked about so many things. Since Washington, however, you've been . . . well, different. I even heard from some of the others that you've taken to drinking."

He fixed her with a stern look. "What I do is none of your business. I'm not a drunkard, if that's what has you worried."

Mary felt as if he'd slapped her. She had always been a strong woman, able to hold her emotions in check without difficulty, but Chris's harsh comment made her feel like crying. She fought back tears and took a moment to control her feelings.

Chris got to his feet. "Now, if you'll excuse me, I want to finish writing my thoughts."

Mary stood as well. "I thought we were friends. Close friends, even. Over the weeks since you joined us, I thought our friendship had grown into something special."

"Why? Because I spent time with you? I'm a writer. I was getting to know you—to know everyone."

"And you don't want my friendship?" Mary knew it would be better to just stop the conversation, but she couldn't help herself. She'd done nothing wrong, and yet Chris was suddenly treating her like a stranger.

He gave an exasperated huff. "In my business I find friendships to be a liability more than an asset."

"But why?"

"Friends put demands on me that often interfere with my writing. Now, I must take my leave."

She watched him go, feeling as if she'd suffered a great loss. It wasn't quite as bad as learning about August's death, but the pain was there all the same. Why was he acting this way? What had happened to make him change from the open and kind-hearted man he'd been to this moody stranger? She felt tears well up and decided it would be best to seek the solace of her bunk and what little privacy she could have there. If someone saw her crying, she'd just tell them she was thinking of August.

Chris hated himself for the way he'd treated Mary, but it was for the best in the long run. He knew she'd come to care for him—that her friendship could easily develop into something stronger. And that, he couldn't let happen. His past was too much to put on anyone, which was the reason he had promised himself he'd never get involved with a young woman. He would never marry and, that way, never have to explain the secrets of his childhood and the sorrows that followed him, even now. He'd never have to worry about passing down the shame that haunted him.

Still, he hated that he'd hurt her. He did care for her, and it had never been his desire to cause her pain. She was a special woman, one he could have easily fallen in love with.

As he entered the men's car, he found Wes sitting at the small table, staring out the window into the night.

"Contemplating life?" Chris asked, doing his best to sound lighthearted.

"Just troubled at the idea of pretending to propose to Lizzy in front of hundreds of people when I've already proposed. I don't like the idea of making a mockery out of something that means so much to me."

Chris nodded and took the chair opposite him. He glanced over his shoulder toward the berths before looking back at Wes. "No one says you have to do it. It would be a pretty spectacular thing for the audience to witness, but if it doesn't suit you, then don't do it."

Wes sighed. "Then I'd be the bad guy."

"Yeah, well, that happens in life."

"You sound like you're speaking from experience," Wes replied, putting his full attention on Chris.

For a moment Chris thought about denying it and going to bed, but something deep within him wanted to talk—to figure out a way to let go of the past.

"I just hurt Mary's feelings. So I suppose I deserve to be the bad guy."

"Why not go apologize to her, then, instead of sitting here talking to me?" Wes asked with a smile.

Chris shrugged. "There are a lot of things I can't explain." He fell silent. After a time, he glanced up to find Wes just watching and waiting. Something in his expression put Chris at ease. He felt safe. "Tell me more about God. I remember hearing that He punishes the children for the sins of the fathers, going down sometimes three or four generations."

Wes pulled his Bible from the shelf over the table. "That's in the Old Testament. I remember reading it too. But while I believe the consequences of a father's sin will travel down multiple generations—or can—there's also a verse in Ezekiel, which is also Old Testament, that says this." Wes flipped through the pages until he came to the one he wanted. "This is the eighteenth chapter. It says, 'The word of the Lord came unto me again, saying, What mean ye, that ye use this proverb concerning the land of Israel, saying, The fathers have eaten sour grapes, and the children's teeth are set on edge? As I live, saith the Lord God, ye shall not have occasion any more to use this proverb in Israel. Behold, all souls are mine; as the soul of the father, so also the soul of the son is mine: the soul that sinneth, it shall die.'"

"So God changed His mind about sin?" Chris asked.

"Not exactly. Sin is sin. It came into the world by way of one man—Adam—and it's been dealt with by way of one man—God's Son, Jesus. See, the Bible says we're all sinners and that the cost of that is death. But Jesus came and offered Himself up to pay that cost. So while I think children often bear up under the consequences of their father's actions, I believe we are each responsible for our own sin. Without Jesus, we are doomed to be forever separated from God because of it."

"But with Jesus, I don't have to account for the sins of my father?"

"No, you don't. It doesn't change the fact that your father is still your father. If he's done something that everyone knows about, then it's likely they are going to worry that you'll do the same. Or it's even possible that they could believe you had a part in whatever he did. But in Christ you are a new person—redeemed. He forgives your sins, and even though that doesn't guarantee you won't have to bear consequences, it does mean you'll spend eternity with God." He smiled. "Which sure beats the alternative."

"I suppose it would. I've heard many a preacher speak on hellfire and eternal damnation. It doesn't sound at all pleasant."

Wes crossed his arms. "You know, a lot of folks haven't had the blessing of a good father like I did. It makes it hard for them to believe that God is good and loving. Especially when they had neither good nor love from their earthly father."

"Exactly. My father was a terrible man. My brothers too." Chris shook his head. "It has always left me feeling hesitant to trust anyone or to want them in my life. Especially if there is a chance I could turn out to be like my pa and brothers." He kept his voice a bare whisper, hoping no one else could hear their conversation above the rattle and clanking of the train.

"Take it to the Lord, Chris. Seek Jesus as Savior. He can give you forgiveness and the strength to make your own life—a life that is honorable. It's as simple as going to Him in prayer—just apologizing for your sinful ways and asking Him to save you."

"And He does it . . . just like that? What if I'm not on His list to save?" Chris could hardly believe it was that simple.

"The Bible says that God loved the whole world so much, He sent His Son to die in their place. You're a part of the world, and while it's true that not everyone is going to be saved, it's evident that God's Holy Ghost is working on your heart, or you wouldn't be here asking me these questions. I think you're tired of carrying the deeds of your father and brothers on your shoulders, along with everything you know yourself to be guilty of. Why not lay it down at the cross?"

Chris shook his head and gave a long sigh. "Why not indeed?"

Jason stood on the open platform between train cars after discussing details for their time in New York with Oliver. The old man was a good sort and welcomed Jason's ideas easily, but Jason would just as soon be rid of him. A thought kept flitting through his head that without Oliver and Wes, Jason could pretty much take over and keep Lizzy in the show. She loved what she did, and he knew that if Wes wasn't influencing her to return to the ranch, she would stay on. Jason could even get her mother to return to the tour, and then he was sure to keep Lizzy. Perhaps if he told her how much they'd suffered without her cooking and mothering of each member, Rebecca Brookstone would be won over. It was worth consideration.

The other idea that had come to mind to rid them of Wesley was to pit Lizzy and Wes against each other. She wasn't easily offended, so when the idea had come to mind to have them stage their engagement for the audience, Jason had known it would be a topic that would put Lizzy and Wes in a difficult position. Wesley was old-fashioned and private. He would hate the idea of having to perform like a trained monkey. Jason knew it could become a bone of contention between them, and the idea pleased him. He would have to think of ways to further the irritation on Wesley's part. If he got them fighting—so much the better. Then, when he sent Wesley back to the ranch, he would leave with anger and harsh feelings. Those had a way of growing in the absence of dealing with the problem.

The train rocked sharply to the right, and Jason grabbed the railing. He had never cared much for train travel, and even with the comfort of private cars, his opinion hadn't improved much. But it was a necessary evil, and he would do what he had to do.

"Well, I see you had the same idea I did," Oliver Brookstone said, joining Jason on the platform.

Jason turned and smiled. "I needed a little air—even smoky, it's better than the staleness of the car."

"I agree." Oliver came to stand beside him. "This whole area is fast asleep while we make our sojourn. Still, I can't help but wonder at the people and places out there. Especially the ones who are still awake at this hour. Are they contemplating us as we contemplate them?"

"You're turning into quite the philosopher, Oliver. I never really think of those people at all. They're just out there, and I am here. They don't enter into my world unless I choose for them to, and seldom do I allow that. Why complicate matters?"

Oliver laughed. "My brother would chide you for having no compassion or interest in mankind. He was tenderhearted when it came to others. He would have given the shirt off his back to a stranger in need. I've seen him do nearly that. Thankfully, he only gave his outer coat, but Mark was a true humanitarian, unlike me."

"I know you miss him." An idea came to mind. Jason knew the older man still grieved the loss of his brother. He was also given to drinking when his sorrows became too great. If he drank enough, Oliver Brookstone would become easy to manipulate. Jason smiled. "He must have been quite the man."

"Oh, he was." Oliver shook his head. "I don't know why God took him from this world when He could have just as easily removed me."

"I know such thoughts often leave me sleepless," Jason said, trying his best to sound sympathetic.

"But you're a young man. You shouldn't have a care in the world." Oliver gave him a look of envy. "I sometimes think we don't appreciate our youth until it's too late."

"My father has often said that you and your brother were very close. Was that true when you were young?"

"Without a doubt," Oliver replied. "Mark and I were like two sides to the same coin. We had our viewpoints and dreams— some the same, some different—but always they complemented each other in some way. Mark took a wife and had a child, while I remained single. Mark loved ranch life and I the show. Together we were able to help one another have it all."

"But now he's gone. That must make you feel such a void in your life."

Oliver's expression saddened. "It does indeed."

Jason nodded. "If I had such a brother, I'm not sure I would have the strength to go on without him. You are a brave soul, Oliver Brookstone."

The old man frowned and looked off into the black night skies. "No. I'm not brave at all. In fact, I'm quite the coward."

⊷⊱ EIGHT ⊰⊶

The next day, Mary sat cleaning her Stevens Crackshot rifle and sharing her heart with Lizzy in one of the staging rooms off the main hall of Madison Square Garden. They'd already learned that the massive arena with seating for eight thousand people was sold out for their one-night performance.

"Something isn't right. Chris was obviously upset, but he won't talk about it."

"Men aren't generally given to discussing their troubles," Lizzy replied. "That's been true of most of the men in my life. They think they're saving their womenfolk from worry, but their silence is the most troubling of all."

The scent of gun oil wafted on the air. It was a smell Mary loved. It reminded her of her father and grandfather. "I know you're right. Opa never talks about his troubles, and Papa didn't either." Mary set down her rag. "I really like him, Lizzy. I just want him to know that he can trust me to be a good friend."

"Or more?" Lizzy asked, grinning. She was braiding ribbons that they would tie into the manes and tails of the horses for their performance.

"Or more." Mary sighed. "Although if I can't even get his friendship, I'm sure to be unable to win his love." She looked down the barrel of her rifle to make certain she was satisfied with her cleaning job. "He will stand in front of my rifle and trust his heart to me, but not where friendship and romance are concerned."

"I hope I'm not interrupting," Ella said, opening the door just enough to pop her head inside. Her long blond hair had been neatly pinned up. She looked like a delicate china doll.

"No, come in," Mary said, lowering the barrel. She picked up the stock and put the two pieces back together before picking up the screw that held them in place.

"I'm glad you're both here. I need to speak to you about something important." Ella stepped into the room, dressed for an outing.

"Are you going somewhere?"

"Yes, but I'm hoping you two might join me. You see, my brother, Robert, is in town. He came to see me a little while ago. He has a meeting, but then he wants me to join him for lunch at the restaurant across the street."

Mary perked up at this. "What did he say? Why does he want to meet?"

"I fear he'll try to convince me to return home. Perhaps even try to strong-arm me. I don't know why else he would want to meet me for lunch. He could have said what he wanted to say when he was here earlier." Ella was clearly worried.

"I'll go with you," Mary said.

"So will I," Lizzy said, putting her braiding aside. "When are you supposed to meet him?"

"In two hours." Ella chewed her lower lip.

"Well, no matter his reason for being here, we'll go with you, and then you won't have to fear him trying to force you home." Mary finished securing her rifle.

"Did he say anything about your father also being in New York?" Lizzy asked.

Ella sat down as she pulled off her gloves. "No. He did say there won't be any charges brought against Father or Jefferson for August's death. Apparently, because of the Montana law officials requesting information, our county sheriff gave pretense of investigating further. It was no doubt a sham, but he declared the matter closed."

Mary felt her throat tighten. Sometimes she wished she could be a powerful man for just a few minutes so she might enact justice for all the wrongs of the world.

Lizzy gave Mary no chance to pose the question they were both wondering. "Was that all he had to say about it?"

"No." Ella shook her head and turned her gaze to the table. "He told me not to cause further trouble."

"What? You?" Mary was outraged. "You haven't caused any trouble. They brought this on themselves."

"I know, but to their way of thinking, I'm to blame." Ella refused to look Mary in the eye. "Robert said that Father is willing to forget what's happened but still wants me to return home and marry Jefferson."

"But, of course, you won't." Lizzy made such a matter-of-fact statement that Ella couldn't help but look up. Lizzy patted her arm. "We won't let you go, no matter what they say."

"Thank you. I've been worried about what trouble Father and Jefferson might cause the show."

Lizzy gave an unladylike snort. "They've not managed to cause us much trouble at all. We had those shows in Kentucky cancel, but other locations were quickly found. The shows were all sold-out with standing room only, and now we're headed to England, where I'm certain those two hold much less influence than they do here."

Mary found her voice returning. "I think we should confront your brother at lunch and learn exactly what he knows. Something caused them to kill my brother. Whatever it was that he saw cost him his life, and I intend to know what that something was."

"We can ask," Ella said, nodding, "but don't be too disappointed if he refuses to say. He might not even know. Father has always been very particular about what anyone knows regarding his business. Robert is often gone selling horses and recently even moved from the family farm to his new property."

"Nevertheless, we can ask." Mary began collecting her things. "I'll get this stuff put away and change my clothes. I certainly can't go to the restaurant dressed like this." She waved her hand over her simple blouse and navy-blue skirt.

At exactly twelve thirty, the trio entered the restaurant and were taken to Robert's table. If he was surprised to see that Ella had brought Lizzy and Mary, he didn't say anything as he rose in greeting.

"Robert, you already know Elizabeth Brookstone, and this is Mary Reichert." Ella turned to the ladies. "This is my brother, Robert Fleming."

He gave a slight bow. "My pleasure, ladies." The ladies were seated, and he took his place before continuing. "You all look very lovely."

"Thank you," Lizzy said before either Mary or Ella could reply. "I hope you don't mind our coming along. We're happy to pay for our portion, but we didn't want Ella going about the city without companions."

"I quite agree, Miss Brookstone. I'm glad that you care so much for her safety and reputation," Robert replied. "Furthermore, I wouldn't hear of you paying for your dinner. I'm happy to make you my guest. However, I think perhaps this also has more to do with you wanting to hear firsthand about the investigation regarding Miss Reichert's brother." He looked to the waiter who stood patiently with menus in hand. "Perhaps we might order first?"

"Of course," the ladies murmured in unison.

Mary looked over the menu and found the selection rather intimidating. Her mind was certainly not on food.

"What do you recommend?" Robert asked the waiter.

The man gave a slight nod. "We have a delectable stewed veal done in a provincial manner and served over white rice."

"That sounds fine. I'll have that." Robert looked to the women. "What about you ladies?"

"I agree," Lizzy said, setting her menu aside. "The veal sounds fine." The other two settled on the same.

"Might I also recommend starting with the sorrel soup and then a chilled shrimp salad prior to your entrée?" the waiter asked.

"Yes, bring it for all of us," Robert replied. "And perhaps tea for everyone?"

Mary nodded, as did Lizzy and Ella. Her mind was still a million miles away from food and drink.

Once the waiter had gone, Robert eased back in his chair. He seemed not the least bit concerned about his company.

"Ella tells us that you moved away from the family farm," Lizzy began.

"Yes. I was fortunate enough to purchase a grand old place not six miles from my father's property. It was in disrepair and took some renovation, but it was completed last May, and we were finally able to move in."

"I remember you have two sons, is that right?" Lizzy asked. "How do they like the new place?"

"Nathanael and Beaufort are delighted," Robert replied. "Thank you for remembering them. In return, I will share a bit of news that even Ella doesn't know."

Ella straightened. "Do tell."

"Virginia is with child. She will be delivered in October."

"Congratulations," Lizzy said before Ella could reply. "And is your wife happy with the new place?"

"She is. I believe every woman prefers to be mistress of her own home, don't you?"

Lizzy shrugged. "I've always enjoyed living with family. Of course, they are my own and not my in-laws."

Mary listened to the conversation continue and wondered how she might pose a question about the type of things going on at Fleming Farm that merited death upon their discovery. Nothing came to mind, however.

They were well into the entrée before Mary finally interrupted the polite conversation. "I don't wish to sour our dinner, Mr. Fleming, but you must know that I have questions."

Robert dabbed his mouth with his napkin. "I do. I presume you wish to ask me something in regard to your brother's death."

"Yes." Mary put her fork aside. "What in the world could he have seen that got him murdered?"

She was blunt and to the point and knew that her words probably shocked him, but to his merit, Robert Fleming only nodded.

"I know you believe him to have been murdered. Ella informed me of what she overheard, and frankly, I am of a mind to believe, along with my sister, that your brother met with foul play."

This shocked Mary so much that she couldn't even speak. She stared at him wide-eyed. He believed that August had been murdered?

"I can see that surprises you," Robert said. "But you must understand that I know just how devious my father can be. Our grandfather was even worse, as I hear it. However, you must also understand that I have no idea what might have brought your brother to that end."

"None whatsoever? Not even a guess?"

Robert shook his head. "My father has long been involved with a great many underhanded and illegal activities. As for Jefferson Spiby, well, the list of his offenses is too long to tell.

However, even knowing that, I can say that it doesn't matter in the least to the authorities of our county—and in some cases, our state. You see, both my father and Mr. Spiby wield a great deal of power. They are wealthy and not beyond buying the support and defense of anyone deemed useful. Those who won't be bought are soon buried beneath a mountain of problems and ostracized by one and all."

"So Ella has told us." Mary feared that no matter what she asked, she would never get the answers she desired. "But someone must know."

"Look, I intended to tell Ella this when we were alone, but I will state it for one and all, because I believe it's important that you understand. Our father was greatly embarrassed by Ella's accusations. It caused him to tighten ranks with Spiby all the more. Whatever those two are up to, I wouldn't put it past them to make difficulties not only for Ella but also for the Brookstones."

"They can try," Lizzy said in a snide tone. "We aren't without our own influence."

Robert nodded. "Be that as it may, I feel it only fair to warn you. It would be in your own best interests to do nothing further to draw attention to your complaints."

"But they killed my brother." Mary felt her stomach knot so tightly that she feared she'd be sick. "My brother was a good man—a kind, God-fearing man—and they killed him." She saw sympathy in Robert's expression but knew his response would offer no comfort.

"I'm sure you take solace in knowing he's in a better place," he answered.

"She'd take more solace if Daddy and Jefferson were put behind bars," Ella retorted.

"Perhaps, but it wouldn't bring her brother back."

Mary pushed away from the table. "No, but it might keep it

from happening to someone else's brother. If you'll excuse me, I need some air."

She left the dining room and walked toward the exit. She had no real destination in mind but knew that she didn't want to continue speaking to Robert Fleming when there was no hope of him doing anything to aid her cause.

"I am sorry for your friend," Robert told Lizzy and Ella. "I wish there was something I could do, but I won't risk my family."

"Do you honestly think they're at risk?" Ella asked. "Would our father truly allow anything to happen to his own grand-children?"

Her brother gave a shrug of his broad shoulders. "You know him as well as I do. You know too the influence Spiby has over him. Personally, I'm glad you got away from him. He is the lowest of sorts, and I have no doubt he killed Miss Reichert's brother. Worse still, it was probably not his first nor his last murder. That's why I'm begging you to say and do nothing more. I will continue to look for an opportunity to set matters right."

"Truly?" This was the first time she'd heard him say anything that suggested he wanted to right the wrong.

"Ella, you don't know what goes on in there. You're a woman, and women are not a part of the business world. As a man, I've long detested the way Father treats others. I have few true friends because of him. Spiby too. Folks in our area have long planned on your marriage to him, and together, those two men are a formidable force to be reckoned with. As I said, I have no doubts of Spiby's ability to cause harm—even death. I don't know what happened that night with Miss Reichert's brother, but I am keeping my ears open. My eyes too."

"And you will share anything you learn with me?"

"I promise I will, but for now, we must let this lie. Otherwise

Father and Spiby will tighten their own security in whatever measures they deem necessary."

Ella drew a long breath and let it go. "I've been such a fool all these years not to know what they are capable of. I knew Jefferson is a womanizer, but nothing more."

"That's just as they desired. I doubt Mother knows even a fraction of it. She certainly would have no knowledge of anything underhanded, and while her circle of ladies at church might have their opinions of Jefferson Spiby, they would be careful discussing anything negative for fear it would get back to their husbands."

"Husbands who are no doubt in debt to your father and former fiancé," Lizzy threw out.

"No doubt." Ella couldn't believe how naïve she'd been. "I feel so bad for Mary. She loved her brother dearly. Losing him was hard on her. I know it would be hard on me to lose you."

Robert smiled. "I don't plan for you to lose me, but neither do I want to lose you. For all of our sakes, please be careful and let this matter go . . . for now. God won't be mocked. The truth will eventually be known."

"But who else will have to pay before the truth comes out?" Ella asked, shaking her head. "Who else might die at the hands of Jefferson Spiby before someone finally stands up to him and puts him away for good?"

❖❖ NINE ❖❖

T hings were arranged in a different fashion for the New York show. Given the huge venue and the large crowd, Oliver Brookstone felt they needed to go above and beyond. To stretch the show a bit, he and Jason hired a full orchestra to perform between acts. The crowd seemed enthralled.

When it came time for the trick shooting portion of the evening, Mary and Alice came out together and did a variety of simple tricks, with Mary using her rifle and Alice her bow. As the act continued, the tricks grew progressively more difficult, and the performers separated, with Alice continuing while Mary arranged for her riskier numbers. While they had allowed for their shooting competition at the beginning of the show as usual, it had been agreed that they wouldn't choose someone from the New York audience for Mary to shoot at. The last two performances had nearly been disastrous when the men chosen to assist Mary proved unable or unwilling to obey directions. Jason feared legal ramifications and suggested they use one of the crew. Phillip DeShazer had eagerly volunteered, and so he would be selected from the audience as if he were a complete stranger.

Alice earned a standing ovation as she stood on the back of

her horse and shot flaming arrows at a variety of targets. When the targets were hit, the arrows set fire to the structures that had been created in various designs. They quickly lit and burned out, and the crowds loved them.

When Mary came back to the focus of the act, she rode around the oval ring they'd created and fired her rifle at glass balls that Carson and Wes slung high. A special sling was used by each man to get the balls as high in the air as possible. As Mary pushed the horse to go faster and faster, so too were the men required to produce the targets quicker. All the while, Oliver urged the audience to applaud and marvel at her abilities.

"Isn't she amazing?" he cried out. "Surely no one can best our Mary!"

Despite the distraction, Mary never missed, and after fifty in a row, she slowed the horse and took a bow. The crowd loved her. She gave a wave of her red Stetson and dismounted as Oliver announced that her next tricks would further prove her amazing skills.

"Now our Mary will show you just what a deadeye she truly is. We will choose a volunteer from the audience."

Hands went up, and many men jumped to their feet as well. Oliver gave Mary a nod, and she did a slow walk, circling the arena. After a careful perusal, she pointed, and Phillip ran out to join her. There were boos from the disappointed gentlemen but cheers overall.

Phillip had donned a fancy suit and hat—both loans from Jason Adler. He looked quite dashing, Mary thought, and beamed him a smile of approval. As she took him to stand in the appropriate place, Oliver announced that she would be putting on a most deadly display.

"Our Mary is going to shoot the buttons off this gentleman's vest—a feat that requires a very even hand and absolute silence."

Mary helped Phillip from his coat. "You put the padding beneath your shirt like I suggested, didn't you?"

"I did." He grinned. "But I'm betting you could have managed without it."

"Oh, of course, but it gives you a little extra protection." She smiled. "Usually I can just clip the buttons off, but I warned Jason that sometimes a bit of material goes with them as well. The padding will make the buttons stand out a bit more, as well as keep you from any accidental injury. The important thing is that you stand absolutely still."

"You can count on me, Mary. It won't be the first time I've been shot at—but it will be the first time I won't move a muscle." He laughed.

She lined him up in front of a custom-made, two-inch thick curtain. The weave was something special that easily absorbed the spent bullets. In the very center was a tightly woven bamboo sheet to offer further protection.

Once Phillip was in place, Mary gave each of the buttons a tug just to make sure they were separated from the vest. Next, she stepped to her place. She carefully laid out her bullets and picked up her rifle.

Oliver cued the orchestra, and they began to play a low hum of strings and muffled snare drums. Mary lowered the lever of her Stevens Crackshot and chambered a round before returning the lever to its original position. She pulled back the hammer just as Oliver silenced the orchestra and asked everyone to be completely still. The arena went quiet.

Mary smiled and drew the rifle to her shoulder. She could have shot those buttons off in a hurricane, but the drama made for more excitement. She took careful aim and fired. The first button popped from the vest, and the audience applauded as she reloaded. The next four buttons followed, and the crowd went wild with cheers and applause. A few gifts of flowers even rained down.

After taking a bow and thanking Phillip for his bravery, Mary did a series of other tricks with targets, using her rifle and her pistol. The crowd was particularly excited when she shot the center out of pennies that Oliver himself threw in the air. He handed these out as souvenirs to various people in the audience.

"Isn't she wonderful?" Oliver asked as Mary hurried from the arena to change into her fancy dress and jewelry. "Mary's own dear father, God rest his soul, was once a participant in Buffalo Bill Cody's show. Mary has long loved performing and learned to shoot practically before she could walk. While we wait for her, I have a special surprise. Our own Gertie is going to sing."

Mary rushed to the dressing room where Ella stood ready, as did Alice. They helped Mary from her western outfit and into a beautiful mauve silk gown. The Edwardian fashion was the very latest, with a squared neckline and draped ivory lace for sleeves. The body of the dress was long and straight with only the ivory lace to embellish it at the waist. As Alice finished with the buttons up the back, Ella secured a beautiful necklace of paste diamonds and pearls while Mary attached matching earrings onto her lobes. The final task was to style her hair atop her head in a wave of pinned curls.

"Here," Alice said, handing Mary long ivory gloves.

"Do I look all right?" she asked, pulling them on.

"You're perfect," Ella said, fastening a diamond paste bracelet before stepping back with Alice. "Now, go thrill them."

Mary returned to the arena entrance so Oliver could see that she was ready just as Gertie finished the final refrains of the popular song "A Bird in a Gilded Cage." Many of the women in the audience were dabbing away tears. The song was always a huge hit.

"Thank you, Gertie," Oliver said. "That was beautiful and heartwarming all at the same time. Ladies, may you never marry without love."

The audience applauded once again.

Oliver smiled and allowed a few moments for the din to die down. "And now, ladies and gentlemen, just to show you what a beautiful and talented lady our Mary truly is—she will show you further skill while dressed for a night of elegant dining and dancing. Perhaps you thought her talent was due to her western style of dress, but the most elegant fashion dictates are now observed, and I believe you will be just as impressed."

The crowd remained silent until Mary stepped forward and the spotlight found her. She glittered and sparkled as she waved and then curtsied deeply, as if she stood before a king or queen. The crowd clapped with wild abandon.

Mary went into her final act, again using Phillip as her target. He held a lit cigar in his mouth for Mary to shoot. Then he stood facing her with a target screen behind him and a bevy of balloons secured around him. Mary took up her rifle and mirror and turned her back to Phillip for her final shots. One by one, she popped the balloons while the audience exclaimed in awe.

Finally, her act was complete, and she exited the arena to wait for the final parade of performers.

"Mary?"

She turned to find Chris emerging from the shadows and felt conflicted. Part of her wanted to smile, and another wanted to snub him. He made it easier on her, however.

"Look, I know I don't deserve your kindness, but I want to apologize."

She relaxed a bit. He seemed more like his old self. Ella and the other Roman riders went by as they rode their teams into the arena. The applause momentarily made it impossible to hear anything Chris might have to say.

"I know now is not a good time, but I was hoping you'd let me take you to dinner after the show. I want to talk to you in private."

Mary nodded. "I'd like that."

He smiled. "Thank you. And by the way . . . you look beautiful." He glanced to his right as Jason Adler approached. "Until then."

He gave Jason a nod and then left without another word. Mary wondered if Chris would finally tell her what was causing his ill temper.

"Mary, you were superb as usual," Jason Adler said. "Do you by any chance know where I can find Wesley?" His tone and expression suggested something was weighing heavy on his mind.

"Is there a problem?" Mary asked.

"I'm afraid so. I've had a telegram from the ranch."

Mary frowned. Telegrams were hardly ever good news. "The Brookstone ranch?"

"Yes. I'm afraid Mrs. Brookstone has had some trouble and needs Wesley's immediate return."

"But we're leaving tonight for England."

"Yes, I know. It's all rather inconvenient." Jason shrugged. "I suppose, however, that Mrs. Brookstone's needs must come first. Carson and Phillip can surely manage the horses."

"Yes, I would imagine, but Lizzy can't be as easily replaced."

Jason shook his head. "Lizzy wasn't asked to return. It's just ranching business, not a personal issue with her mother."

"Yes, but I don't know that she'll see it that way."

"But her mother insists she continue with the show." Jason looked momentarily shaken. "And you know the Brookstones have always been firm on the show coming first."

Mary thought his attitude was strange. "Yes, but I also know Lizzy would do anything for her mother. Not only that, but Wesley won't be eager to let her go to England without him."

"I'm sure whatever is going on at the ranch can be cleared up quickly, and then Wesley can rejoin the troupe. I'll make sure he has a ticket to cross over when he is able to return to New

York." Jason smiled as if that had resolved the entire matter. "It will be harder without him, but I'm sure we'll manage."

"Especially when it comes to managing Lizzy."

"What?" Jason asked, looking surprised.

Mary put her hands on her hips. "I know how you feel about Lizzy. You'll be glad to have Wes gone so you can work on her feelings, but it will be a waste of time. Lizzy has loved Wes for a great many years."

Jason smiled. "While I won't do you the injustice of lying, I will say that my feelings for Elizabeth Brookstone are of no concern to you."

"They most certainly are. Lizzy's feelings will affect the entire show because, as you so often put it, Lizzy is the heart of this show. If she's upset, just remember that will play out in her performance. Therefore, it might behoove you to refrain from trying to come between her and Wes."

Jason shrugged. "I believe in the adage that all is fair in love and war."

Mary shook her head, knowing without a doubt that he was only going to cause further trouble. "You may come to regret that."

Chris sat across from Mary at the impeccably set table. She was still wearing the lovely gown of mauve silk with ivory lace. She'd rid herself of the fancy jewelry but still looked every bit the grand lady.

With their orders placed, Mary sat in silence, waiting for him to begin the conversation. Chris tugged at his collar, then gave a nod. "I need to say what I must and stop worrying about what you might think of me."

"I really don't know what to think," Mary admitted. "You've been dark and brooding for days."

"Yes, and for that I am sorry. I want to try to explain, but I'm afraid there is still a great deal I'd rather not say."

Mary frowned. "Christopher Williams, I don't recall ever trying to force you to speak on any topic that you didn't want to share with me. I have asked for an explanation of your treatment but made no demands."

"I know that, and I suppose that only serves to make me all the more regretful."

"Then why don't you just say what you wish to say, and if I question you on something that you don't want to discuss—tell me. I'm not a child, and I too have things I don't wish to share with others."

"Seems simple enough." He toyed with his fork. "I was born near Washington, D.C., and being there brought out the worst of memories. Being there, in fact, left me feeling ill both of mind and body."

"And why was that so hard to explain?" Mary asked as the waiter placed a bowl of French onion soup in front of her.

Chris waited until the waiter had finished serving them both before continuing. "There's a lot I can't say . . . or rather that I don't want to talk about. Suffice it to say, my father and brothers didn't have the best reputation, and I didn't want to be confronted by anyone who knew them and would associate my behavior with theirs."

"I knew you were troubled, so I prayed for you," Mary said, smiling. She picked up her spoon and shrugged. "I pray for you often, even though I suppose by some standards my faith is not all that great."

"Nor mine. I've had a fair exposure to church teachings but have struggled to make any real acquaintance with God. Until lately, in fact, it wasn't in the forefront of my mind."

"For me it's just always been there. I've always attended church with my family, but I suppose I haven't ever worried about a personal understanding. My grandparents encouraged me and prayed for me. I suppose I thought that was enough. Although, since losing my brother, I have sought to better know God in order to seek answers."

"And has God given you those answers?"

"Not exactly." Mary sampled the soup and smiled. "It's good. You should try it."

Chris did just that, and for a while they ate in silence while he pondered all the questions and doubts that swirled through his head.

"As far as the past is concerned," Mary said as she put her spoon aside, "you needn't worry about what I will think. Nor anyone else here, for that matter. I think Oliver Brookstone and Lizzy are two of the most compassionate and forgiving people I've ever known. They would never hold the wrongdoings of others against a child who had no say."

"I can see that just in knowing them this short time. Nevertheless, I'm haunted by the past, and it often causes me regret and even . . . bitterness."

"Bitterness I understand." Mary dabbed the napkin to her lips. "I shared a lunch with Ella and her brother today. Lizzy was there as well. Robert Fleming said that nothing will be done regarding my brother's death. Apparently, just as Ella stated, people are either too afraid of her father and Jefferson Spiby or too indebted to them to speak out against them. He told Ella to do nothing further to interfere, but I'm hoping you were serious about getting someone to go to the farm to investigate."

Chris met her worried expression. "Of course I was serious."

"I'd like you to move forward with that. Even though Robert Fleming asked Ella to do nothing more, this wouldn't involve Ella. No one would think her involved at all."

"It's already been done. I put things in motion when I met with my editor yesterday. He doesn't know the extent of why I wanted him to include Fleming Farm as the focus of the story, but the reporter who will write the story is a good friend of mine. I explained to him in some detail that something underhanded and dangerous is going on there."

Mary leaned forward. "And he was all right with risking his life to investigate?"

Chris grinned. "All right with it? He jumped at the chance. He loves a challenge, and the more dangerous, the better. He'll ferret it out. You just wait and see."

She shook her head and eased back in her chair. "Thank you. I'm so grateful. I was beginning to fear that nothing could be done."

Chris felt a strong urge to protect this beautiful young woman. He wanted to assure her that he would set her world to rights—that he would never let anything hurt her again. But how could he do that when his own world was in such disarray?

For a long while they ate and said nothing more. All around them the world continued, unaware of their thoughts and unconcerned with their troubles. Chris had seen so much in life— talked to people from all walks and heard their goals, troubles, trials, and victories. He'd done what he could to capture in words the deepest desires of mankind, and yet for all of that, he still couldn't figure out his own heart.

"Mary," he finally said, putting down his fork and knife, "I don't feel like I can be completely open about my past or the things that are troubling me now, but I want to express my regret for making you feel bad. It wasn't fair of me to put that on you. The truth is, I don't deserve your friendship. Worse still . . . it frightens me."

"Frightens you?" she said in surprise. "Why in the world should my friendship frighten you?"

"Because I have spent my entire life avoiding such relationships. I know the dangers it would expose me to . . . and expose

110

the other person to. I've worked hard not to entangle myself in anyone else's life, and then I met a beautiful young woman who has a way of drawing me out of myself." He shrugged.

In the candlelight he could see her cheeks flush. "I accept your apology and in return give you one of my own. I forget that just because I tend to be outspoken, I expect everyone else to be the same. I don't want to force you to tell me your secrets, Chris. I just want you to know that you can—that I care enough to ask. But I want you to know that I also care enough to refrain from asking. If that's the price for our friendship, then I'm willing to pay it."

He was touched by her sincerity and gentle expression. She did care about him. Something deep within his heart told him the past wouldn't matter to her. She would never hold it against him. But just as quickly, a steel band surrounded his heart, and his thoughts betrayed him.

But I hold it against myself. The past is my burden to bear, no one else's, and I won't put it on her. I can't.

⭢⇌ TEN ⇌⭠

With her horses safely in Wesley's care, Lizzy made her way to the wagon where her things were being loaded. They were departing soon for the ship that would carry them to England. It was thrilling to imagine the long voyage. Lizzy had never been abroad, and the thought of traveling across the ocean and seeing foreign places was beyond her wildest expectations. The fact that Wes would be with her made it all the better. How she wished they were already married.

Carson stood atop the wagon, tying down the tall stack of trunks. He gave Lizzy a wave. "I think we have everything."

"I'll make one more run through the cars, just to make sure." She hiked up the skirt of her fine gown to avoid the dirt and oil on the tracks. Jason had insisted the performers dress formally, as he had arranged first-class passage for them. Lizzy and the others had come back to the train after the performance to find a new outfit for each and every person. Her own gold gown was regally trimmed in lace and fringe. She felt as if she were queen of the show.

The climb into the commons car was a little more difficult in a fancy dress and delicate heeled shoes. While Lizzy appreciated the custom fit of finery, she was also a great deal more inhibited.

The undergarments alone were confining in a way that made her want to tug and twist to free herself from their grip. And the dainty shoes that matched her gown could hardly stand up to a sturdy pair of boots. Still, as her mother would have said, everything had its place. And first class on a luxury liner was not the place for split skirts and boots.

She looked around the room to make sure all necessary articles had been packed, but the car had been thoroughly emptied. She found Alice in the costume room collecting the last of the items there. Alice's reddish-brown hair had been carefully curled and pinned into place to complement the icy-blue silk gown she wore.

"You look beautiful."

"So do you," Alice replied, smiling. "I've never had anything this fine." She stopped to give a twirl. "When I was a little girl, I dreamed of owning beautiful clothes like this. Well . . . maybe not exactly like this. Styles were different back then. I always wanted a bustle."

"I know what you mean." Lizzy looked around the room. "I thought bustles were so glamorous, the way they stuck out in the back, but it was the hooped skirts that I wanted. I saw pictures of them in my mother's old copies of *Godey's Lady's Book.*"

"Yes, I loved those too," Alice declared. "I thought they made the dresses look like big bells. What fun to remember that. The clothes these days are beautiful but seem far less creative."

"Perhaps we should dream up something and then introduce it in the show." Lizzy chuckled. "Uncle Oliver said he's always asked by women where they can purchase the split skirts we wear. I swear, if we sold those along with our little flags, we'd make a bundle of money."

"Everybody wants what seems novel." Alice went back to packing the few remaining articles on her bed.

Lizzy went to the sewing table. "I've come to help, since Jason already put Agnes and Brigette on the train home."

"Will they rejoin us when we return to America?"

"I hope so. No one can sew as well as Agnes, and Brigette has learned to be nearly as good. I suppose it helps to have such a talented aunt." Lizzy picked up a spool of thread. "Still, I wish they were going with us. I know Jason said he'd have plenty of help for us there, but I like our little family. Now, what can I do?"

"There's not much left, as you can see. I'm just trying to make sure the last of the sewing supplies gets packed. I know we can probably buy more in England, but since they're here anyway, it seems foolish not to take them." Alice tucked a handful of material into one of the open carpetbags.

"You must be especially thrilled with this adventure," Lizzy said, picking up the only other stack of material still on the desk. She handed it to Alice. "I was just thinking how I envy you and Carson being married. I wish Wes and I were. I think it would be the most romantic of trips."

"Like a honeymoon," Alice offered. "That's how Carson and I are viewing it. A genuine wedding trip."

"Yes. I had thought of that." Lizzy picked up a large sewing kit. "Where do you want this?"

"The trunk." Alice pointed to the end of the bed.

Lizzy deposited the basket there and straightened. "I'm a little afraid of traveling by ship across the ocean. I wonder what it will be like."

"Well, you're soon to find out," Alice said with a grin. "And I wouldn't fret too much about not being married. At least you and Wes will have a lot of time together."

"If only Jason would leave us be." Lizzy shook her head. "I don't understand why he won't accept that I'm in love with Wesley. He can be such a sweet man—very thoughtful—but I love Wes."

"It doesn't seem like Jason believes that matters. I think he's convinced he can change your mind."

"But I've told him otherwise. I've made it quite clear."

"Some men refuse to give in until a woman is legally bound. Jason strikes me as that sort."

Lizzy sighed. "I hope not." She glanced around the room. "Well, it looks like you have everything under control here. Do you need help getting it out to the wagon?"

"No, Carson will be in directly. In fact, I'm surprised he hasn't already made an appearance. If you want, go check out the men's car. I think that will be the end of it."

"I'll do that. You never know—something might have been overlooked. Uncle Oliver is terrible about forgetting things."

Lizzy left the commons car and went to the men's. She had no sooner stepped through the connecting door, however, than she caught sight of her uncle and Phillip sitting at the small table. A bottle and two glasses sat between them, and Uncle Oliver was pouring what looked to be another round.

"What's going on?" she demanded.

Phillip grinned. "We were just celebrating."

Uncle Oliver looked apologetic but happy. "We made more money tonight than we've ever made before, Lizzy girl."

"That's wonderful news, but Uncle Oliver, you know we don't allow liquor."

"It's just a little celebratory drink. Nothing more."

Lizzy looked at the half-empty bottle. "How many celebratory drinks?"

Phillip laughed. "She's too smart for us, Oliver." He held up his glass. "To Lizzy Brookstone!"

"Don't drink to me." She made her disgust no secret. "I can't believe you two. This is uncalled for. Uncle Oliver, you promised Mother you wouldn't drink."

He nodded and put a cork in the bottle. "I did. I'm sorry. It's just . . . sometimes a fella has to celebrate. You take this." He handed her the bottle.

Wes entered the car. He looked at his brother and Oliver and then turned to Lizzy. "What's going on here?"

Lizzy held up the whiskey. "This is what was going on. Apparently, a celebration for all the success we had tonight."

Wesley frowned and turned to his brother. "There's work to be done. Get over to the tack car and see that everything is loaded properly. I'll speak with you about this later."

Phillip had the decency to lower his head and say nothing. Whether he was embarrassed or sorry for his actions, Lizzy couldn't say, but she was sure the last thing he wanted was to hear a lecture from his big brother.

"Uncle Oliver," Lizzy started after Phillip had gone, "you know this stuff makes you ill. You must stay away from it."

"Don't worry about me, child. It was just one drink. Now, tell me how the packing is going. Are we ready to head out for the ship?"

"Oh, there you all are. I'm so glad to have found you," Jason said, holding up a piece of paper. "We've had a telegram from the ranch."

"Is Mother all right?" Lizzy asked, putting the bottle back on the table.

"Apparently she's fine, but there are some ranch problems that have her requesting Wesley come home to lend a hand."

"What kind of problems?" Wes asked, taking the telegram from Jason. He read it quickly. "It doesn't say, just that it's urgent I come now."

"But we're leaving for England," Lizzy said, looking at Jason. "If Wes goes back to Montana, he won't be able to accompany us. We need him."

"Yes, I did think of that," Jason said with a slight nod. "There won't be much for him to worry with on the ship, and once we're in England, my people can take over. I'll wire ahead and let them know."

"If Rebecca bothered to send a telegram requesting Wes, then you know it must be important," Oliver said, looking at Lizzy.

"Then I'm going back with him. Something might be wrong with Mother. She might need me."

"The telegram says she's fine, that it's just ranch business," Wes said, looking up from the slip of paper. "I don't think your mother is in danger."

"And you know what Rebecca would say about the show and your obligations to it," Oliver said, getting up from the table.

Lizzy noticed he was none too steady. Perhaps it was best that she remain with the show and keep an eye on her uncle. She sighed. "But I was really looking forward to our time together." She looked at Wes and knew he understood.

"Wes can join us as soon as the ranch business is dealt with, and he can wire us at my father's estate to let us know what's happened," Jason interjected. "It surely won't take long to figure out. At least I wouldn't think so. I'll see to it that he has a ticket waiting for him at the ship's office. Once he finishes with his duties in Montana, he can simply telegraph me. I'll have my people waiting to take care of his needs when he reaches England. We'll all be together again soon. You'll see."

Lizzy nodded. It seemed there was nothing else to be done.

Jason turned to Oliver. "I have a few matters for you to sign off on," he said. "If you would accompany me, we can take care of it now."

"Certainly." Oliver went to Lizzy and kissed her on the cheek. "Try not to fret, my dear. I'm sure nothing is amiss. I'll wire your mother myself and make sure she knows how to reach us in England if there's further need."

"Thank you." Lizzy hugged her uncle, then waited until he and Jason had gone to go to Wes. He opened his arms to her, and she cherished his embrace despite the heat of the evening. "I don't want to go without you."

"I know. I'm not happy about sending you to England with Jason. He's always up to something where you're concerned."

Lizzy pulled back and looked up into his worried expression. "You know he means nothing to me."

"That doesn't stop him from trying to entice you."

"And you think I'll give in to him?" She raised a brow as she studied his face. "Wesley DeShazer, are you that uncertain of my love?"

"Of course not." He sighed and pushed back a strand of her brown hair. "But I am uncertain of him." He frowned. "I know he'll try anything to win your heart."

"But he can't, because you have possession of it." She smiled. "It's no longer mine to give."

He looked down at her for a moment, and then the frustration left his expression and was replaced with the love Lizzy had come to expect. He lowered his mouth to hers and kissed her. Lizzy sighed, wrapped her arms around his neck, and held him tight.

Later at the pier, Wes kissed Lizzy again just before she and the rest of the troupe boarded the ship. He had a bad feeling about the entire situation but knew that to express his thoughts would only worry her.

"I love you, Wes. Never forget that," she whispered as he pulled away.

"I won't. Don't forget that I love you—that you are mine." She smiled. "Never."

He released her and watched her go up the gangplank with her uncle and Jason Adler. It was all he could do to remain in place. The heavy night air seemed to weigh him down, along with the discomfort of letting her go. For a moment, Wes felt as though he were being pulled to the bottom of the harbor.

"You heading out tonight, brother?" Phillip asked, coming alongside him.

"No. First thing in the morning." Wes watched Lizzy turn as she reached the top. She gave him one final wave and blew him a kiss. Wes waved in return and fought the urge to tell her not to go.

"She'll be all right, Wes. I'll keep an eye on her."

"You'd better." Wes turned to face Phillip once Lizzy disappeared from sight. "I have a feeling Adler will take every advantage of my absence. He still intends to have her for his own."

Phillip shook his head. "Lizzy loves you, Wes. She's crazy about you. I wish Ella Fleming felt even half as much for me." He grinned. "You don't have to worry about Lizzy."

"I'm not. I'm troubled by Adler."

"I'll stick to Lizzy like glue," Phillip promised.

"And stay away from the liquor," Wes demanded. "We've had this talk before, Phillip. You won't be any good to anybody if you're drinking."

"Don't you worry about it, brother. I'll be just fine. I doubt those Englishmen have anything I'd want to drink."

Wes knew better but didn't want to end their farewell on a negative note. "I'll be praying for you, Phillip. I know there are things that bother you, trouble you. I'm always here to talk. You know that, don't you?"

For a moment, sadness crossed his little brother's face, but it left just as quickly, and Phillip again laughed. "Of course I know that. You just get the ranch business settled and get back to us. It's a pity the Brookstones don't have a phone and you can't just call Mrs. Brookstone up and settle things from here."

"I doubt I could even get a call into Miles City. You know how unpredictable the lines are. We're lucky the telegraph works.

I wired back to let her know I'm coming, but unless someone from the ranch is in town or has the time to ride out, she won't even know that much." Wes shrugged. "I love the isolation there except for times like this."

Phillip nodded. "Well, guess I'd better join the fellas and get myself onboard." He gave Wes a hug. "Don't waste any time."

Wes shook his head. "You can be sure I won't."

Jason watched Lizzy as she stood at the rail, waving to Wesley. His chest tightened as jealousy washed over him. Why couldn't she see that he was truly the better man?

A uniformed officer passed, and Jason called out to him. "I wonder, my good man, could you direct me to the radio office? I'd like to speak to the operator."

"Of course. I'll take you down right now, if you like."

"That would be wonderful," Jason said with a nod. With any luck, he'd manage to steer the operator to deliver all telegrams to him—no matter whom they were addressed to. Jason had a list of all the room numbers in his coat pocket, and soon the radio operator would as well. Any messages that made their way to the ship would pass through him first. If they were from Montana or Wesley, they would meet with a convenient demise. He couldn't have something so trivial interfering with his plans.

Then, once they were in England, he would see to it that all telegrams and letters that came to his father's estate passed through his hands in a similar manner. That way, when Wesley realized he'd been duped and sent Lizzy a telegram or letter, as he would no doubt do, Jason would be able to get rid of that as well.

"Here we are, sir," the officer declared.

Jason looked at the sign on the door. *Radio Room.* He smiled. "Thank you ever so much."

ELEVEN

H ave you ever seen the likes, Lizzy?" Mary asked, looking in wonder at all the finery hanging in her wardrobe. "Jason must have felt we were all too poorly dressed to hobnob in his society."

"I'm stunned," Lizzy admitted. "He mentioned purchasing a few things for us, but I didn't expect to find an entire new wardrobe."

"It's not just the clothes," Ella threw in. "He's purchased shoes and purses, as well as paste jewelry to go with our new outfits."

"I hardly see how that's saving the show money." Mary fingered through the new outfits, shaking her head. "But the clothes are beautiful. I must admit he has good taste."

"Still, it's hardly proper for him to arrange all of this," Lizzy stated.

"The rooms alone must have cost a fortune," Ella mused. "I remember my father saying something similar when he took us abroad. Goodness, I can't even imagine the money that has been spent for us to have such lovely staterooms." She crossed the suite to one of the closed doors. Opening it, she peered inside. "It's a bedroom, and there are two large beds."

Lizzy walked to the opposite side of the suite and opened the door. "The same here," she called.

"I imagine Debbie, Gertie, and Jessie's cabin is like ours, and Jason mentioned Alice and Carson have a suite to themselves." Ella ran her hand along the back of a chaise lounge.

"I heard my uncle say that the magazine arranged for Chris, while he, Jason, and Phillip are sharing something similar to what we have here. I suppose they meant for Wesley to be in the same suite." She sighed. "I'm going to miss him so much. I can't tell you what a disappointment it is that he won't be with us."

Ella's expression saddened. "I was sorry about that too. I know how much you were looking forward to seeing London with him."

"You can spend your time with us so as to avoid Jason." Mary began to remove her costume jewelry. "No doubt Jason is delighted to have Wesley gone."

"No doubt," Ella replied. "I don't understand the games men play. I would think chasing after someone who has no interest in you would be exhausting and self-defeating."

"Still," Lizzy countered, "the heart often desires what it shouldn't. I fell in love with Wesley long before he fell in love with me. He was even married to someone else for part of that time. I did everything in my power to bury my feelings for him. I didn't want to sin against God by being so desperately in love with a married man."

"Yes, but your love for Wesley was there long before he married another. And furthermore, you handled yourself admirably. All the time I saw you two working together during his married years, you did nothing to be ashamed of."

Lizzy plopped down on the lounge. "I used to pray and pray that God would take away my feelings for Wes. I'm certainly glad He didn't."

Mary yawned. "I don't know about either of you, but I'm completely worn out. We've been busy all day, and now it's nearly midnight."

A knock sounded on the door to the suite, and Lizzy went to answer it. When she opened the door, two uniformed maids curtsied. "Mr. Adler sent us."

Lizzy shrugged. "For what purpose?"

The girls exchanged a look of confusion. "Why . . . for the purpose," the taller one began, "of seeing to your needs. We'll be your maids during the crossing."

Ella and Mary joined Lizzy at the door. "It seems Jason has arranged for us to have two lady's maids," Lizzy explained.

"Somehow that doesn't surprise me." Mary looked at the two women. "I suppose we should let them come in and help us rather than keep them out in the hallway."

Lizzy nodded and stepped back. "Come in."

The two young women stepped inside. "We will ready you and your rooms and turn down the beds. The ship will sail soon, but you will no doubt be fast asleep before that happens," the tall woman declared. "I'm Sarah, and this is Miriam."

"I'm Elizabeth Brookstone, but you can call me Lizzy."

"Oh, no. That wouldn't be acceptable. We'll call you Miss Brookstone," Sarah replied, giving a curtsy that Miriam quickly mimicked. They looked to Mary.

"Ah . . . I'm Mary Reichert."

"Miss Reichert." They both bobbed again.

"And I'm Ella Fleming," the petite blonde declared.

"Miss Fleming." They curtsied one final time. "We are very happy to make your acquaintance and will endeavor to see that your every need is met." Again this came from Sarah, who was clearly in charge. "Would you care for a bath this evening before retiring?"

Lizzy shook her head. "No. I'd fall asleep in the tub. I'm happy just to wash up. If you can bring a basin of hot water and some soap, I'll be just fine."

Mary nodded. "That goes for me as well. A hot bath sounds wonderful, but perhaps tomorrow."

"Very good." Sarah turned to Ella. "And for you?"

"The same." Ella covered her mouth to hide a yawn.

"We will return shortly with all that you need. Please feel free to relax until then. If you have no objection, we will use our own key to enter and exit."

Lizzy spoke for the trio. "I'm sure that's fine." She looked to Mary and Ella for their approval. They nodded.

The two maids left the room, and Mary turned to Lizzy. "I didn't expect to be waited on hand and foot. This has turned into quite a grand affair for this little ol' Kansas farm girl."

Ella giggled.

Lizzy shook her head. "It's a bit overwhelming for this Montana ranch girl too. I'm going to bed as soon as possible, and I intend to sleep late." She sighed. "I sure hope Wesley doesn't have any trouble getting home."

Mary hugged her. "I'm sure he'll be just fine. Try not to worry."

An hour later, Mary stretched out in the luxurious bed. She couldn't remember ever having slept in such a sumptuous bed. The mattress seemed to wrap itself around her as if hugging her close. She sighed. They would be a week at sea, and she could get used to all this finery.

She thought back to her dinner with Chris. She felt they had gotten their relationship back to an even and comfortable place. She didn't understand why he felt he couldn't speak about his family and whatever it was that shamed him so deeply. Or worse still—what frightened him so much about having friends.

Lord, I know my faith in You is growing, because I feel Your peace about this. Please just give me wisdom to do the right thing.

She thought of Lizzy and how she was always saying that there was nothing too small or too great for God to care about. Mary also remembered many a time in Sunday school when her teachers had said that even the prayers of a child were heard by God.

A small sigh escaped her. *Lord, I put my trust in You. I know that You love me and that You love Chris too. Please help him see that I care about him and want to help him in any way I can. Amen.*

She felt she'd barely closed her eyes when a knock sounded on the bedroom door and Miriam appeared to bid her and Ella good morning. The shapely redhead went to the windows and pulled open the drapes.

"Mr. Brookstone and Mr. Adler ask that you ladies join them for breakfast. They will come for you in one hour."

Mary yawned and sat up. She felt the rocking of the ship and wondered suddenly if she might be one of those unfortunate people who suffered from seasickness. Thankfully she felt perfectly fine. From the other bed, however, Ella gave a deep moan. Perhaps she wasn't as lucky.

"Are you all right?" Mary got to her feet and moved to Ella's side.

The blonde lay curled up on her side. "No. I'm absolutely green. Sea travel has never agreed with me, but I was hoping I'd outgrown it."

"I'll bring some broth for you, Miss Fleming," Miriam promised. "You just stay in bed. You'll be right as rain soon enough."

"I'll explain to Oliver and Jason what's happened." Mary gave her friend a sympathetic smile. "Just rest."

Another moan was all that Ella managed.

"What would you care to wear today, Miss Reichert?" Miriam asked as Mary made her way into the sitting room.

"I hardly know. The wardrobe you will find is all new to me.

You probably know better than I do. Pick out something appropriate, and I shall be content."

Miriam went to the wardrobe and opened it. After a few moments she pulled out a suit that sported a dove-colored skirt and coat trimmed in dark lilac cording. "This should serve you well for the morning." She hung the ensemble on a wardrobe stand, then fished through the drawers to find the appropriate undergarments.

Mary was impressed by how efficient Miriam was in her work. In no time at all, the redhead had brushed Mary's long brown tresses into a fashionable coiffure suitable for a princess. She was just securing the final touch—a cameo at the base of Mary's throat, when Lizzy emerged from her room fully dressed and ready for the day.

"Just look at you," Lizzy declared. "Aren't you beautiful."

"I could say the same for you. That is a lovely shade of blue—almost robin's egg." Mary stood once Miriam completed pinning the cameo in place. She gave a whirl. "And this fits like it was made for me."

"It probably was. Knowing how much attention Jason gives to detail, he probably got all the measurements from Agnes before sending her home." Lizzy went to view herself in the cheval mirror. "Goodness, but I can't imagine what Mother or Wes would say if they saw me like this."

"They'd say you were beautiful." Mary came to stand beside her. "We're both quite elegant."

Lizzy frowned. "A bit overdressed for breakfast, wouldn't you say?"

"Not at all, Miss Brookstone," Miriam declared. "You will be quite content when you view the other dining room passengers."

"That's exactly what Sarah told me," Lizzy replied. She smoothed the lace inset of the bodice. A knock sounded at the door to the cabin, and Lizzy shrugged. "I suppose we shall soon see for ourselves."

Miriam answered the door and gave a curtsy. Jason Adler and Oliver Brookstone stood smiling in the hallway.

"Come in, Uncle," Lizzy said, giving a twirl. "Come see what your money has bought us."

He chuckled and looked from Lizzy to Mary. "Jason assured me this was money well spent, and I can't agree more." He went to Lizzy and kissed her cheek. "You look like one of those dainty cakes we had with tea the other day."

Lizzy laughed and gave him a hug. "I thought as much myself."

"You're both lovely," Jason said with a smile. "You should always be dressed so beautifully."

Mary watched him as he kept his gaze on Lizzy. She wondered how far he would go to win Lizzy away from Wes. She didn't trust him. Not because he was a bad person, but because his interest in Lizzy clearly blinded him to much of anything else.

"Where's Ella?" Oliver asked, glancing around the room. "Surely she's not going to keep us waiting."

"She's ill," Mary offered. She hadn't had a chance to tell Lizzy yet. "Seasick," she added at Lizzy's questioning look.

"Pity. Well, I daresay they know how to deal with such matters on the ship," Jason assured them. "I'll make certain they take good care of her. Now, however, we should head to our private dining room."

"Are the others joining us?" Lizzy asked.

"Mr. Williams will be, but otherwise we thought a more intimate meal would be nice," Jason replied. "The rest of your troupe will be cared for in the main dining room. Now, why don't you let me escort you?"

Mary slipped in front of Lizzy and took Jason's arm. "I'm happy to let you lead the way. We wouldn't want to keep Mr. Williams waiting, and I, for one, am famished." She smiled up at him. They both knew what she was doing.

Lizzy took her uncle's arm. "That leaves us," she said sweetly. "I hope you don't mind."

"Mind having one of the prettiest gals on my arm for all the world to see?" her uncle replied. "Why, I'm honored." They led the way from the cabin.

Mary looked to Jason. "Well?"

He nodded, but Mary could see he wasn't pleased. She hoped he wouldn't be further insulted, but she felt it necessary to state her thoughts. "You know, I am making it one of my tasks to look after Lizzy for Wes. I don't intend to be parted from her."

For several long moments, Jason said nothing. Mary thought about adding on to what she'd already declared, but it seemed unneeded. Jason was smart.

"I find your devotion both charming and unnecessary. You will all be well looked after on this journey. I assure you my father wants only the best for each of you and was willing to pay out of his own pocket in order to see to each person's comfort and well-being on the ship."

They arrived at a private saloon and were ushered in with great formality. Two uniformed stewards seated Mary and Lizzy while Chris joined the other gentlemen.

"I thought perhaps I'd misunderstood your directions," Chris explained. "I must say, you ladies are quite the spectacle. You brighten the day."

"Thanks to my uncle and Jason, we have an entirely new wardrobe," Lizzy declared. "In fact, I've seen nothing of my other clothing."

"It's safely packed in storage," Jason assured her. "You'll have everything returned to you when we reach my father's estate."

"Personally, I was glad for a new suit," Oliver said, patting Chris on the back. "How did you sleep?"

"Quite well, thank you." Chris looked at Mary. "I hope you passed the night as well."

"I did. I've never slept in anything quite as plush as that bed," Mary admitted. "I found it hard to leave this morning."

Chris chuckled and took the chair on her right, while Jason took a seat to Lizzy's right and Oliver chose her left. The table had been elegantly prepared for six, which begged Oliver's explanation of Ella's illness.

"I'm sure she'll be able to join us soon," he said. "Hopefully for supper."

"I hope so," Chris replied.

Breakfast was a veritable feast, and before Mary could scarcely approve or disapprove one dish, a servant appeared with another. By the time the staff had made their rounds, Mary had eaten grilled codfish fillets in parsley butter, basted eggs, steamed figs in syrup, and hot croissants. It was unlike any breakfast she'd ever had in Kansas.

The conversation was casual and refreshing. Jason kept to the topic of London and his father's estate, while the others marveled at the ship's furnishings and food. Mary was glad to have Chris at her side.

"Our estate is just outside London," Jason explained, "but we also have a flat in town. Part of the time we'll stay at the apartments in London to avoid the trip back and forth, but when there is more than a day's rest between acts, we will be at the estate. It's much more relaxing there, and I think you'll agree that rest is important."

"Of course," Oliver agreed.

"Where will the horses be kept?" Lizzy asked.

Jason gave her a warm smile. "We have arranged beautiful stalls at Earls Court. I think you'll be very pleased. There is also a large park not far away where they can be exercised, as well as the exhibition hall itself, if the weather is bad."

Lizzy picked up a knife to butter her toast. "I'll want to be near them."

"My father will no doubt have arranged everything perfectly, so you needn't worry," Jason replied.

The conversation continued, but Mary was far more interested in Chris than anything Jason had to say. While the others were caught up in the details of the country estate, Mary leaned closer to Chris.

"I wondered if maybe later you would be willing to explore the ship with me," she said in a whisper.

He gave her a casual smile, only the left side of his lips rising. It made him look so appealing, and Mary felt her heart skip a beat.

"I'd be honored, Mary. I find ships fascinating."

"I sometimes wonder what it would have been like aboard one of the great clipper ships with all those sails," Mary admitted. "Having grown up landlocked, I rarely heard anything about ocean travel and ships. But once, when we were performing in Boston, I saw a large clipper ship in the harbor. She was just setting sail, and it was one of the most amazing things I've ever seen."

"I can imagine," Chris replied, smiling. He seemed more like his old self. "I've been on smaller sailing ships, but never the truly great clippers."

"I'm not sure you heard me, Mary and Chris," Jason interrupted, "but I was just telling the others that there will be a welcoming party at my father's estate on our first night there. He's invited all of his important friends. Some are noblemen and others are politically connected. All will be useful to us, especially in planning for next year."

"I suppose that's why you bought us all those fancy clothes." Mary fixed Jason with a smile. "And they are lovely."

"We felt you deserved them," Oliver interjected. "We want to impress London's society, after all."

"I'm sure their performance will go much further toward impressing than will their outfits," Chris countered. "After all, you can put an expensive dress on any woman, but these ladies are able to do things that few others can even dream of." He gave Mary a wink, then refocused on his breakfast.

"I agree," Jason said, looking put out by Chris's comment. "But what one wears is important in my society. I wouldn't want any of our beautiful ladies embarrassed."

"Nor would *you* want to be embarrassed," Mary said, smiling. "I'm sure that's even more important, since London is your town."

Jason was clearly uncomfortable with the way the conversation had gone. He fell silent, and gradually the topic turned to the horses and Lizzy's concerns for them while traveling by sea.

"I would like to check on them after breakfast," she declared.

"That would hardly be appropriate," Jason said, shaking his head. "Mr. DeShazer and Mr. Hopkins will be able to see to them and let you know if they are distressed."

Lizzy nodded. "I'm sure that's true, but I still intend to check on them myself."

Mary almost laughed at the look on Jason's face, but she didn't want to cause a bigger scene. It was gratifying enough to see Lizzy put him in his place.

"Are you enjoying ocean travel?" Chris asked as he escorted Mary around the sun deck.

"I'm fascinated by it," she admitted. "I find even the uncertainty of my steps captivating. It reminds me of watching a drunk man try to navigate from room to room." She giggled. "I have to admit, I'm grateful for the railing when things get rough."

Chris chuckled. "I promise to be here as well. I can't have you falling all over the deck, now, can I?"

Mary stopped and turned to face him. "I'm here for you as well. I hope you realize there's nothing you can't talk to me about."

He frowned. "Why do you suppose I need to talk about something?"

"Well, you said the past troubles you and that you can't talk about some of those things."

"Exactly. I can't talk about them." His tone grew reserved. "Shall we continue our walk?"

Mary realized the matter was closed to discussion, but she'd never been easily deterred. She'd find a way to get him to trust her. Maybe the simplest would be to ignore his offense and just talk about herself. Sooner or later he'd have no choice but to join in.

"When I was a little girl, I used to climb up into the barn's loft. There was a big door up there through which Opa hauled hay bales with a pulley. He'd hook the bales onto the pulley by the wire and then hoist them up with a rope by hand, and someone would be up there to pull them inside and stack them for the winter. I used to climb up there and pretend I was on a big ship looking out at the ocean, and when the wheat was thick and tall, I could almost pretend it was water waving in the wind." She turned her gaze back to the ocean. "Of course, the two look very different, but as a little girl, I didn't know any better."

"It sounds like you had a very creative imagination." His words were still clipped and edgy.

"I did. Of course, my father helped with that. When he came home from traveling with the wild west show, he was always full of stories to entertain August and me. Kate was too little to appreciate his stories." She moved along the rail with the fall and rise of the ocean. She had what Sarah the maid said were her "sea legs" and found the fresh salt air invigorating. "I suppose since father was participating in a show that re-created so many imaginative things, it was easy for him to re-create it for us. Sometimes he pretended to be a cavalryman, and other times he was a buffalo hunter on the plains. He had some really good friends among the Indians in the show. I even met a few of them."

"I did too, as you might recall. I probably even met your father."

"No, he died in 1885. You were no doubt living with your grandmother in London then."

"Yes."

Chris didn't bother to elaborate, and Mary knew it was sense-less to press for more. He had buried his past deep. He had hidden it away and covered it with years of pain and sorrow and had no intention of ever allowing it to see the light of day again.

"I'm glad for my memories of my father. You see, I don't remember much of anything about my mother. Sometimes I catch a whiff of a scent and it makes me think of her, so I have to wonder if she wore that scent." Mary stopped as they reached the place where they'd started, and braved the question. "Do you remember your mother?"

"Some. She was very loving and very gentle." He stopped abruptly, as if he'd said too much.

Mary saved him the need to once again make clear that the past wasn't up for discussion. "Well, thank you for walking with me. I had no idea this ship was so big. I think I'll go take a rest now before lunch."

It was the hardest thing in the world to walk away. She wanted nothing more than to stay and demand answers . . . or at least coax them. How was she supposed to earn his trust and confidence when he was determined never to give them?

<hr />

Eight days later, the troupe was luxuriously settled on the Adler estate just outside of London. Lizzy had to admit that much attention had been given to each person's needs and no one could find the slightest thing to complain about.

"I'm sorry we don't have an indoor arena," Jason offered as they stood talking to the Adler's party guests.

Lizzy gave a gracious smile. "It's unimportant. You've provided so much that I couldn't possibly ask for more."

An older woman put a lorgnette to her eyes and gave Lizzy a once-over. "I am told you do tricks on horseback."

"Yes. I am a trick rider. I have been since I was a little girl."

"I say, that must have worried your parents considerably."

Lizzy chuckled. "No, not exactly. My father was my teacher."

"The entire Brookstone family is involved in wild west shows," Jason offered. "Very talented people. Now, if you'll excuse us, I must introduce Miss Brookstone to my uncle."

He took hold of Lizzy possessively and led her across the room to where a much older man stood arguing with Jason's father, Henry Adler.

"Marcus, you won't convince me to give you any more money, so don't embarrass yourself by asking," Mr. Adler was saying.

Lizzy pretended she hadn't heard a word. "Mr. Adler, thank you for the lovely party."

Jason didn't give his father time to respond. "Uncle Marcus, I want you to meet Miss Brookstone, the star performer of the Brookstone Wild West Extravaganza. She's become quite special to me."

The older man with muttonchop whiskers and dull blue eyes looked at her as if she were something he'd picked up on the bottom of his shoes. "We were having a rather important conversation," he replied, finally fixing his gaze on Jason. "If you'll excuse us." He took Henry Adler's arm and pulled him toward the door of an adjoining room.

"I must apologize. My uncle can be quite rude. He's no doubt trying to entice my father into loaning him money."

Lizzy shook her head. "But he's an earl. Surely he must be rich."

Jason laughed. "You will learn that there are many titled people in this room who have less money than your family. A lot less. Having a title doesn't guarantee having money. My uncle married well enough, but the earldom was already impoverished, and a great deal of money went into making improvements to the estate. Especially the house."

Lizzy let him walk her out into the gardens, where lights had been strewn and a small group of musicians played in contrast to those performing in the house.

"My father always knew he'd have to marry into money and help restore the family fortune before he could focus on making his own."

"That must have been hard for him. I mean, finding a way to make a great deal of money is hard enough, but having then to turn it over to your father or brother rather than benefit your own dreams . . . Well, I would think it could make a person bitter."

"It was expected of him, and he knew that from a young age. He knew he needed to marry a woman with a lot of money, and here in England that wasn't likely, since he couldn't return the favor in kind and give his wife a titled position."

"So he went wife hunting in America," Lizzy stated rather than questioned. "And married for money rather than love."

"He did exactly that, but love grew. My father and mother are happily matched, and Father has been far more successful than any of my uncles."

"That must be especially hard on your uncle who inherited the title."

"People come to Uncle Marcus all the time, asking him to invest in one thing or another. Because of the way the family has managed things, people naturally presume he is successfully wealthy, but nothing could be further from the truth. He doesn't understand the first thing about . . . well, much of anything. Father had to advise him regarding the estate and how to modernize it and make it beneficial to the family. Father had to explain to him about the proper investments and what would be good for the future and what was no longer wise to hold on to. Of course, in this country, it's normal to hold on to the past."

Lizzy nodded, grateful that the conversation was about his family rather than his feelings for her. But she had come out here with him in the hope of convincing him to stop his attempts to woo her away from Wesley. She wasn't at all sure, however, how to bring up the matter without having to deal with his adoration.

Still trying to figure that out, Lizzy posed what she hoped was a neutral question. "Are your father and uncle otherwise close?"

Jason frowned. "What do you mean?"

"Well, my uncle and father were the best of friends. We all lived together in Montana, and Uncle Oliver is like a second father to me. Are your father and his brothers close like that, or is this issue of money the only thing that brings them together?"

"Ah, yes." Jason nodded. "Mostly it's the money. My grandfather was a cold and indifferent man. He sent all his boys to different boarding schools. Didn't want them together, lest they conspire against him."

"How terrible. That's no way to have a family."

"I'm afraid my grandfather wasn't all that concerned with family. The name and the estate were what mattered. His standing with his peers and the royal house were far more important than whether his family loved him—or each other, for that matter."

"So you're not close to any of them?" How very sad it would be to grow up without the love of family.

"Not really. I'm not even that close to my sisters."

"Sisters? I didn't know you had sisters."

"I'm the eldest of four children and the only son. My sisters are married and live in various places. As my father's only son, it is his deepest desire that I follow in his footsteps and continue to expand his fortune. And since it's his fortune I will one day inherit, I am motivated to do as he wishes."

"So making more money is what he wishes of you?"

"That and settling down with the proper wife." He stepped closer and took her gloved hand.

Lizzy pulled her hand away. "I would remind you that I'm engaged to Wesley."

"But that doesn't mean I might not have a chance to win you for myself. You aren't yet married, and many a woman realizes she is improperly matched before she takes her vows. That could be said for you."

She shook her head. So much for worrying about how to introduce the topic. "No. It can't be said for me, because it isn't true. I've loved Wes for a very long time, and while I admire you, I do not love you."

Several other partygoers strolled through the gardens. They murmured *hello* and moved on before Jason continued.

"Lizzy, you haven't even given me a chance. Let me try to convince you. Spend time with me and let me escort you around London. I know I can make you love me."

She frowned. "Why would anyone want a love that had to be forced? I'm sorry, Jason, but I can't betray Wes. My love for him runs too deep. He's as much a part of me as the air I breathe."

"I think you're afraid to know the truth," Jason countered. "You've never even attempted to fall in love with another. I think you're afraid of what that outcome might be."

Lizzy looked at him for a moment. She could see that he was fully convinced he was right. "You're entitled to your opinion, Jason, but you are very wrong. You see, Wesley was married once before, and as a Christian woman, I knew that I had to let go of my love for him. Since I couldn't be a good Christian and covet another woman's husband, I did what I could to turn my attentions elsewhere, but no one interested me."

"You hadn't yet met me. I believe we're destined to be together. Perhaps since you're so certain that God ordains every step you take, you could say that He hadn't yet brought us together, and so He was saving you for me."

"I could say that, but it wouldn't be true. When Wesley was married, I focused on anything and everything else in order to be free of my feelings for him. I learned more daring tricks and sought more adventurous routines. I threw myself into working, and in doing so, I got very good at what I do. However, my father and mother knew I was heartbroken and did their best to counsel me as I sought to get beyond my love for Wes. The thing was, I couldn't get beyond it, and I believe that is because *we* were destined to be together."

"But he was in love with another."

"No. He married only because she was in need and he felt sorry for her. She might have met with a terrible fate had Wesley not stepped in to help her. And while I don't think a person should marry for anything less than love, I admire what he did. It makes me love him all the more."

Jason looked as if he might say something, but then he shook his head. She could see how much she'd hurt him, but lying and giving false hope would have been crueler.

"Now, if you'll excuse me, you have a party to help with, and I want to be alone for a bit." Without another word, she walked away and headed from the gardens toward the stables. Despite wearing a gown that no doubt cost a small fortune, Lizzy knew she'd feel better once she was with her horses. She could only hope and pray Jason didn't follow her.

Lizzy hadn't quite reached the stables when she heard Ella arguing with someone. Lizzy went in search of the younger woman and found her trying to drag Phillip toward the servants' quarters.

"What's going on, Ella? Phillip?"

The twosome stopped, and Phillip straightened and grinned. "Evenin', Miss Lizzy."

The scene was almost comical. Ella stood a head shorter than Phillip. She was dressed beautifully in a pale green gown trimmed in pink rosettes. Her hair was done up high atop her head, and she was adorned with costume jewelry and full-length gloves. Phillip, on the other hand, was dressed to work with the horses.

"I asked what was going on," Lizzy repeated.

"It's nothing," Ella assured her. "Phillip isn't feeling well and I was helping him back to the servants' quarters so he could rest."

"Are you sick, Phillip?" Lizzy's concern grew as she approached them.

"I'm jussss' fine." He wobbled a bit before patting Ella on the shoulder. "Ella's ssso pretty. Don't cha think?"

"You're drunk, aren't you?" But Lizzy didn't need his reply to know the truth. She sighed. "You promised Wesley that you wouldn't drink. What in the world is wrong with you? Can't you keep your word for even a few weeks?"

Phillip frowned. "Sorry, Lizzy. Some—some fellasssss . . . gave me a bottle and . . . well, isssa party."

Lizzy shook her head. "Let me help you, Ella. We'd better get him to bed before Uncle Oliver sees him. Otherwise he'll probably want to join in and have a drink as well."

She put her arm around Phillip's waist while Ella did likewise on his other side. Together they helped him to the door of the servants' quarters. To their surprise, one of the Adler footmen appeared. He eyed Phillip with contempt but straightened and gave Lizzy a nod.

"Can you see that he gets to bed safely?" Lizzy asked.

"Of course, ma'am." He grasped Phillip by the shoulder. "Good evening, ma'am." He closed the door as soon as Phillip was inside.

"Well, that was quite the ordeal."

Ella nodded. "I found him drinking in the garden and figured it would be best to get him out of sight. I didn't want him embarrassing the Adlers or you."

"That was kind of you, but you needn't worry. I have a feeling just our presence here is enough of an embarrassment." Lizzy put her arm around Ella. "I know this is probably more in keeping with the life you've known, but I'd just as soon be back in Montana, riding with the wind in my hair, instead of fending off Jason's lovesick proposals."

"It's too bad Wesley isn't here," Ella murmured.

"Yes." Lizzy gazed across the gardens. "It is too bad he's not here. Both for my sake and yours. If he were here, Phillip would know better than to get carried away with alcohol and Jason would know better than to try to court me. We'd neither one have to worry about what was coming next."

·✦= TWELVE =✦·

T o Mary's surprise, Henry Adler arranged for a highly publicized shooting contest to begin days before their first London performance. He also arranged for a very large cash prize. Each man who wanted to be a part of the competition had to pay to enter, but the fee was minimal, so the crowds were large.

Most of the men were only fair at shooting. In England it was the gentry who owned guns. The poorer common folk who were attracted to the large purse didn't generally possess firearms, much less have time and extra ammunition to practice. Henry Adler took that into consideration and made both guns and ammunition available for the preliminary rounds. If necessary, he pledged to furnish the same if a man advanced through the competition but had no rifle. In the first day alone, four hundred men were eliminated from the competition.

Each day Mary was present while the men were put into groups and various targets and goals were presented. She was something like the queen of the festivities. Jason Adler and Oliver Brookstone paraded her around to encourage and entice the men to compete. By the end of the competition, with the numbers narrowed down to five men who were quite proficient with their rifles, Mary was anxious just to be done with it all.

"You look tired, Mary," Chris said, joining her as she sat watching the final five men vie for top position.

"I am. I'm weary of this affair. Some of those poor boys in the early rounds could hardly sight the target, much less hope to shoot a bull's-eye. These final contestants at least know how to handle their rifles."

"They're from a wealthier set. I interviewed them, and two are even in line to inherit titles. Something like this is a novelty to them and no doubt an embarrassment to their parents. They've probably gotten involved just to poke fun at their station and the rules that come with it."

"Well, I'll be glad when it's done. I imagine all these people who've come out to watch will be glad too."

A man across the way gave a wave.

Mary narrowed her eyes. "Who's that waving?"

Chris glanced in the same direction. "Looks like a man I used to know. If you'll excuse me, I'll go see what he wants."

Mary knew Chris had grown up in London, but since their arrival, he'd said nothing about his time there. He didn't talk about friends he'd known or even about the grandmother who'd raised him. At least he wasn't sullen, as he had been in America, but he was still guarded. She had hoped to entice him to at least take her around the city and point out things that played a role in his youth. She thought he might even find it a good compromise to their situation, since he had been happy living with his grandmother. But the opportunity never seemed to arise. Adler kept her much too busy, and Chris was caught up in his own work.

"Well, what do you think of our final contestants?" Oliver Brookstone asked, taking the chair beside Mary.

"I have to admit they seem capable of giving me a run for the win."

Oliver chuckled. "I doubt they'll be able to stand up to you. Your beauty alone will have them flustered. It's always been that way. I'll expect you to sally up to each one and endear yourself to them in such a way that they'll be more concentrated on you than the target."

"That seems rather unfair, Oliver."

"Nonsense. A man has to be able to shoot under any and all circumstances. A woman too. Would you allow a handsome fellow to distract you from your shooting?"

"No, I suppose not."

"Exactly," he replied with a grin.

"How old were you when you first began to shoot, Oliver?"

"I was just a boy. Four, I believe. My father had a very small .22 rifle that he used to show both Mark and me how to shoot. We loved it from the start, but I was never as good as you."

"Chris has never shot a gun," Mary said without thinking. "I started to show him, but it just didn't come together. Maybe while we're here I can teach him something."

"Perhaps. Of course, a fella's got to want to learn. In this modern age, learning to shoot is no longer the necessity it once was. I think a great many people are relieved not to have to shed blood to support their families."

"So much is changing. August used to say that soon people would no longer ride horses for transportation. He said the new automobiles were bound to get bigger and better, and people would see it was much easier to use a machine than an animal."

"I suppose he made a good point, but I'd much rather trust a horse to see me through in minus-forty degrees back home than a machine." Oliver shook his head. "Of course—and you aren't allowed to repeat this—I'm finding I prefer city life."

"City life? Truly?" Mary was surprised by this. She had often heard Lizzy say that Oliver had little interest in the running of the ranch, but she'd never mentioned him wanting to leave it.

"It's easier in the city. You want something, you pick up the phone and call for it. Or you walk down the block and get it. Or send someone else for it." Oliver rubbed his hands together. "When you get older, you'll understand the charm of that. Now, where is that young man of yours?"

Mary felt her cheeks flush. "Chris is hardly my young man."

Oliver laughed. "Maybe not, but you knew exactly who I meant."

He had her there. "Well, he was here a moment ago, but then someone caught his attention and he went to speak to him."

"Perhaps it's about an article in the paper. I heard some representatives from *The Times* would be here."

Mary nodded. She hadn't considered that possibility. "You may be right. He did seem all business about it. I'm glad Chris has been able to write about the show. He tells me it will definitely bolster sales next year."

"I hope so. We've enjoyed a hefty profit this year, but there was the added expense of coming to England. A series of magazine articles enticing people to come see the show might well secure us for a while. Jason already has the schedule lined up for next year. Isn't that something?"

"It is. I suppose someone like him would know the best way to go about it. Still, you mustn't be hard on yourself. As we were saying, times have definitely changed with the turn of the century. People and their interests have evolved, and even the way of doing things is moving at a much faster pace."

"Indeed. Still, I think there's something to be said about the past. I think folks in the city are attracted to this connection to times long forgotten, even if they want the modern amenities and comforts. Added to that are the risks being taken and the thrill of it all, and I'm hopeful that the show will go on for years to come. At least so long as I go on."

Mary turned to look at the older man. "Why do you say that?"

He shrugged. "The show is my life. It's what I love. The ranch has never interested me the way it did my brother. Life there is hard and isolated. I prefer the city, and I need the thrill of the crowd—the audience's enthusiasm. I suppose I'm just a performer at heart."

"We all have our passions."

"What of you, my lovely Mary? Are you still passionate about shooting? Will you stay with us?"

She frowned and looked back at the men on the field. "I don't know. Losing August took a great deal from me. He might still be alive but for the show and his participation in it. I'd hoped that by coming along I would be able to seek justice for him, as well as deal with his death. Lizzy keeps telling me to take it back to God, but I don't know that God is listening."

"I can understand that. I don't know that He's listening to me either."

Mary nodded. "Lizzy told me maybe it was more important that I listen for Him. So I'm trying. I'm reading my Bible each night and trying to listen for Him to speak, to tell me what I need to do to let go of the past and embrace the future."

"I must say that sounds like the wisest of solutions."

Mary smiled and shrugged. "I hope so. I truly want to know the answer. Sometimes I feel so lost, so sad. I think Chris feels much the same, which is why I find myself intrigued by him."

"He does appear to bear a heavy burden," Oliver admitted. "Do you have any idea what it is?"

"Some. It's mostly to do with his family and the past. So we have that in common to a degree. But he isn't inclined to speak about it. I know he needs a stronger faith in God. He's said as much. I think he was speaking with Wes about God, but now there's no one to talk to." She straightened. "Maybe you could share with him, Oliver. You've long had faith in God, and you know more about such things than I do."

Oliver's expression grew sad. "I'm afraid I'm a big disappointment to the Lord. I've failed more times than succeeded in doing what He wanted me to do."

"So . . . does God reject us after we fail a certain number of times?" She asked the question in all sincerity.

"Of course not. I didn't mean it that way." Oliver shifted uncomfortably. "I just mean . . . well, I think when a person ignores God and does as he pleases, God turns him over to his own devices."

"And never has anything to do with him again?"

"No . . . not exactly. God is infinitely patient with us, and I suppose because He is love and He loves us that He forgives us our sins over and over." Oliver shook his head and gave a chuckle. "You have a way of convicting me, Mary, without even realizing it."

She laughed. "That wasn't my intention, but perhaps it is God's."

"Out of the mouths of babes," he murmured and got to his feet. "I don't believe I'm the man to help Chris, but I will keep it in mind, and should the moment present itself, perhaps God will also give me the words."

Mary nodded. "Maybe He'll give us both the words."

<hr />

"Ladies and gentlemen, this is the moment we've all waited for," Oliver announced to a large audience. "Mary Reichert has never been bested in these competitions, but then again, she has never competed against Englishmen."

The crowd's applause was more subdued than what they had from American audiences. Jason and Henry Adler had warned the Brookstone performers of this, however, so Oliver took it in stride.

"Our winning finalist from the competition is Henry Sanbourne. Mr. Sanbourne will now compete against Mary in shooting glass orbs from the sky. One by one the orbs will be catapulted into the air. The first one to miss is the loser. Now I will introduce you to our fair Mary. Mary hails from the small farm state of Kansas. I know a lady doesn't usually reveal her age, but our Mary doesn't care. She's twenty-five, and I tell you that because she's been shooting competitively for over fifteen years, either at county fairs or with our show."

There were some exclamations at this announcement. Mary stood just out of sight, dressed regally in one of her formal costumes. It was funny how the outfits created for the show were so much roomier in the shoulders and arms than the clothes Jason had arranged for her. Why a woman wouldn't demand the more maneuverable gowns for everyday wear was beyond her.

"So without further ado, may I introduce you to the one . . . the only . . . Brookstone's Wild West Extravaganza's Mary Reichert!"

The audience applauded, and Mary entered the arena. She waved and blew kisses. When she reached the competition area, she paused and unfastened the frogs that held her cloak closed. She let the cloak fall to the ground to reveal a beautiful yellow gown trimmed in black velvet piping and lace. At her throat was a choker of rhinestones, and matching earrings dangled from her earlobes. A household maid had done Mary's hair up in a fanciful weave of curls with a few well-placed rhinestones to give her even more sparkle.

"Mr. Sanbourne," she said, turning to the gentleman who stood at the end of the table. "Are you ready to compete against me?"

He gave her a once-over and smiled in a leering manner. "I can think of a dozen things I'd like to do with you, and none of them involve any form of competition."

She was used to men who tried to break her concentration

with either idle talk of love or lewdness. She gave him a smile. "Well, I can only think of how embarrassing it's going to be when your friends tease you because a woman bested you at shooting."

He cocked a brow. "I say, you haven't bested me at anything."

"Not yet. But it's just a matter of a few glass orbs. Shall we get to it?"

She saw the flicker of hesitation in his eyes and knew that his false bravado was failing him.

Oliver called for silence and then ordered the crew to prepare for the first throw. Mary went first and blasted the glass ball to pieces without much effort. Henry went next, and although he only grazed the side of the ball, it too burst and allowed him to move on to the next round. The competition continued with one ball after another. In America, Mary had never had a competition go past fifteen orbs, but after twenty balls had been released and shot, she could only wonder how long this would continue.

Around their twenty-fifth ball, she spied Chris standing in the corner of the arena, speaking to someone. Perhaps it was *The Times* man. Chris seemed chatty enough and didn't appear at all uncomfortable. Perhaps the man was even an old friend. With any luck at all, maybe Chris would introduce her.

The next shot was hers to take, and Mary found herself thinking of Chris and nearly missed her mark. She knew she needed to focus, but she couldn't help but wish she knew what was going on with Chris. She cared about him.

A gasp from the crowd along with a moan of disappointment drew Mary's attention back to the competition. Henry had missed. The ball had fallen to land on the tarp below, and only then did it break.

"And Mary Reichert wins again!" Oliver declared. "Let's give the little lady a hand, folks."

The audience overcame their surprise and began to clap, and

then a few began to cheer, and before long there was a standing ovation to celebrate Mary's win. Gone was the English reserve, as they seemed more than a little impressed with Mary's contribution to the entertainment.

She cradled her rifle with her left hand and waved with her right. She'd nearly lost the competition by letting her thoughts dwell on Chris and what he was up to. She'd have to be especially careful as the show continued.

Turning to Henry Sanbourne, she extended her hand. "Very good competition, Mr. Sanbourne. You were a worthy opponent."

He shook her hand but said nothing. Sulking, he walked away with his expensive rifle, leaving Mary surprised by his attitude. If he'd thought this would be an easy win, he apparently hadn't considered her reputation.

She looked back at where Chris had been. He was gone, and so was the other man.

❖⟜ THIRTEEN ⟞❖

The Adlers hosted another grand party, this one at their London home, three weeks after the Brookstone show went abroad. England was in half mourning for Queen Victoria, who had died in January, although many felt full mourning had been set aside much too soon. King Edward, however, was a man who craved entertainment and socializing. He was known for his mistresses and extravagant lifestyle, and the death of his mother wasn't going to keep him from living life to its fullest. Much of the nobility disagreed with this, while others rejoiced. The last few decades under Queen Victoria had been dark and void of joy as she maintained a permanent state of mourning for her husband, Albert.

Lizzy had no feelings toward the dead queen one way or another but was instead put off by all the snobbish attitudes and wasteful spending. Jason had assured her that it was his father's money to spend and she shouldn't care, but she did. She was also worried about Wesley and her mother. She hadn't had so much as a telegram to tell her he'd gotten to the ranch safely. Already she had sent two letters to her mother and three to Wes, and while she did know it would take time for them to get to America and then to Montana, she had hoped for at least some word. She had no way of knowing what was happening back at the ranch. Was everything all right? Was her mother truly healthy and well?

"I should have gone with Wes, no matter what Jason said," she murmured.

Now, she was stuck in England, waiting and wondering when Wesley might join them. To add to her worry, Phillip and her uncle had taken to leaving for hours on end. She had no idea where they went or when they returned, but she knew they were both drinking. She'd asked Carson to keep watch over them, but he reported that often her uncle would simply order him to work elsewhere, and when Carson went to check on them later, Oliver and Phillip would be long gone. He had seen them both drunk on more than one occasion but found it impossible to keep them from imbibing.

"You don't look as if you're enjoying yourself."

Lizzy looked up to find Jason watching her from only a few feet away. "I'm not. I don't like parties and the opportunity they give my uncle to drink."

"Your uncle is just fine. I saw him not ten minutes ago. He wasn't at all intoxicated," Jason assured her.

"That would be a first, then." Lizzy frowned. "Jason, I want to send a telegram to Wesley. It's not right that I haven't heard from him."

"I would imagine you haven't heard from him because he's on his way to join you here."

Lizzy blinked. "What do you mean?"

"It would have taken him at least ten days to travel to and from the ranch, and that is only if he could secure a seat on the necessary trains. Then there is the passage from New York to London. That's another week. Under the most ideal circumstances, he needs at least three weeks to conclude all of that travel."

"I suppose you're right, and that's not even allowing for the time he'll need to resolve the issues at the ranch."

"Ah . . . right. That would add to the schedule."

"Still, he could have sent me a note." Lizzy sighed. "I need him here with me. To help me. I can't keep his brother from drinking, and despite what you think about my uncle, his health is not good, and drinking only makes it worse."

Jason gave her a gentle smile and touched her shoulder. "Lizzy, I wish you wouldn't worry. My heart's desire is to keep you from such misery. I want only to give you a wonderful life here in London. I want to show you off and show you the beauty that can be had. I want you to fall in love with this town and with me."

She pushed him back. "I will never fall in love with you!"

His eyes widened, but he said nothing. Lizzy stormed past him, knowing it was futile to explain it to him once again. She had mentioned his nagging interest to her uncle, but the older man had told her not to be insulted or offended. Jason was simply a young man in love.

"Lizzy, wait." Jason had followed her outside to the gardens.

"I have no desire to listen to you speak of love. We've talked about this over and over. I think you are a very fine man, but I am in love with Wesley."

"But you haven't even given me a chance."

Lizzy shook her head. "I don't want to give you or anyone else a chance. I love Wes, and that's the final word." She could see the disappointment in his eyes. "Jason, you're a good man, and you will find a woman one day who will love you as much as you love her, but I'm not that woman. Even if Wes were to die, God forbid, I would still not marry you."

"But why?" He held out his hands. "I can give you so much."

"I wish I could make you understand."

She hurried back toward the house. Uncle Oliver was standing near the open French doors with a nearly empty champagne glass in his hands. Without stopping to say a word, Lizzy yanked the glass from his hands and threw it on the cobblestones behind her. The crystal shattered.

Lizzy knew it was wrong, but at that moment she didn't care. She'd pay for it herself if need be, but she had to get her point across.

"You know you aren't to be drinking. You know what you promised my mother." Her tone was accusatory, but she didn't care. "If you continue to drink, Uncle Oliver, then I'm going home." She glanced around the room. Thankfully everyone else was on the other side of the room and paid them no attention.

Oliver recovered from his shock and laughed. "Lizzy, you darling child, you remind me of my stepmother. She could lose her temper when my father broke his promises. But honestly, you mustn't fret so." Oliver followed her into the hall. "It was just half a glass, and as you saw, I hadn't even finished it."

"I'm tired of worrying about you. You drink to forget your sorrow at losing Father, but you still have me." Tears came to her eyes. "I don't want to lose you too."

Uncle Oliver's brow furrowed as his expression grew concerned. "I am sorry. I didn't mean to cause you pain. Sometimes, I . . . well, I know you don't understand."

Lizzy's heart softened. "But I want to. I want to help you overcome this. Tell me what I can do."

Oliver shook his head. "There's nothing anyone can do . . . except me. I wish I were stronger. I wish I could stand up against the demons."

"God will give you the strength you need, Uncle Oliver. He promised He'd never leave nor forsake us. You can trust Him to help you." Tears streamed down her cheeks. She wished Wes was there to help encourage her uncle. Often a man wouldn't listen to the pleas of a woman—especially one they considered little more than a child.

"Uncle Oliver, I love you. You're all I have left of Father. Please don't leave me to face the world without you."

For a moment her uncle seemed stunned by her words, but after several long seconds, he gave her a weak smile and a nod. "I'll do what I can, child. For you. For you I will try."

Lizzy shook her head. "You must do it for yourself, Uncle Oliver."

His expression grew sad, and he shook his head. "Then I don't think it will ever happen, for I am not worth the effort."

Jason felt the telegram in his pocket. It had arrived precisely two weeks after they'd left Wesley behind in New York. Jason could imagine DeShazer seething when he learned that there was no emergency at the ranch. His telegram to Lizzy spoke of Jason's deceit and warned her to stay away from him. The very nerve of that American cowboy.

Of course, Lizzy would never see this telegram, nor the one that was sent from New York. She'd never see the letters her mother sent either, because Jason didn't trust Rebecca Brookstone not to warn Lizzy against him. He hadn't opened the letters because it would serve no purpose. If they were innocent, he couldn't very well give them to Lizzy opened. And if they spoke against him, as Jason very much feared they might, then he didn't want her to see them. Instead he had burned them in the kitchen stove. Later, after Lizzy was his and Wesley was all but forgotten, he might confess his actions, but for now it was better she didn't know.

"What do you mean?" Ella asked the footman.

"Miss, I only know that I was given this missive for you."

Ella opened the letter and read the barely legible script.

Need your help. Please come.
  —Phillip

"Who brought this?"

"A young boy. He's waiting on the street for you." The footman gave an exasperated sigh and turned to go.

Ella considered calling him back, but he was already in such a snit about the matter that she felt it would do her little good. She didn't know what had happened to Phillip, but it probably involved alcohol. Perhaps he was hurt or had been arrested. Neither would bode well for him. She ran upstairs to the bedroom she shared with Mary to retrieve her cloak and purse. If he was in trouble, she'd no doubt need money.

Without speaking to anyone, Ella slipped from the house and made her way down the front stairs. The young boy waiting for her couldn't have been more than ten. He was hopelessly filthy but of good spirits.

"Are you Miss Ella?"

"I am," she said, smiling despite the situation.

"I'm to take you to me mum. She's helping your friend."

"Very well."

They began walking, but after a quick clip for at least ten blocks, Ella glanced around for a taxi.

"I'm afraid I can't go much farther in these shoes," she told the boy.

He stopped and looked at her oddly, then gave a shrug. "Take 'em off. That's what I do when they pinch."

She shook her head. "I'd rather hire us a cab. Can you find one?" She looked up and down the mostly residential street. The lamplight gave her some comfort, but only minimal. The feeling of being very alone washed over her, and Ella bit her lower lip.

"You wait here." The boy disappeared without another word, shooting down a side street as fast as his legs could carry him.

Ella pulled her cloak close and realized the foolishness of what she'd done. She had no idea how to find her way back to the Adler house should the boy not return. She looked up and down the street and saw lights in most of the windows but no real sign of people.

The damp air seemed to settle on her like a blanket. She remembered the terrible talk about Jack the Ripper—a man who killed women he found on the streets. That was years ago, however. She'd heard about it when her family visited England in 1895. It was still fresh in everyone's mind then. The biggest concern was that the killer had not been caught. Had he ever been found?

Ella backed up a few steps and nearly jumped out of her skin as her body came in contact with something hard. She shrieked and leapt forward, whirling around at the same time. It was just an iron post.

The minutes hung like hours, and yet Ella wasn't sure what to do. She felt frozen in place. She could see a bit of traffic about two blocks ahead where the street intersected. Perhaps that was a better place to be.

She started to walk but hadn't gotten even a block when she heard the sound of a horse clipping along behind her.

"Miss Ella! Miss Ella!" She turned and saw the boy sitting up with the driver. "I found a ride, Miss Ella."

She wanted to cry and felt her knees start to buckle. Forcing herself to be strong, she drew a deep breath.

The driver brought the cab to a stop, then jumped down and tipped his hat. "Miss, this lad says you need a ride. I told him I'd box his ears if he were lyin'."

"He's not. I sent him. Thank you so much for coming to my rescue."

"Ah, you'd be from America, from the sounds of it."

Ella nodded and let him help her into the carriage. "I am." She settled into the smooth leather, still feeling shaken.

"Where would you be wanting to go?" the driver asked.

"The boy knows. You'll have to ask him. I'm supposed to retrieve a sick friend. I'll need you to drive me back to the Adler
house, but I'm not exactly sure where that is either. The boy
hopefully can direct you."

The man tipped his hat and climbed back into the driver's
seat. Ella chided herself for not at least getting the address of
the Adler house.

They weren't all that long on the road before Ella heard the
boy telling the driver to pull over. When the carriage came to a
stop, the driver assisted Ella from the carriage.

"Will you wait for me?" she asked, watching as the boy headed
into a well-lit tavern. Several drunk customers bounded out
the front door, singing at the top of their lungs. Ella shivered.
"Better still, could you maybe accompany me?"

"Of course, miss."

Ella nodded and headed toward the establishment.

The boy waited at the door. "He's upstairs. Me mum is takin'
care of him."

They passed into the pub, and immediately Ella was as-
saulted by the smell of food and drink and sweaty bodies. People
around the room seemed to be working class. At least it appeared to be a decent establishment.

The boy led the way around the side of the room and up a
set of stairs that were all but hidden from view at first glance.
The steps were steep and narrow and the passageway dark, but
Ella was determined to continue. All she could think was that
Phillip had been injured or was too drunk to get home on his
own. Once they reached the top, the stairs opened onto a long
dimly lit hall. Doors lined the hall at regular intervals.

"Where is he, boy?" the driver asked.

"Third door on the right." The boy hurried to it and threw it open
without knocking. "Mum, she's come. She's come to take him."

Ella moved to the open door and looked inside the small space. A short woman with mousy brown hair and a baby on her hip walked toward her.

"Your friend got into a wee bit of trouble. Some fellas roughed him up a bit out back, and I managed to get him up here. I found a piece of paper in his pocket with an address, and he keeps askin' for you. That is, if you're Ella."

"I am."

The woman nodded. "He's well into his cups, so he's not feelin' much pain, but he will soon enough."

Ella bit her lip. It wasn't the first time she'd helped Phillip out after he'd been drinking. It was, however, the first time he'd suffered a beating. At least that she knew about.

"This man is going to drive us home," she said, gesturing to the cabbie. "I think he can help me get Phillip downstairs and loaded into the carriage."

"Come this way," the woman told the driver. The baby began to fuss, and she jostled him to the opposite hip.

The cabbie followed her, disappearing behind a small partition. "Ah, here now, gov'nah, lemme help you," Ella heard the old man declare.

"Where's Ella? Ella's gonna take me home," Phillip slurred.

"She's just on the other side of the screen. Come on with ya now," the woman commanded.

Within a few seconds the driver reappeared with Phillip tucked under his arm. Poor Phillip. His clothes were torn and dirty, and his face was bruised and scratched. There was a cut above his right eye that had left caked blood rivulets down the side of his face. Ella's heart went out to him.

"Oh, Phillip. What have they done to you?"

He smiled. "You should ask what I did to them."

Ella shook her head and looked to the driver. "Please take him down. I'll be right there."

The man nodded. "Boy, you go before me and make sure the stairs are clear."

Ella turned to the woman. "Thank you for sending your son." She fished a few coins from her purse and held them out. "Please take this for your trouble."

"Oh, I couldn't do that," the woman said, pushing the money back. The baby reached for his mother's face. She kissed his fingers before smiling at Ella. "It was my way of bein' a good Christian."

"And this is my way of thanking you, as a good Christian." Ella smiled at the infant, then tucked the coins in the woman's apron pocket.

Hurrying to catch up with the driver and Phillip, Ella found they were already heading out the front door of the tavern. She followed them, glad no one seemed of a mind to stop her. She hated what had happened to Phillip and yet knew he'd brought it on himself. What would Lizzy say when she saw him? Would he be fired—sent home in disgrace? What if they fired him and didn't even bother to send him back to America, but left him to figure out things on his own?

She waited until the driver got Phillip in the carriage before letting him help her inside. It wasn't until they were on their way down the street that she remembered she didn't know where they were going. Apparently the driver did. Hopefully the little boy had told him the Adlers' address.

"Phillip, whatever happened to you?"

He had his head back and his eyes closed. She expected one of his humorous replies, but instead he sounded sadder than she had ever heard him.

"I'm no good, Ella. No good . . . at all."

"That's not true, Phillip. You are a good man. You just need to leave the bottle alone. You and drink don't get along so well."

"I can't . . . stop, Ella. I . . . I can't stop drinking." His head lolled to one side as the driver made a sharp turn. With what looked to be great effort, Phillip sat up and straightened. "I can't stop." He looked at her and shook his head. "I . . . need it." His words were slurred and stammered. His head fell forward until his chin touched his chest, but his eyes were raised to hers.

"But why, Phillip? Why do you need it?" She wanted to understand his pain.

"To forget. I . . . I have to forget."

This time he did close his eyes, and for a second she thought maybe he had passed out. Nevertheless she pressed him for answers.

"Forget what, Phillip? What do you need to forget?"

The question seemed to startle him, and he jerked back with such force that Ella gasped. He looked at her for a moment, his eyes not seeming to see her.

"I need to forget. . . ." He stopped and ran his tongue over his teeth as if his mouth had grown too dry. He licked his lips and then closed his eyes and fell back against the seat. "Forget I killed him."

Ella shivered and clutched her cloak close. "Killed who?" she barely whispered, but it was enough.

"My father. I killed my father."

Ella was so stunned by this revelation that she was afraid to press for more. Not that it would have helped. Phillip had passed out.

When they reached the Adler house, Ella had the presence of mind to go to the servants' entrance. She found one of the footmen and asked him to find Mr. Hopkins.

Once Carson was found and brought to her, Ella explained the situation, and they managed to sneak Phillip up the back stairs as the drunk man tried to rally.

"Where are we goin'?" Phillip asked.

"We're getting you to bed so you can sober up before anyone else sees you in this state," Ella told him. "Where's your room?"

"Top . . . top of the stairs." Phillip rolled his head over onto Carson's shoulder. "Howdy, Carssson."

"Keep you voice down, Phillip," Carson countered. "You don't want to stir up attention."

Phillip gave a cough and nodded. He tripped over his own feet, and if Carson hadn't been helping him, he would have landed on the stairs.

"I'm so afraid he'll get in trouble for this." Ella tried to help Carson, but he was all but carrying Phillip at this point.

"Don't worry. I'll see he gets sobered up. Alice and I are headed back to Adler's country place first thing in the morning. We'll take Phillip with us. Can you get the door?"

"Of course." Ella scooted past Carson to the room at the top of the stairs. She opened the door and found the light. It was hardly more than a broom closet. One tiny bed was positioned along the length of the room, and at the foot of that was Phillip's trunk. The width of the room barely left two feet of passageway beside the bed.

Ella stepped out of the way to let Carson and Phillip in the room. "Help me get him undressed," Carson said.

Ella hesitated only a moment. She took Phillip's coat from Carson as he worked to maneuver it off Phillip's body. Next he took off the tie that had already been unknotted and unbuttoned the bloodstained shirt. Ella worked on the cuffs while Carson began to pull Phillip's arms from the sleeves.

"I'll leave him his pants and save his modesty and yours," Carson said. With a little push, he had Phillip sitting on the edge of the bed. "If I let go of him, he's going to fall back. Can you get his boots off while I hang onto him?"

Ella glanced down at Phillip's feet. "Of course." She quickly lifted his left leg and pulled his boot off, then did likewise for the right. Once this was accomplished, Carson carefully pushed Phillip back and then reached down and raised his legs.

"He'll have a powerful headache in the morning, but I'm bettin' he's had worse."

"Thank you for helping me." She glanced at Phillip stretched out on the bed. He'd managed to sleep through most of the ordeal. She wondered about his past and what he'd done to cause the death of his father, but it wasn't the time to seek answers. She looked back at Carson. "I hope he won't get in too much trouble."

"Well, it was a night of celebration, and he wasn't on duty. Still, I know how the Brookstones feel about their people drinking."

Ella recalled Lizzy's concerns about her uncle and didn't see how he could condemn the poor wrangler for a sin he too shared.

"Hopefully they'll understand. Like you said, it was a night of celebration."

Ella walked away shaking her head. Phillip hadn't been drinking for the fun of it. He was trying to wash away a burden of pain and sorrow. He was drinking to forget his past.

⋄⊱ FOURTEEN ⊰⋄

Wes counted the minutes until the train would finally arrive at his London stop. He repeatedly pulled out his pocket watch and checked the time, then replaced the watch in his pocket. He had mulled over and over what he would do the minute he found Jason Adler, and none of his thoughts were good. He glanced out the window, hardly seeing the brick row houses, and wondered how anyone could be so despicable. He huffed for at least the tenth time since taking his seat.

"The burden you're carrying seems to weigh you down, son. And while I no longer hold the pulpit, I still consider myself a man of God, if you wish to unburden yourself."

Wes had ridden in this train compartment with the small, balding man for over twenty minutes. Why had he chosen now to speak up?

The old man smiled. "I suppose you think that rather presumptuous of me, but I can't bear to see one of God's creatures suffering."

Wes smiled. "I didn't know my problems were so visible."

"I say, you're an American." The man seemed positively delighted. "I thought you were by the hat. It's the style cowboys wear, isn't it?"

"Yes." Wes laughed. "And I wear it because I am a cowboy. From Montana—one of the western ranching states." He extended his hand. "Wesley DeShazer."

The old man smiled and shook his hand. "You can just call me Father Paul. Everyone does."

"It's nice to meet you, Father Paul."

"Likewise." The man took off his gold wire-rimmed glasses and then pulled a handkerchief from his suit pocket. Wiping his glasses, he waited for Wesley to continue.

"You are very astute, I have to say. I'm in a bad way."

"And what—or maybe I should ask *who* has brought about this bad way?"

"An Englishman who hopes to steal my fiancée." Then, without thinking twice, Wes spilled the entire story. He told Father Paul about the Brookstone show and Lizzy's part in it and then explained Jason Adler's dirty deeds. "By the time I got back to the ranch and realized Mrs. Brookstone had never sent the telegram, the rest of the troupe was well on its way to London. It's probably a good thing it's taken all this time to catch up with them, because I might have beat Adler to death."

Father Paul nodded, finished cleaning his glasses, and tucked the handkerchief back into his pocket. "Anger has a way of controlling us, to be sure. We often do things in angry haste that we'd never consider in calmer times."

"Well, I still intend to confront him and remove my fiancée from his presence."

"You say she's a performer with this wild west show. Will she accept your demand that she leave the show?"

The question took the wind from Wes's sails. "No. Probably not. She has been taught from the time she was young that the show must go on under all circumstances. She won't approve of what Jason did, but she will feel obligated to stay."

The old man nodded and put on his glasses. "She sounds

like a remarkable young woman. So few young people seem to care about commitments these days. They pledge themselves to one thing or another, without any real intention of honoring their promises."

Wes felt a momentary stab of guilt. "And if I insist she leave, it will cause no end of problems for the troupe and her family . . . not to mention us."

"Yet it will be hard to continue doing business with a man who obviously stoops to untold depths to get what he wants."

"Yes."

The train rolled over a rough spot in the tracks, and the men were jostled hard toward the window. The old man smiled and straightened as if nothing had happened. "Life is full of unexpected discomforts."

Wes rubbed the spot where his elbow had hit the armrest. "More than I ever expected. Definitely more than I wanted."

"And yet you're so young and full of life. Some might even call you blessed."

"I am blessed."

The older man smiled at this declaration.

Wes stopped rubbing his elbow and smiled. "I am blessed."

"Just remember, son—God never promised His children a life without complications. The devil may be trying you, but he had to get God's permission to do so, just as he did with Job. Satan isn't all-powerful, and even if God allows him to try you, that doesn't mean God ever leaves you unprotected. Jesus told Peter that Satan had asked to sift him like wheat, but Jesus had prayed that his faith wouldn't fail. He wasn't leaving Peter without help, and He's not leaving you without help either. This man may well be the devil in human form, but that doesn't mean God ever intends for you to face him on your own."

"That's the thing—I don't think this man is the devil." Wes

felt his anger ease. "He's been honorable in every other way. The problem is, he's in love with Lizzy. I can't fault him for that. She's a wonderful woman. I fault him for not honoring the relationship we have. I fault him for lying and cheating to try to steal her from me." He chuckled. "Maybe he is the devil."

Father Paul laughed too. "Well, he's doing the enemy's work nevertheless, so you must not give him any room for a foothold. The real battle isn't with this man, but with the one who influences him to act in such an underhanded fashion. Remember what Ephesians six says. 'For we wrestle not against flesh and blood, but against principalities, against powers, against the rulers of the darkness of this world, against spiritual wickedness in high places.' This battle is beyond you and can only be won with Christ."

The train began to jerk and slow as they approached the station. Wes considered Father Paul's words. They were like a calming balm upon his soul. Perhaps because most of what he said was taken directly from the Bible. "Thank you, Father Paul. I guess I needed that reminder."

"We all do from time to time. Therein lies the value of spiritual counsel and ecumenical services. But where that cannot be found through God's servants, God Himself will provide through His Word and Holy Spirit. I will be praying for you, Wesley." Father Paul dusted off the front of his brown tweed suit. "And just so you know, I plan to attend the performance of the Brookstone troupe. I had it planned even before I met you."

Wes grinned. "Well, be sure to come back to where the performers and animals are prior to the show. I'll be there with the horses . . . or with Lizzy. I'd love to introduce you to her."

Father Paul smiled. "I'll do my best to locate you."

⸻ ✦✧✦ ⸻

Lizzy found Uncle Oliver doubled over and heaving into a chamber pot. His skin had a pasty yellow hue, and his eyes were bloodshot. No doubt alcohol had played a role in this.

"Oh, Uncle Oliver, what can I do?"

He tried to wave her off. "It's nothing. Just a stomach complaint. I'm sure I'll be fit as a fiddle in an hour or so." He moaned and pressed a hand to his abdomen.

Lizzy sat beside him on the bed. "My father once told me how you pulled him from the Yellowstone River one June when the floodwaters were raging and he'd gone after a calf."

Oliver nodded. "It nearly got the best of us both. Your father had roped the calf, but the current was so strong that it started pulling him and his horse into the river."

"Father said you were on dry ground, and you roped his horse and started pulling him back from the water."

"Yes. It wasn't easy, because the pull of the river was so violent. But gradually, inch by inch, we were successful. I pulled your father to safety, and he pulled the calf."

Lizzy put her arm around his shoulders. "Well, maybe I can return the favor. Maybe I can rope you this time and pull you to safety."

Oliver studied her face for a moment, and tears came to his eyes. "Oh, Lizzy. I don't think you can pull against this current." He threw up again but had nothing left to expel.

"I'm calling for a doctor, Uncle Oliver. We'll start there. Now, let me help you back into bed."

"But there's a show tonight. I must be well."

"We'll make Jason play your part. He'll do it very poorly, but it will teach him your value." Lizzy stood and pulled back the covers. Uncle Oliver had never looked smaller or weaker—so helpless. She wanted to burst into tears but forced a strength she didn't really have. "Now, come on."

"I suppose I've little choice. Do you really think Jason can manage?"

"He'll do just fine, or I'll do it myself," Lizzy said, pulling the covers up to his chin. "Now, don't leave this bed. I'll be back shortly."

An hour later, Lizzy listened as the doctor rendered his verdict. "Your uncle, as I understand it, spent a good deal of his youth and adult life drinking heavily. I am of the opinion that he is suffering several maladies related to that and his age."

"What maladies?" Lizzy asked.

"I believe he is having a buildup of bile and other toxic fluids in his abdomen," the doctor declared. "It is also of my opinion that he has a cirrhosis of the liver, which is causing a failure of his vital organs."

Lizzy fisted her hands to steady her nerves. "What can be done?"

"He must rest, and he must cease drinking alcohol." The doctor's words were said firmly, without room for question. "There is no other hope. If you will not heed my warning, sir, it is my opinion that you will be dead within the month."

"No!" Lizzy went to her uncle's side. "Is there nothing else to be done? No surgeries or medicines?" She took Oliver's cold hand.

"Nothing. He must remain in bed for the next six weeks."

"I can't do that. I have a job to do," Oliver protested.

"You can and you will, Uncle. I'll tie you to this bed if I have to." Lizzy saw the shock in the doctor's face but didn't care. "I will see that he does as he's told."

"Very well. I will leave some powders that, when mixed with water and even a bit of honey, should settle his stomach and help with detoxification. There must be no more alcohol."

"Do you hear that, Uncle? No more drinking or you'll die."

"I hear you," Uncle Oliver said with resignation.

Lizzy turned back to the doctor. "Thank you for coming. What do I owe you?"

"Mr. Adler told me that he will see to my bill. Good day."

Lizzy gave the doctor a final nod, then waited until he'd left the room. She knew the others were waiting downstairs to hear what was going on with Oliver, but first she wanted to speak with her uncle.

"You heard him, Uncle Oliver. This is serious. I believe we should end the show and return home immediately." She sat down beside him, still holding his hand.

"No. You can't do that, Lizzy."

"But our time here is nearly done. We haven't that many more shows anyway. I'm sure Mr. Adler can manage the cancellations and arrange our passage home."

"No, you don't understand." Uncle Oliver looked embarrassed and lowered his gaze to the bed. "We have an obligation, and to fail to see it through will forfeit everything."

"Everything?"

"Yes." His voice was weak. "Adler tied it all together. If we leave now, we'll lose the money owed to us and perhaps even suffer penalties."

"But how can that be?"

"It's just the way Jason set things up. We were able to get last-minute accommodations onto the schedule that way. I thought at the time it was a risk but not overly dangerous to our welfare."

"But now it is. It's dangerous to *your* welfare." Lizzy shook her head. "Why did you ever agree to that?"

"I had to, Lizzy. We needed the money, and the shows in England were bound to pay out even better than those at home. Especially with Henry supplying our room and board. Say nothing to anyone. I'm ashamed that it's come to this."

"I won't say anything," Lizzy promised. She drew a deep breath.

"But in return, you're going to promise me that you'll stay in bed the next six weeks."

A knock sounded on the door, and Jason Adler and his father entered the room. "We spoke with the doctor," Henry announced. "I understand this is quite serious."

"It's a matter of life and death," Lizzy replied. "I was just suggesting we return immediately to America. . . ." She stopped short of revealing that she knew the truth of the financial arrangement.

Jason gave her a sympathetic smile. "Now, now. We needn't cancel the show. The doctor said that your uncle needs rest for at least six weeks. He can remain here and recover from his sickness while you finish the performances. Once that is complete, we will take him by ambulance to the ship and then back to America, if he's up to it. Otherwise he can continue to convalesce here. I will oversee it all."

"And I will help," Henry added. "Oliver, you have been a dear friend, and I will spare no expense to see you have what you need. In fact, I'll accompany you back to the States. I have business there anyway."

"The show still needs an announcer," Oliver reminded them.

"I've already thought of that," Henry admitted. "I believe that between Jason and me, we can make those announcements. Elizabeth can help us put together a script with details about each performance."

The idea struck Lizzy as completely feasible. "Yes. That will work. We'll never be as good as you are, Uncle, but it will see us through and allow you to rest."

"I suppose there is nothing more to be done," Oliver said, closing his eyes. "I hate letting you down, Lizzy."

She leaned over and kissed his forehead. "You aren't. You're going to rest and get well, and that will be your gift to me." She looked at Henry. "Will you let the others know what's happening? I know they're very worried."

"Of course." He came to Lizzy's side and took her hand. "I don't want you to worry about a single thing. Your uncle is dearer to me than my own brothers. I will see that he has every comfort."

"Thank you, Mr. Adler. I appreciate your heart in this."

"Be reassured that I have it under control." With that, he left the room, though Jason remained.

"You'll see, Oliver. You'll be on the mend in no time. I'm confident of your recovery," Jason declared. "Lizzy and I will see that you want for nothing."

She didn't like the way he linked her name with his, but she said nothing. "Jason, you must make it clear to your staff that my uncle is, under no circumstances, to receive any alcohol."

"Of course. I'm certain Father has already addressed the matter, but you can be confident that it will be done."

"No one needs to fuss over me," Oliver declared. "I realize I've caused a scene, but I think the doctor is a bit of an alarmist, and I don't want the two of you fretting."

"We won't fret, Uncle," Lizzy assured him, "but we will be vigilant."

An elderly woman dressed in black with a white pinafore apron entered, pushing a tea cart loaded with all sorts of things. Lizzy frowned, wondering if she was actually going to serve tea.

Jason offered an explanation. "Father asked Mrs. Platte to sit with your uncle and act as his nurse. I hope you approve. She's quite competent and in fact was a nurse in her youth, serving with Florence Nightingale in the Crimean War."

Lizzy felt a new respect for the older woman. She had read about such nurses. "I'm grateful for your help, Mrs. Platte. Did the doctor inform you that my uncle is not to have anything alcoholic?"

"Indeed he did, miss," the older woman replied as she began sorting through the cart.

Lizzy turned back to her uncle. "I'm going to leave you for

the time being, then. We're leaving shortly for tonight's performance, and I need to prepare a script for Jason and his father."

"I'll be praying for you," Uncle Oliver said.

Despite his bravado, he was so weak that Lizzy hated to leave his side. How she wished her mother and Wes were there. Perhaps she could have Jason send for them.

She kissed her uncle again and got up from the bed. "If he needs anything, Mrs. Platte, please see that he gets it . . . with the exception of alcohol. I'm afraid that has been the cause of this problem."

"You may rest assured that there will be no alcohol used in my service," the older woman declared.

"I'm glad."

Lizzy looked to Jason, who offered her his arm. He drew her out into the hall and had barely closed the door before Lizzy broke down into tears. She hadn't meant to cry in front of Jason, but she had exhausted her resolve. She didn't even fight when he took her in his arms.

"Poor Lizzy. I'm so sorry, but rest assured we will do everything possible to see him through this. I am confident that he will recover."

She forced herself to calm and straightened, pushing away from Jason's comforting hold. "I want my mother to come. Wesley too, if he isn't already on his way. I don't know why I haven't heard from them, but I must have them here. Can you arrange it?"

Jason looked momentarily surprised, then nodded. "Of course."

"My uncle will listen to Mother, and she has a way with him that no one else does. I believe his recovery will be much improved if she's here."

"Then I will see to it immediately. You know I only want whatever will offer you peace of mind and heart. I love you, Lizzy, and I hate seeing you suffer like this."

"I don't have the energy to chide you again for your declaration of love. Just get my mother here as soon as possible. If anything should happen . . . if he should fail . . ." She sniffed back tears and shook her head.

Jason put his arm around her again. "Lizzy, let me comfort you. Let me be the one to see you through this." He lowered his face to kiss her, but Lizzy turned away.

"Leave me alone!"

"You heard her, Adler."

Both Lizzy and Jason startled as Wes's voice echoed in the hall. When Lizzy caught sight of him, she burst into tears anew and ran into his arms.

⊶⊱ FIFTEEN ⊰⊷

Lizzy didn't think she'd ever been happier at the sight of someone. Resting in Wesley's comforting arms, she thanked God over and over for this moment. Now, somehow, she felt certain things would be all right. She felt confident that she could face whatever was to come.

"Oh, Wes. I prayed you'd come. I prayed, and here you are." She looked up at him, assuming she'd find his expression sympathetic and loving. But instead he wore a fierce scowl. She pulled back. "What's wrong?" Then she remembered that he'd just found her in Jason's arms. "Oh," she murmured.

"I say, it's good to see you again, Wesley," Jason said from behind her. He sounded anything but sincere.

"I'll just bet." Wes let go of Lizzy and all but pushed her aside.

She turned and saw that Jason was smiling. Wes seemed to forget she even existed as he stalked toward Jason. She expected a harsh exchange—perhaps even a threat of violence. She didn't expect Wesley to swing his fist into Jason's jaw.

"Wes!" She hurried to his side before he could punch the Englishman again. "What are you doing? Why did you hit him?"

"Didn't you get my telegram?"

She shook her head. "No. I've been beside myself, not hearing from you or Mother about what was going on at the ranch. I've sent letters but heard nothing."

Wes turned back to Jason, who held his hand to his face. "Why don't you tell her, Adler? Tell her what happened to her letters and my telegram. Tell her about the telegram that started this whole charade."

Jason lowered his hand and gave Lizzy a look of regret. His entire countenance seemed withered. Had Wes hit him too hard?

"What is this all about?" Lizzy couldn't stand the tension between the two men. It was worse than it had ever been. "What is he talking about, Jason?"

"Tell her. Tell her or I will," Wes declared. He crossed his arms and fixed Jason with a glare. "And then so help me, I'll hit you again just for being a coward."

Jason shrugged. "What Mr. DeShazer is alluding to is the fact that I sent him on a wild goose chase." His chin was red where Wes had clipped him. "I know what I did was wrong, but I felt I had to do it. I had to have time alone with you in order to win you for myself. I felt certain I could make you love me, but I knew I would never be successful unless I got Wesley out of the picture so you could see my good attributes."

Lizzy backed up a step. "What are you saying, Jason?"

"Go on, Adler. Tell her about your deception." Wes held his stance, but his voice was angry.

Jason looked at the carpeted hall floor. "Your mother didn't send a telegram asking Wes to come back to the ranch. I did. I wanted to get rid of him long enough to show you that I could make you happy. I wanted to show you my world and how beautiful it is and how I could give you all that your heart desires."

Lizzy felt ill. She looked at Wes. "Mother didn't ask for you?"

"No. In fact, she was very alarmed that I had left you and Oliver. I turned right around to get here as fast as I could. Thankfully, I thought to get money from my bank before leaving

Montana, because Adler didn't even have the decency to leave me a ticket as he promised."

She turned to Jason. "And Wesley's telegram? My letters?"

Jason gave a shrug as he rubbed his jaw. "I'm afraid I did away with them."

"Oh, Jason! How could you?"

He had the decency to look regretful. "As I said, I'm in love with you. I would go to any lengths to win your heart. I thought perhaps you had just never considered the possibility of loving someone else since you grew up with . . . him." He glanced only a moment in Wesley's direction, then returned his gaze to Lizzy. "I know it was wrong, but I was desperate. I know you hold great store in your Christian faith, so I'm asking you to forgive me."

Lizzy shook her head. "It isn't that simple, Jason. My uncle is sick . . . perhaps dying." She had to force the words from her mouth. "This might have been avoided if Wes were here. He would have been able to keep my uncle company. Uncle Oliver might not have struggled so much with his sadness, and even if he had, Wes could have helped keep him from drinking. Now, if my uncle dies . . . it will be as much your fault as the alcohol's."

"That's hardly fair," Jason started, but Wes wouldn't let him finish.

"We're going home," he announced.

"Don't do that on my account," Jason said quickly. "Remember, Oliver needs to rest. If you move him, it could be to his detriment."

Lizzy remembered what her uncle had said about the show and their payments. "Dead men hardly need money," she muttered.

"What was that?" Jason asked.

She shook her head and looked at Wes. "I'm afraid we must stay. The doctor just saw Uncle Oliver and said he needs bed rest for six weeks."

"You must see reason," Jason interjected.

"Reason," Wes said, putting his arm around her. "You want us to see reason? The time for that has passed. We can hire a nurse, Lizzy. She can take care of Oliver on the trip home."

"No. No, we can't." Lizzy knew Wes wouldn't understand, but she had made her uncle a promise and couldn't tell him why it was necessary to remain.

Wes stared at her. "Do you mean to tell me that after all this man has done, you feel obligated to honor your commitment? He forfeited any loyalty you might have felt was owed."

"It isn't about that."

Wes shook his head. "Then what? Give me a reason why we can't just close down the show and walk away."

"There's only a few more weeks," Jason interjected. "It's hardly fair to punish the entire crew for what I did. I promise—and if my word means nothing, then my father will pledge to see that Oliver has the best of care. You know how my father favors him. By the time the show finishes, Oliver will be better able to travel."

"Complete your show, Adler, but do it without Lizzy. She and I are going to take Oliver home."

"No." Lizzy prayed Wes could somehow understand. "Please listen to me. There are only a few weeks left. Let's honor our commitment and give Oliver the time he needs to rest, and then we'll leave."

"But you still have the performance in America as well," Wes replied. "And then it will be one more thing after that. I say we go now and forget this lying schemer."

"I'd like to, but I can't, and I'm asking you to accept that."

"It's really to everyone's benefit that you stay. My father is going to be furious with me, and believe me, his punishment will be worse than what you have in mind," Jason said.

"I don't know," Wes answered in a low, husky tone. "I had in mind to put an end to your scheming permanently."

Jason blanched.

"We're staying and finishing the contract." Lizzy kept her gaze on Jason, unable to bear the fact that Wes would see this as a betrayal.

Jason gave a hint of a smile. "And you'll forgive me?"

"I'll forgive you, but I'm not going to forget this. I won't trust you again. You've proven you can't be trusted. Not only that, but I'm not the main person you've wronged in this. You should seek Wesley's forgiveness even more than mine."

Jason looked at Wesley. "I am sorry, chap. I've always been of a mind that until a woman is wed, she's fair game."

Wes tensed at Lizzy's side, and she figured she'd better intercede before Jason ended up with another punch to the face.

"Enough. Wes, I want you to come see Uncle Oliver. He's quite ill."

"I know," Wes all but growled.

Lizzy feared he might well spring like a cat. She took hold of his arm. "Jason, for your own benefit, I suggest you leave us now."

Jason hesitated only a moment, then gave a slight bow of his head and went off in the direction of the stairs. Lizzy shook her head. What Jason had done was unthinkable. How terribly betrayed Wesley must feel.

"I'm so sorry, Wes. I had no idea he'd done this."

"I know."

She turned and wrapped her arms around him, hugging him close. "I missed you so much and needed you so dearly. It's been overwhelming at times, and now with Uncle Oliver desperately ill, I'm beside myself."

She felt him begin to calm as his muscles relaxed and he rubbed her back. "I wish I'd been here for you."

"You're here now, and that's all that matters."

"But it's foolish to stay here and finish out the show. Your uncle needs to be in America—home, where he can be with people who love him and have his best interests at heart."

Lizzy didn't know what to say. She knew if she argued for honoring their obligations, Wesley would think her heartless, yet she'd made Oliver a promise.

"Wes, do you trust me?" she asked, pulling away from him.

"You know I do." His brows knit. "What are you getting at?"

"There are things that complicate us leaving. I'm asking you to trust me. I can't talk about them . . . but we have to stay and finish out the show. We have to finish the season. Uncle Oliver has constant nursing care here, and when we leave, the Adlers will see that he has care on the ship. Once we're back in America, hopefully Mother will have joined us by then, and she can take care of Uncle Oliver's needs. We can send them both home and finish with the Expo in Buffalo."

"I don't see why you're being so stubborn," Wes said, shaking his head. "What good is it for the show to go on if it kills your uncle?"

"It won't. He'll have no further part in it—at least not this season. Jason and his father are going to share the master of ceremonies' duties, and I'm going to write them a script." She drew a deep breath. "I'm asking you to trust me. Pray about it, and I'm sure God will show you the right way."

She could see in his expression that he didn't like the idea, but after a few moments, he nodded. At least that would buy her some time.

A few days after Lizzy told Mary and Ella that her uncle was facing death, Ella received another plea for help from Phillip. He was in trouble again, and this time he wasn't in the comfort of a public house, but rather a jail. She shook her head. What could she do? She knew nothing about English jails, and even if she did, she could hardly go there and demand they set him free.

She thought about talking to Wes, but Phillip had begged her to say nothing to anyone. Telling his big brother would be the worst thing she could do—at least in Phillip's eyes.

"But I must do something."

Ella paced the beautiful bedroom she'd been given at the Adlers' country estate. It was much bigger than their place in the heart of London and done in hues of gold and blue. And whereas her bedroom in London had been shared with Mary, here there were enough rooms for everyone to have their own. The mansion was like a palace, with dozens and dozens of rooms that could never be explored in a single day. Each of those rooms was filled to the brim with antiques and beautiful tapestries, as well as precious artwork by artists Ella actually recognized. Jason had told her over dinner one evening that his father and mother used to go on trips throughout Europe with the sole intention of finding treasures for the estate. She remembered a time when she was quite young that her parents had done the same.

"This house grieves my uncle to no end," Jason had admitted. "Which in turn delights my father. He may never have the title of earl, but he has amassed a fortune my uncle can never hope to match."

Ella remembered Jason's words. It saddened her to think of the rivalry between brothers when they might have been close instead. She thought of her own family's division, and even of Wes and Phillip. If Phillip didn't know the disappointment he would cause his brother, he might have reached out to him instead of her.

She loved being a part of the Brookstone show, but Phillip's constant problems were beginning to weigh her down. She wasn't sure how she'd become his keeper. It was impossible to forget what he'd said the night she'd retrieved him from the tavern. That he'd killed his father. Was he serious? He seemed to be, but the opportunity to question him further had never arisen, and Ella kept what she knew to herself for fear of getting Phillip in trouble.

"Oh, Phillip, what am I to do?"

Sadly, Ella was attracted to the troubled man. She loved his dark brown eyes and the way they lit up when he was truly amused. He had such a sweet and gentle spirit, but there was a darkness in his soul that threatened to destroy him. Now he was in trouble, and all she wanted to do was save him.

"What do I do?" she asked the room.

She went to the massive window and gazed out on the lawns below. She was surprised to see Jason Adler playing with two of his father's Irish wolfhounds—gifts from King Edward VII when he was still the Prince of Wales. Jason was the epitome of propriety, and yet he seemed to genuinely care about the show and its people. Perhaps if she went to him and explained, he could figure out what to do about Phillip. Especially since it might well take an Englishman to get Phillip released from an English jail.

Making her way downstairs, Ella tried to think of what she would say and how she might gain his promise to say nothing to Lizzy and Wes. Of course, there was no guarantee he would keep that promise even if he gave it, but it was a risk she had to take.

By the time she reached Jason, he was speaking to a servant who had both dogs on a leash. She waited to approach until the man had bowed and led the dogs away.

"Miss Fleming, don't you look pretty today. Like a beautiful flower," Jason said, smiling as she approached.

This pink gauzy gown was her favorite of the new wardrobe. "Thank you. You're very kind to say so."

"What can I do for you today?"

Ella bit her lip and looked at the stone walk. "I . . . there's a delicate matter that I need help with, but first I must impose upon you a promise of secrecy."

Jason didn't hesitate. "Of course. You have my word. But please tell me what has you troubled. I do love to play the rescuing prince."

She looked up to find him smiling and smiled in return despite her worries. "Might we walk while I tell you? I don't want to be overheard."

He extended his arm, and Ella took it. They walked for several yards before she finally stopped and turned to face him. "Are you sure you promise to keep this just between us?"

Jason's expression softened. "My dear, I would never betray your confidence. I've made a number of mistakes and done things I'm not proud of, as you may know, but I am a man of my word."

She wasn't sure what he was talking about, but she nodded. "Very well. I have received a note from Phillip."

"Wesley's brother?" He looked confused. "Why the formality of a note?"

"He's in jail." She handed him the note. "I don't know what to do. I've helped him before but never had to get him out of jail, much less an English jail."

Jason read the note. "He's being incarcerated not far from here. I know the people in charge, so don't worry. I will retrieve him immediately."

"Just like that?" Ella asked.

He smiled and surprised her by putting his hand on her shoulder. "My dear, what are friends for? I feel, after the mess I've made of things, that I must redeem myself, and to do something kind for Wesley's brother is just the thing."

Ella nodded. "I'm so grateful. Should I come with you?"

His smile broadened. "Would you like to? I can show you some of the village. I think you'd find it quite charming."

She considered it for only a few seconds. "I'll go. Phillip might feel better with me along."

———◆◆×◆◆———

Wes had looked all over for Phillip, but he was nowhere to be found. He knew from Lizzy that Phillip had been faithful to his duties, and for that, Wes was grateful. But according to Carson, Phillip was also drinking, and often it had been with Oliver.

As he moved through the Adler stables, Wes had to admire the setup. There were at least a dozen men working with the horses and even a team who looked after the hunting dogs. Wes would like to experience an English hunting adventure after listening to some of the men speak about their experiences. He had never hunted on horseback—at least not in the same manner that the English did, chasing after their dogs and a fox. He saw hunting as a means to provide meat for the table, not a game. Still, the thrill of the chase, jumping streams and fences, racing through forests and such, all sounded rather interesting.

He stopped a young groom. "Excuse me. I wonder if you've seen my brother, Phillip. He's about as tall as me, but skinnier . . . more like you."

"Sorry, I haven't seen him," the boy replied. He didn't wait to converse further but went on his way without so much as a nod.

Wes was about to give up when he saw two of the stable boys making their way outside and toward the house. He watched from the stable as a carriage pulled up and Jason Adler stepped down. The driver waited as Jason helped Ella from the carriage and then, to Wesley's surprise, Phillip jumped down. Wes started for the carriage, then stopped. Phillip shook hands with Jason and then turned and said something to Ella. He nodded and smiled, then offered Ella his arm, and the threesome headed for the house.

Wes decided now was the time to find out what was going on. He crossed the grounds in long strides and made it to the house just after Jason and the others had gone inside. Following them, Wes wondered why the three had been together. Had Jason taken his brother to town to drink? Wes certainly wouldn't put it past Adler.

He shook his head and made his way into the deserted foyer. Where had they gone? He glanced at the large open drawing rooms on either side of the foyer and listened for voices. There was nothing. He pressed on down the hall and stopped when he heard Adler speaking.

"As I promised Ella, I'll say nothing about this particular matter, but if it happens again, I'm afraid I'll be forced to tell Mr. Brookstone what's going on."

"I appreciate that, Mr. Adler. I do. And you'll see. I won't let it happen again. I don't want to end up back in jail."

Wes frowned. Phillip had been in jail?

"You've got a good friend in Miss Fleming, but I think you're taking advantage of her kind and generous nature," Adler continued. "A gentleman should never put a lady in such a position, and yet you've done it numerous times. Phillip, no matter your woes from the past, a gentleman keeps such things to himself and never puts his family or friends at risk."

"I am sorry for that too."

Wes could hear the regret in his brother's voice. Why couldn't regret be enough to tame him? Why couldn't he understand how he was hurting other people?

"Very well. I suggest you return to your quarters. We have a show tonight and will need to load up and get to the arena in a little over an hour."

"I'll be ready."

"As will I," Ella promised. "I'm going to change my clothes right now."

Wesley pulled back into an alcove and hoped he wouldn't be discovered. Jason had apparently done his brother a great service. He might hate the man's deception regarding Lizzy, but keeping Phillip out of legal troubles in a foreign land was something Wes couldn't ignore. For whatever reason Jason had done it, Wes was grateful.

◈⇒ SIXTEEN ⇐◈

On the seventh of September, word came via the evening papers that President McKinley had been shot. Worse still, it had happened at the Pan-American Exposition where the Brookstone Wild West Extravaganza was to perform its final show. Everyone immediately wondered if the Expo would be closed.

"I can't imagine it would be kept open," Alice said.

"I don't understand why anyone would shoot at the president. They say he's still alive, although gravely ill," Lizzy commented. "I've been praying for his recovery." Wes patted her arm, and she shook her head. "There's such evil in this world. They said the man was an anarchist."

"I read that he'd lost his job," Alice offered.

"And his mind," her husband countered. "They said he was mentally unstable."

Lizzy was still shaking her head. "I just can't believe he would try to kill the president of the United States."

"Here we are. We call this Trafalgar Square," Jason declared with a wave of his hand. "Majors, let us out here."

The carriage came to a stop, and everyone disembarked. Jason led the way to a pedestaled white column.

"This is a memorial to Admiral Horatio Nelson who died at the Battle of Trafalgar. And if you look over there"—he pointed to the right—"you'll see the National Gallery. That's our final destination. I think you'll be amazed by the impressive collection of art."

Mary only half listened to Jason's ramblings. She wanted to know about the history of London, but she was more interested in Chris taking her around town. She craned her neck to look first one way and then another to see if there was any sign of him. He had promised to join them after a meeting.

"Miss Reichert, I'm sure your young man will be along shortly. He told me he would be tied up until shortly after ten o'clock, and as you can see, it's just now ten fifteen." Jason gave her a sympathetic smile.

Mary nodded. "I'll just wait here with your Admiral Nelson. Chris mentioned this place, and I'm sure he'll come here first."

"I don't like to leave you alone," Jason declared.

Wes and Carson exchanged a glance. "Why don't you stay here with Mary, and we'll head over to the gallery," Wes suggested. "We won't get lost in such an easy crossing."

"Capital idea," Jason declared. "I should have thought of it myself."

Alice and Carson followed Wes and Lizzy as they led the way to the National Gallery. Jason stood next to Mary, who smoothed the front of her peacock-blue walking suit. She wasn't good at waiting, and lately she felt more and more curious about Chris and his life in London.

"I realize you know that Mr. Williams grew up here," Jason said. "Did you know that his grandmother was married to a man who served in the government?"

Mary nodded. "Chris told me something about it, but I don't really remember."

"Your country's ambassador brought Chris's step-grandfather

here to serve as one of his secretaries. His grandmother was quite the entertainer. My father told me that she was such an endearing soul that the stuffier upper crust of London was hard-pressed to ignore or dislike her."

"But why should they dislike her?"

Jason shrugged. "Because she was an American, and it had been less than fifty years since war between us. But Mrs. Lamb was charming and soon had London eating out of her hand. My father even remembers meeting her once and thinking her quite handsome. He told me that my own grandmother, who seldom left her home for anything less than an invitation to a royal affair, would always attend Mrs. Lamb's parties. There was just something about her."

Mary smiled. "Like Chris. People just have a way of opening up to him and enjoying his company."

"Of course, neither one was very open about their past and the life they led in America."

"Why should they be? It's no one else's business. That's one thing I've never understood about people. Why dwell in the past when the future is infinitely more important?"

Jason shook his head and smiled. "My dear, in the nobler set of London—and England in general—the past is everyone's business. This city thrives on its foundations and gossip. Why, the past is often far more important than the future."

Mary caught sight of Chris and waved. She didn't know if that went against social rules or not, but she really didn't care.

"I'm sorry to be late," Chris declared, "but I arranged a bit of a surprise." He looked at Jason and gave a nod.

"I suppose I shall go join the others." Jason looked as if he wished Mary or Chris would ask him to stay, but neither did.

"Thank you for staying with me, Mr. Adler." Mary didn't even wait for his reply but hooked her arm through Chris's. "Where are we headed?"

"We'll start with a walk," Chris said, leading her away from the square and a dejected Jason Adler. They headed down a road that Mary didn't recognize. "So Adler felt it was his job to watch over you, eh?" He cast her a sideways smile. "Does he know that you have your pistol in your purse?"

Mary giggled. "I doubt it."

Chris chuckled and began pointing out various buildings, and Mary devoted herself to learning all she could.

The day was damp, and the overcast skies threatened rain as they often did, but thankfully the bad weather held off. Even if it had poured, Mary wouldn't have cared. She enjoyed being on the arm of such a handsome man—a man she cared for a great deal. A man she hoped cared for her.

"I arrived here when I was six years old," he began without her prompting. "My grandmother was encouraging, and as I've told you, she loved London. This was one of the first walks she took me on. We often walked for the pure pleasure of exploring."

"She sounds like a wonderful grandmother. My oma is that way. She always loved to show me things and teach me in the process. Although our walks were usually more rural and dealt with identifying plants and their medicinal properties."

"Learning is important, and that was my grandmother's goal as well. She wanted to teach me. She wanted to make me into a better person, and for that I am eternally grateful."

They continued down a long street with what appeared to be parks on either side of them. Mary started to ask Chris a question and decided better of it. Maybe with him it was best to be silent and let him feel the freedom to share what he would.

"That's Buckingham Palace ahead of us," he said.

As they neared, Mary was impressed. "I know a lot of little girls dream of being a queen or at least a princess, but I never did. I was too much of a tomboy—or hoyden, as my teachers usually called me."

Chris chuckled. "I can imagine."

She elbowed him. "You aren't supposed to agree with those who insult me."

"Was it an insult?"

"Well, *hoyden* certainly has negative connotations." Mary smiled and shrugged. "But no, I don't suppose it matters to me. I loved riding and shooting."

"There are a great many women in England who love the same. Hunting is popular, as you've heard the Adlers mention."

Mary continued studying the cream-colored palace as they walked closer. "I doubt I could ever be happy in such a place."

"Why?"

"I just imagine that a place such as Buckingham Palace comes with a great many rules. I was never much good with rules, except when it came to firearms." She halted their walk and shook her head. "Don't get me wrong, I wasn't completely without civility." She laughed. "In fact, I once won a Sunday school award for comportment."

Chris laughed and pulled her back in step. "I'll just bet you did."

They walked past the palace and continued for a long time in silence. Mary didn't care. She so enjoyed just being beside Chris and watching the world around her. For the moment she didn't have to impress anyone with her performance or skills. She didn't have to explain her thoughts or feelings. She was just able to walk and appreciate her surroundings.

Chris took her down several streets, turning at one block and then another. To Mary, the stone buildings looked mostly residential now. Many were ornately trimmed, but most had a simplistic stateliness that suggested wealth and entitlement.

After a time, Chris stopped in front of a brick building. There was a long series of doors and windows, suggesting a great many families resided here.

"This was where I grew up," he said, turning to Mary.

She was so surprised by his announcement that she could say nothing. Instead she looked again at the four-story building. It was a connected series of homes, as best she could tell. She tried to imagine a child growing up here.

Looking around her, Mary spied a small park across the street. "And did you play there?"

"I did on occasion, but only when my grandmother could take me. She was particular about me." He smiled. "Would you like to see inside the house?"

Her mouth dropped open. "But I thought you sold it."

"I did, but to a good friend. The man who purchased it came to see me the other day. He invited me to call and take lunch, and I asked if I might bring you. He approved, and so here we are. Now, I ask again, would you like to see inside the house?"

"I would very much enjoy that. Oh, Chris, thank you. Thank you for sharing this with me. I know talking about the past doesn't come easy."

He sobered. "No, it doesn't, but you've been a good friend, and I want you to know more about me."

She surprised them both by jumping forward to kiss him on the cheek. Realizing what she'd done, Mary bowed her head. Her cheeks grew hot. "Sorry. I suppose that was just my Kansas farm girl enthusiasm."

He chuckled and tucked her arm against his side. "I think I shall enjoy Kansas farm girl enthusiasm."

She swallowed her embarrassment and managed to raise her gaze to his. His blue eyes seemed to twinkle in delight— something she so seldom saw them do.

Mary couldn't help but smile. "I don't know about you, but I'm starved."

———————◆◆◆◆◆◆———————

Chris had known Horace Middleton since they were in short pants together. Leaving American poverty, where shoes had been a rare luxury, Chris had come to London and found himself plunged into a life of strict rules. Mary had been correct in imagining Buckingham Palace as a house of regulations, but so too were the houses of more common folk.

"I'm honored that you would allow me into your home to see where Christopher grew up," Mary said as a footman offered her a platter of grilled fish.

"As I'm sure he must have told you, Christopher and I go way back. It was only through his brilliance that I managed to get through school." Horace, tall and redheaded, gave her a smile. "Of course, I repaid him by seeing he was invited to all the best parties."

Chris rolled his eyes. "Parties where we often drank too much and gamed too long."

"Yes, but what else is youth for?"

They enjoyed a casual conversation, and Chris relaxed in spite of the talk being focused on the past. After dinner, Horace gave them a tour of the house, leaving no door unopened. It hadn't been so long since Chris had been here, but the memories seemed to pour out of every corner. Maybe it was due to the stories being told. Maybe it was because Mary made him feel things he'd never thought possible. With her, Chris could be himself without fear of condemnation.

Soon it was time to depart, and Chris thanked Horace for his consideration. "We certainly don't need to take up your entire day."

"Do come again to see the show," Mary encouraged. "I'll see that you can attend as many as you like for free."

"I just might take you up on that offer. I've never seen anyone shoot like you do, Miss Reichert. It's been a study in fascination for me."

They followed Horace to the foyer. Chris cast one more look around. He could almost smell his grandmother's rose scent, and he half expected her to come sweeping out of the intimate drawing room where she received her guests. He missed her. She had been a mother to him when he was little and a confidante and counselor when he was grown.

"Are you ready?" Mary asked, interrupting his thoughts. "Horace says his driver is waiting to take us to the station."

Chris nodded. "I'm ready. Thank you again, Horace. It was nice to see the place again, and you were right. Your cook is gifted."

Horace laughed. "Don't let it get around. I had to pay a premium to bring him here. I'm afraid to host a dinner party for fear of our friends finding out just how good he is."

Chris chuckled and offered Mary his arm. "Shall we?"

They made their way outside and down the few stairs to the street. Horace's driver was waiting, and once they were safely seated, he started them through the busy streets to the station where they would catch their train. They were to meet up with Adler and the others and travel back to the country estate, since there wouldn't be another performance until the following evening.

"Did you enjoy yourself?" Chris asked.

Mary gave him a look that suggested she'd never been happier. "I'm so deeply touched that you arranged this for me. It says to me that you trust me with your memories."

Her words seemed to pierce through the walls he'd built to protect himself from the ugly opinions of others. "I do trust you, Mary. I trust you as I've never trusted anyone else. In time I hope to answer all those questions you have about me and the

198

past. For now, however, I keep those answers to myself as much for my sake as yours."

Mary's expression altered to a sad sort of sobriety. "Chris, you never have to worry about what I'll think. Frankly, if remembering those things causes you pain, then I'd just as soon you forget. I think you know I've come to care for you."

Chris felt a tightening in his chest. "I do know that. I just hope you won't regret it."

She shook her head. "How could I ever regret knowing you—caring about you? We're friends, Chris, and I hope we always will be, if not . . ." She fell silent as the carriage came to a stop.

Chris wondered what she might have said if their journey had been just a little longer. Would she have declared her love for him? Did he want her to? It had been a long time since he'd felt loved, and that had come only from his grandmother. He had never allowed himself to fall in love because of his past, but now it seemed his heart had other ideas. He had a feeling that wherever Mary went, his heart would go also.

That evening, long after everyone else had retired, Chris and Wes sat reading newspapers in front of a large fireplace in the Adler library. Chris yawned and put the paper aside at about the same time Wes put his paper down.

"It seems everyone else has gone to bed. I suppose we should too," Wes commented. "Tomorrow's a performance day."

"Before you go, I wonder if I might talk to you about something."

Wesley eased back in his leather chair. "Of course. What did you have in mind?"

Chris steepled his fingers and rested his elbows on the cushioned arms of the chair. "I care very deeply for Mary."

"I think we can all see that," Wes replied, grinning.

"The thing is . . . I haven't been completely open with her

about my past. In particular things that my father and brothers did that earned them a terrible reputation."

"Why should Mary care about that?"

"Well, even if God doesn't hold me to blame for the sins of my father, many in human form do. Not only that, but I think I also fear I'll turn out to be just like him and my brothers. After all, I have quite a temper. I've just learned to keep it under control."

"Which, I'm guessing, is more than your father did."

"True."

Wes shrugged. "Then I would also guess that you're at least one step ahead of him. You care about controlling your temper and work to get along with folks. Your father didn't care about such things, and it got him in trouble. At least I'm guessin' it did."

"You're right again."

"So just the fact that you have similar traits doesn't mean you're going to end up being like him. God can transform people with the worst of pasts. It's about the heart and what condition you want it to be in."

"But it's not just my heart I'm thinking about."

Wes stretched his legs. "I'm not a betting man, but if I were, I'd bet that Mary would never care about such things. All the time I've known her, Mary Reichert has never been pretentious or shallow in her feelings."

"No. I've never known her to be that way either. In fact, she doesn't even pretend when it comes to God. She's honest about not having all the answers. Her faith has always been more connected to her grandparents, like mine was to my grandmother. I suppose we both have a long way to go where God is concerned."

"You just need to take it step by step," Wes replied. "First you need to believe in Jesus as the Son of God—your Savior. Can you do that? Can you accept that you're a sinner and, without Jesus to intercede, you're bound for hell?"

"Yes. I really don't have a problem accepting that," Chris admitted. "But I just don't see why He cares about me."

"Well, maybe, just for the moment," Wes said, smiling, "don't think about what He's thinking and just concentrate on what you know. You need Him."

Chris sighed and nodded slowly. "I need Him."

·✦≡ SEVENTEEN ≡·✦

As they readied for that night's performance, Mary couldn't help but think back on the day before and the time she'd spent with Chris. He seemed to have enjoyed the day just as much as she had, and yet there was still that point where he always pulled away. Always guarded his heart from her.

Mary pried open a crate of glass orbs. Uncertain they could get them in England, Oliver and Jason had purchased extra before coming abroad. Still, with all the competitions Adler had hosted, they were running low. Mary had pointed this out and asked Jason and Henry Adler to see about getting more balls, but so far she'd heard nothing about it.

She put aside the crate lid and began to retrieve the balls, stacking them in their newsprint wrappings on the table. Each ball had been individually wrapped and carefully packed in straw. The crates were then handled with the utmost care, and usually the orbs arrived unbroken. Still, it was imperative to handle each one delicately.

She had special trays to hold them after they were unwrapped. The trays had cushioned bottoms with silk lining and individual compartments for each ball. There were three trays, and each held twenty orbs. This was what she used for each show unless something else was requested by the Adlers or Oliver Brookstone. Given their low supply, Mary had suggested she do more with vegetables and fruit. These had a nice way of exploding on impact, depending on the load she used, and always impressed the audience—which was, after all, the goal of each act.

After she'd removed all the orbs from the crate, Mary reached for the first ball in her stack and began to unwrap it. It had survived the transatlantic crossing without so much as a crack. The second and third orbs had as well. The fourth had a minor crack, but Mary felt certain she could make it work for one of her tricks.

As she reached for the fifth ball, the word *Williams* on the newspaper caught her eye. She couldn't help but smile. She'd been praying, just as Lizzy had suggested, and asking God what He had in mind for her where Chris was concerned. She hadn't planned to come back to the show and fall in love, but then, she hadn't planned on Chris being part of their tour. Now, as she considered the future and whether or not she'd remain with the show, her heart couldn't keep from considering Christopher Williams as well.

With a sigh, Mary freed the ball from the newsprint, then spread the paper open to see what the article was about. The title read *Williams Gang Put to Death*.

Mary frowned and scanned the short announcement.

Friday, the first of March, the infamous Williams Gang was hanged in a public execution in Baltimore, Maryland. The gang, consisting of father and three sons, was responsible for killing two penitentiary guards during an escape in the spring of 1900. The gang was serving time for having robbed several banks in and around the Washington, D.C., area, the oldest crime occurring in 1880.

Feeling as if her knees might give out, Mary found a bench and sat down with the newspaper. She didn't need Chris to tell her this was his family. She felt certain of it—sickened by it.

Hiram Williams and his sons Luke, Tom, and Ray were serving twenty-year sentences for bank robbery when they made their escape from prison on the evening of April 23rd, 1900. The men had acquired knives and stabbed two guards to death as they made their way from the penitentiary. They waylaid a passerby and forced him to drive them from the area. He later escaped unharmed and was able to tell the authorities the make and model of his automobile so that police could be on the lookout.

The four men were apprehended trying to steal a boat. They were returned to prison and brought to trial for the murder of penitentiary guards Martin Jones and Buford Daily. All four convicts were found guilty and sentenced to death by public hanging. That sentence was carried out without interference or prejudice. The men were not survived by family. The county will be responsible for burial.

Mary reread the article two more times before she could fully comprehend it. Despite the line about the criminals having no family, she was certain this was the horrible secret Chris was trying to keep hidden.

She forgot about her work and carefully tore the article from the paper, leaving the bulk of crumpled paper behind. Then she went to find Lizzy. Maybe she could help Mary figure out how to handle this.

Lizzy and Ella were making practice runs for the evening performance. Lizzy did a run showing Ella one of her drags, then returned and waited for Ella to mimic it. Once the blonde had executed the trick exactly, Lizzy applauded.

"That was perfect, Ella. I couldn't have done it better." Lizzy noticed Mary and rode over. "Hi, Mary. What can I do for you?" she asked, sliding off Thoreau's back.

Mary handed her the newspaper. "I think . . . I feel certain that this article is about Chris's father and brothers."

Lizzy scanned the story and then looked up with a puzzled expression. "Williams is a very common name, Mary. Why do you think these people are related to Chris?"

"He's told me before that his father and brothers were no good. He was much younger than his brothers, and when he was six and his mother died, they were unable to keep him. That's when he came to London to live with his grandmother. He never said anything about them robbing banks, but it just all fits together."

Ella joined them. "What fits together?"

Lizzy looked to Mary for permission to share the article. Mary nodded, and as Lizzy handed Ella the paper, Mary explained, "I found this when I was unwrapping the glass orbs. It was in a crate we purchased from the glass factory just outside of Washington, D.C. I found this article, and I feel confident that it's Chris Williams's father and brothers they're talking about."

Ella read the paper then handed it back to Mary. "That seems an awful far reach."

"No. It's not. I can't explain it, but Chris told me his father and brothers were all that were left of his family when his mother died. Chris couldn't bring himself to tell me what was so terrible that his father and brothers had done or why he didn't want to talk about them. He did tell me he lived near Washington, D.C., in Maryland, however." Mary drew a deep breath and tried to calm her racing heart. "I've been praying and praying about this, begging God to help me understand and to know how I can help. I just know in my heart that this is where God has led me."

"All right, all right." Lizzy put her arm around Mary. "Even if this is true and it is Chris's family . . . he's certainly not to blame."

"I know that. I just . . . I need to know what to do."

Lizzy and Ella exchanged a look and shook their heads. "Do about what?"

"The fact that I know about this. He's been careful to keep all of this hidden from us. But now that I know—"

"You *don't* know that this is his father and brothers," Lizzy interrupted. "You can't just go off the assumption."

Mary folded the paper and pushed it into her skirt pocket. "I know you think I'm wrong, and I understand why. But I've been praying so long about this. Chris is so burdened by his past, and now I feel like God has shown me why."

"Then God needs to show you how to deal with it," Ella said with a shrug. "I agree with Lizzy. You can't be sure it's anything at all related to Chris unless you ask him outright."

"We'll all pray about it, Mary, but I suggest for now you say nothing. I think it might cause unnecessary pain for Chris if it's false, and if it's true . . . well, he obviously doesn't want us to know about it."

"But I thought the truth was always better," Mary declared. "You told me yourself that Jesus said the truth would set us free. I want that freedom for Chris. He deserves it."

"Truth is always best," Lizzy replied. "I'm not asking you to be false or speak lies. I'm simply suggesting that you pray fervently about what to do. I feel confident God will open the door to the truth in this. You need to trust Him, Mary. Trust Him and don't try to force this to come to light."

They were right. Mary knew that, and although she longed to go to Chris and tell him that she knew the truth and that it didn't matter, she knew there was no easy way to do that without causing him pain.

"I suppose it won't hurt to pray about it." Mary put her hand in her pocket and wrapped her fingers around the article. She knew it was only her imagination, but she could have sworn the paper felt hot.

Jason waited patiently as his valet finished brushing the back of his suit coat.

"Will that be all, sir?"

"Yes. Thank you, Westcott."

Once the servant had gone, Jason walked to the window and looked down on the lawns below. It had rained all day, and his mood was as gray as the skies. Lizzy was never free of her companions, and he hadn't found a single opportunity to speak to her privately about what he'd done. Worse still, his father seemed to know what had happened. He hadn't come right out and said anything about it, but there was something in his attitude that suggested he knew Jason had caused problems, and he wasn't happy.

His father was eternally devoted to the Brookstone family, all because the brothers had saved his life on a hunting trip. Jason had listened to him sing their praises, knowing he could never do anything that would impress his father half as much. It was a curse to always be a disappointment to one's father in the Adler family, and Jason was no exception.

Of course, he'd had his share of troubles. School had been difficult, and the only way he'd managed to get through was with a fair amount of creativity. His father had always given him a generous allowance, and often he'd had to part with that money in order to buy his grade. But it had been worth it. He had his education and his social standing, and now it was expected that he would take a wife and add to his father's kingdom. If only Lizzy would cooperate.

Jason knew he was expected to marry someone above his

own station. His father had even hinted at one of the distant relatives of Victoria, a homely young woman with little to offer except that her father held a title and vast lands. Jason's father felt confident that by marrying the right woman, Jason could receive a title that would be ongoing—something he could pass down to his son. But Jason wanted Lizzy, and there was no title that would ever mean as much.

She was all he could think about, and now Wesley was here, keeping Jason from his rightful place at her side. He had considered using Phillip—perhaps threatening the young man's well-being—but as of yet, Jason wasn't sure how to create a situation that would force Wesley to choose between his brother and Lizzy. Worse still, Jason wasn't certain which choice De-Shazer would make.

He began to pace the room, trying to come up with a scheme that would make it so that Lizzy and the others had no choice. Jason didn't like the idea of forcing Lizzy to wed him, but he felt absolutely confident that given time and solitude with him, she would see that his love was dearer than anything Wesley could give her.

The key was isolating her from the others. It hadn't been enough just to get her away from DeShazer. He would have to separate her from her friends and even her uncle. And, of course, the show. She would have to be free of those obligations.

"I know she will love me as I love her. I know she will," he muttered as he came to halt again in front of the window. "I just need the right opportunity. The right place."

He caught sight of the clock. It was time to make his way downstairs to join the others. He wondered which of her ensembles Lizzy would be wearing. He had taken such delight in choosing her wardrobe. Just picturing her beautiful figure draped in creations he had chosen thrilled him like nothing else. He remembered fingering the materials and imagining them lying against her skin. She was the most beautiful woman he'd ever known. Even in her performing clothes, she outshone all others.

He made his way downstairs and found everyone casually gathered in the large drawing room his mother called the Green Room. She had chosen varying tones of green to be the focus, accenting with bric-a-brac, expensive paintings, and a variety of lush materials to draw attention to her favorite color.

"Ah, Jason, I see you are finally here," his father announced.

"I didn't know I was missed," Jason replied, smiling. "Do forgive my delay." He let his gaze travel the room in search of Lizzy. Not seeing her there, he frowned. "I daresay I'm not the only late arrival."

His father glanced toward the others. "If you are looking for Elizabeth and Wesley, they are sharing a meal with her uncle. I understand there were some things they wished to discuss in private."

"It seems there would have been time enough for that later." Jason's mood darkened even more.

His father ushered him to a corner and spoke in a low voice. "I believe you'd do better by seeking another path, Jason." He fixed Jason with a serious gaze. "I hear you've been rather rude toward Mr. DeShazer and the understanding he and Elizabeth have."

"Understanding, indeed. He's a country cowboy setting his sights above his station. Elizabeth feels sorry for him. It's nothing more."

"I was under the impression that their history suggests a great deal more. It would hardly be of use to you to insert yourself in the middle of their courtship. My intentions for you are vastly different, and meddling in their affair serves you no purpose."

Jason narrowed his eyes. "I have my own intentions, Father. I've done as you called me to do in almost every situation. I have been the dutiful son, performing whatever task you put upon me, but do not think that extends to your choosing my bride."

The older man was not in the least bit intimidated, and it caused Jason no end of frustration to watch him lean in and raise his index finger, as he often did to make a point. "I will choose your bride and vocation and anything else that I am of a mind to do. You have nothing but that which I have given you, and I can just as easily take it back. Leave Elizabeth alone and do nothing further to interfere in her relationships. Do you understand me?"

"And if I refuse?" Jason asked, already knowing the answer.

His father's graying brow raised. "If you refuse, you will find yourself very much alone. No future. No family. Nothing."

Ella thought for some time about what Lizzy had said about not forcing Mary's suspicions to come to light. However, she had heard from Phillip's own lips that he had killed his father. That he drank to forget what he had done. Surely if Ella encouraged him to talk about it, Phillip might well find himself set free.

She went into her last routine for the night, performing a variety of acrobatic circus tricks atop a team of four horses with Jessie and Debbie. Jessie was the taller and larger of the trio, while Debbie and Ella were petite and blond. It stood to reason that Jessie acted as an anchor for most of their tricks.

For their last number, Jessie rode the team around the track they'd set up. One by one, Debbie and Ella leapt onto the back of the outside horses and made their way across the team, doing a series of jumps and flips. Ella found it exhilarating to perform. She thrilled to the cheers of the audience and enjoyed their gasps at the dangers.

At one point, Debbie took one of the outside horses and Ella took the other while Jessie continued with her two. They jumped the horses over progressively taller obstacles, to the crowd's delight. When they came back together, Ella and Debbie returned the horses to Jessie's guidance and began their full acrobatic act.

By the time they finished, the audience was clapping and cheering as wildly as if they were Americans. Ella beamed a smile and waved as they circled the arena. She and Debbie had climbed up Jessie's side, secured only by a foothold at Jessie's padded waist, and taken each other's hands. Stretching their remaining limbs out as far to the sides as they could, they held the pose and rode around the arena to the approval of the audience.

Phillip was there to take the horses from them after the performers had completed their final parade to end the evening. The crowds seemed to love that instead of just waving the American flag as she stood atop Thoreau, Lizzy also waved the Union Jack. Wes took the flags from her one at a time, then waited for Lizzy to dismount.

"You all did so well tonight. Oliver will be pleased to hear about it," Jason declared as the performers gathered. "The show was sold-out, and we were even asked to consider doing an extra performance on Sunday."

"We can discuss that later," Wes replied. "Right now everyone is exhausted. I think it's more important we get our things put away and load up for the trip back to your estate. Unless you've changed your mind about staying in town."

"No. We have three days until the next show. It'll be far more restful for the horses to have the freedom of the pasture. Not to mention that it will be more relaxing for the performers as well."

"And I will be better able to keep an eye on Uncle Oliver," Lizzy said.

Ella watched as the trio walked away. She saw Phillip leading the Roman team from the arena and hurried to catch up with him.

"How are you feeling, Phillip?"

"Fit as a fiddle." He threw her a lopsided smile. "I don't know about you, but I'll be glad to get back to America."

"It shouldn't be long now. Were you at breakfast when Mr. Adler announced that the Expo is going to continue despite what happened?"

"I wasn't there, but I got the news. I suppose it might change if the president dies. I heard from Wes that it doesn't look promising. Getting gut shot is never good."

"No, I don't suppose so." Ella pulled off the feathered headpiece she wore for her act. "I can't imagine getting shot anywhere would be a good thing."

"No," Phillip said, shaking his head.

They walked toward the horse stalls in the chilled night air. Ella didn't know how to bring up what was on her heart, but then Phillip saved her from having to figure it out.

"I want to thank you again for getting me out of jail. I wish you hadn't had to involve Mr. Adler, but it seems he's been true to his word. No one has said anything to me about what happened."

"Phillip, you can't let it happen again. The risk is too great. The constables didn't want to let you go. If Jason's family didn't wield the power they do, you would still be there."

"I know."

He looked so remorseful that Ella could hardly continue. The last thing she wanted to do was make him feel bad, but she needed to know the truth. She glanced around to make sure no one else was near.

"Phillip," she finally murmured, "did you really kill your father?"

He stopped mid-step and looked at her with eyes wide and mouth open.

Ella immediately felt guilty for bringing up such a painful

topic, but she couldn't stop now. "I promise it doesn't matter to me, but I think you'd feel much better discussing it."

"Did I say that?" he asked after several long seconds of silence.

She nodded. "When I asked you the other night why you drank. You told me you did it to forget, and when I pressed, you said it was to forget that you had killed your father."

With a small jerk, Phillip turned to the horses and appeared to focus on getting them ready for their trip back to the Adler estate. But Ella could see his mind wasn't on it.

"Phillip, I don't care what you've done in the past. God can forgive anything if you ask Him."

"God is in the forgiving business, but people aren't. People have a hard time forgiving."

"If you're worried about your brother or the Brookstones, I'm sure you needn't. They'll forgive you . . . of that I'm certain."

Phillip shook his head. His expression was so sorrowful that Ella reached out to touch his arm.

"I know they'll forgive," she insisted. "I forgive you—no matter what you've done."

"That's real sweet of you, Ella, but it doesn't matter." He shook his head again. "I can't forgive myself."

⊷⊱ EIGHTEEN ⊰⊶

Chris woke with a start. He'd had the nightmare again. He could still see his father's scowling face sneering at him through the bars of the jail as he awaited his execution. Chris had wrestled with his conscience ever since finding out that his father and brothers were sentenced to die, and had finally given in to go see them and make whatever kind of peace he could.

"You grew up to be the disappointment I thought you'd be," his father had snarled.

Chris had known a void all of his life where his father should have been. Even when he was very young, his mother would hide and protect him from this man—this vicious savage who hated everything and everyone.

"I may be a disappointment," Chris had replied, "but I'm the one on the outside of the bars."

His father had laughed and told him he had no use for Chris unless he had a means to get him out of jail.

Chris, hoping to hurt the old man as much as he had hurt his son, had smiled. "I wouldn't help you even if I could."

The words had come out of his mouth before he realized

it. It was probably the only thing he'd ever said that his father could respect.

The older man had stared at Chris for a moment, then shrugged. "I have no use for you then. Guard! Get him out of here," his father had commanded.

The guard had come and escorted Chris from the room. "Do you still want to see your brothers?" he had asked.

Chris figured since he'd come this far, he might as well see it through. "Show me the way."

The reaction of his two younger brothers had actually been somewhat rewarding. Ray and Tom had told Chris how glad they were that he'd not gone the same way they had. They were sorry to be losing their lives and wished they'd made different choices. Chris had few memories of them, but they shared several they had of him. It was like wiping a spot on a frosted window to peek into the house of strangers. The scenes they painted were interesting, but Chris had no memories or connection to them.

The last person he'd seen was his oldest brother, Luke. Luke was just like their father—hard and bitter through and through. He didn't care at all that Chris had come to say good-bye. As far as he was concerned, he had no brother named Christopher.

"You might as well leave before the hangin'," his brother had told him. "Ain't gonna be anything like you think. It'll damage your delicate sensibilities."

He'd been right on one account. The hanging hadn't been like anything Chris expected. There was nothing dignified about seeing a man put to death—especially hanged.

Chris pushed back the down-filled quilt and got out of the luxurious bed. He had known similar luxury most of his life, but the Adlers were definitely higher up the social ladder than his grandmother had been. They were English, after all, and Henry Adler's father had been an earl. Adler's family were friends with

Queen Victoria's family—both immediate and extended. It was even expected that Henry would receive some form of title—most likely only for his lifetime and not one that could be passed to Jason. But even so, a title was a title, and with Adler's financial and business successes on both sides of the Atlantic, he would no doubt make the best of it.

The valet assigned to Chris appeared from the dressing room. "Good morning, sir. I have your bath ready and your clothes laid out."

Chris had enjoyed a valet's services when he lived with his grandmother, but it was hard to get used to the idea again. Once free of someone shadowing him, Chris found that he didn't like having servants. He wanted privacy most of the time, and servants meant always having someone listening in.

"Thank you, Brumston. It's much appreciated."

"Will there be anything else, sir?"

"No. Feel free to go see to Mr. Brookstone's needs."

"Very good, sir." Brumston didn't have to be encouraged twice. Chris had the feeling the valet didn't like having American guests from a wild west show, much less that he should have to lower himself to wait upon them.

After a quick bath, Chris dressed and made his way downstairs. He was happy to find Mary and Lizzy just sitting down to breakfast. He was even happier to see that they'd chosen the end of the table closest to the fireplace, which glowed with a large blaze.

"Ladies, good morning. How pretty you are today."

They both looked up and smiled, but Lizzy spoke first. "Might we return the compliment?" She looked to Mary, who nodded.

"You look dashing in that navy wool."

"Yes, well, with the chill the air has had, I needed the extra warmth." He went to the buffet and helped himself to the typical breakfast he'd known growing up: grilled tomatoes, poached eggs, sausages, and a rack of toast.

"Mary and I were discussing what to do today," Lizzy announced. "Since we have a nice break between shows, we wondered if it would be possible to take a little side trip."

"To where?" Chris asked, taking a seat opposite them. He immediately reached for the butter and began to slather his toast. When a servant came offering tea, he nodded. "Yes, please."

"What do you suggest? We only have a short time before we leave for home."

"Let's see. You've been to Parliament and Westminster Abbey," he said, thinking aloud.

"I really don't care to do another museum," Mary said, shaking her head.

"Perhaps we could go into London, and I could take you on a walk around the city. We could enjoy a nice lunch while we're out and maybe ride on the tourist omnibus. They drive around to the other sights you haven't seen, like the Tower of London and Tower Bridge."

"That sounds like fun," Lizzy admitted. "Just a nice day out to enjoy the sights."

Chris checked his watch. "After we eat, you ladies can round up all those who wish to come along. I'll check with Henry Adler and see if he has any other suggestions, and we can plan to leave here in time to catch the train at ten. Agreed?"

"Agreed," the ladies said in unison.

Jessie and Debbie entered with Ella. They were discussing something about their act, and when Lizzy posed the question about touring London, Ella shook her head. "We want to work on something new for the routine. Debbie had a wonderful idea, and we want to get right to it after breakfast. Phillip and Carson agreed to help, and Alice plans to practice some new tricks for her act."

"Well, it seems there won't be as many of us as we thought," Chris said with a shrug. "It's no matter. I'm sure we'll have fun nonetheless."

"Wes asked me to give you this," Ella said to Lizzy, handing her a note.

Lizzy read it and shook her head. "It looks like it will be just you and Mary. Wes has plans for us." She smiled and picked up her teacup. "He says I'm to put on old clothes and good boots. Apparently we're going on a long hike."

Mary looked at Chris. "Can we still go?" She looked afraid he might refuse.

"Of course," he said. "I'm keen to go with you alone or with others."

She rewarded him with a smile and dug into her breakfast. "Then I'd better finish this so we won't miss the train."

A few hours later, after walking for miles around the city, Chris suggested they make their way to one of his favorite places for lunch. It was an out-of-the-way shop that served the best fish and chips a person could buy.

When they reached the counter and placed their order, Chris was delighted by Mary's surprise when the owner handed her a newspaper cone with the fried fish and potatoes inside.

"How marvelous," she said, following Chris to a table. "This is charming."

"And delicious." He procured some malt vinegar and two mugs of cider before taking the seat beside her at the tiny table.

Mary warmed her hands on her cider mug. "Brrr." She sampled the beverage and smiled. "This reminds me of my opa's cider. He makes it every year, and we celebrate Oktoberfest with it instead of beer."

"I used to join some of my friends here from time to time. We'd play darts and talk politics." Chris bit into the fish. It was as good as he remembered.

Mary followed suit, picking a piece from the cone and popping it into her mouth. She smiled, her eyes lighting up.

Chris was glad for the time alone with her. He'd enjoyed their afternoon together and found Mary's company soothing after his nightmares. He wondered what she would think if he told her that his father and brothers were convicted killers who'd been hanged the previous spring. Would she be so eager to venture into the city alone with him? Would she dislike sitting this close together—close enough that their shoulders nearly touched?

"I love London," Mary said after another sip of cider, oblivious to his concerns. "It's like a world unto itself. I've never seen anything like it."

He chuckled. "Having seen Kansas farms, I'm sure it's a far cry from growing up there."

"It is, of course, but there's something else. There's something about being surrounded by all these wonderful old buildings. Even the grand way in which they perform their church services makes me think of kings and queens in glorious castles."

"Instead of God?" Chris questioned.

She shook her head. "No, along with Him. It's all formality and pomp. I wouldn't like it all the time, but it makes me more mindful of God's glory." She ate another chip and then shrugged. "It's a sense of walking in the past, yet moving toward the future. I can't really explain it."

"Yet you did, quite eloquently. London has always struck me the same way. Here there is a sense of the old world. Perhaps not as ancient as Rome."

"You've been to Rome?" she asked, looking amazed.

"I have. Grandmother and I traveled quite a bit. When my step-grandfather was alive, he went with us when he could but sometimes had to stay behind. His work for the government kept him busy, and he felt that Grandmother and I should still enjoy ourselves. Each summer he would travel a bit with us and then return to London while we continued."

"That sounds amazing. So have you been all over the world?" Her excitement was almost contagious.

"I have." Chris laughed. "Just about every corner. I've seen India, Egypt, and all of Europe. I think it's what brought out the writer in me. I saw the details of each place and the cultures there, and it all begged to be written about. I kept all sorts of journals."

"I'd love to see them."

He grinned. "Maybe one day I can show them to you."

Mary nibbled on a piece of fried potato, then asked, "What do you plan to do after your travel with the show is complete?"

He shrugged. "I can't really say. I suppose I'll return to New York and continue to write for the magazine. However, lately I've thought about writing a book. Nothing specific, but I'm thinking of the possibilities."

She turned, and suddenly their faces were only inches apart. "With all the experiences, ah, you've had," she stammered, "I-I think it would make a wonderful book. You know . . . for all the people . . . who can't travel around the world as you have."

Chris had considered the idea, but at the moment all he could really think about was Mary and how beautiful she was. She looked equally at ease in the house of a fine family or here at a local pub. There was something enthralling about her, something that made him want to throw caution aside and kiss her.

"Do you trust me?" she asked.

Chris swallowed the lump in his throat. He thought from the look in her eyes that maybe she had read his thoughts.

"I'm sorry. I didn't mean to shock you," Mary said, eyeing him as if trying to gauge whether to go on. "I'm known for speaking my mind, and that just came out without thought." Still, she didn't move.

"I suppose you must have a reason for the question," Chris said, trying to force his quickened breath to calm. He found looking away impossible.

"Oh, I do. Oma always told me that people couldn't be really close . . . friends unless they trusted one another."

Chris nodded. "I believe that's true. I suppose the answer to your question is that I do trust you . . . at least as far as our time together has allowed for trust to build. Now, may I ask you an equally bold question?" Neither one seemed to consider moving apart.

"Of course."

"Why does my trust matter so much?"

She gave him a hint of a smile. "If I'm fully honest," she finally answered, "then I have to say that I care about you and want to be your friend. Your good friend. Perhaps even . . . your best friend."

Her answer took him by surprise. What exactly she meant by "best friend," he couldn't begin to guess. Women were strange creatures. They didn't think the same way men did. Her desire to become his best friend might mean nothing more than keeping each other company throughout their time with the show. It might mean something infinitely more.

As if to prove it did, Mary inched closer, and with her nearness, Chris lost all reason and leaned toward her mouth. He hesitated only a moment, then pressed his lips against hers. The kiss was brief and chaste but very satisfying.

They pulled apart, and only then did Chris realize neither one had closed their eyes. Mary smiled. "I guess that answers my question."

Chris coughed to cover his embarrassment. He'd never allowed himself to act in such a manner before. "Well, to prove my trust in you, I have a surprise."

"You already gave me a surprise." She grinned and picked up another piece of fish. "At least it was a surprise to me."

He shook his head. "I've been working on something since before we left America." He hadn't intended to tell Mary about his secret deals, but since they involved her—or might—he figured he owed her that much. Not only that, but he had to distance himself from the kiss and consider what was happening between them.

She smiled and leaned toward him, as if for another kiss. "What?"

He leaned back and dabbed his mouth with his handkerchief before answering. Good grief, he wanted to kiss her again. "I sent a message to Annie Oakley. I asked if she would consider doing a one-time contest with you."

"What?" Mary repeated the word again, this time in alarm. She shook her head and backed away.

Chris held up his hands. "I spent time, you'll recall, with Buffalo Bill Cody's show and got to know the people there. Annie is a marvelous woman, and I think she might very well enjoy having a shooting contest with you. Sort of the past meets the future. Just like this town."

"Oh, Chris . . . oh, I don't know if that's a very good idea at all. I mean . . . well, of course she's much better than I am. I don't know what Oliver or the Adlers would say."

"They would be thrilled. Annie Oakley's name is known from one end of the country to the other, as well as here in Europe. I think the ticket to such an event could be ten times what we normally charge, maybe twenty times." He grinned. "I think people would pay just about anything to see such a competition. The pictures would be wonderful, and the article could run in the magazine as soon as possible. I know my editor would be delighted."

"Oh my . . ." She swallowed and looked for a moment as if she might be sick. "I never even hoped to meet her. My father knew her. He thought she was the best shooter God ever put on earth. He also told me to strive to be as good as Annie Oakley."

"Well, I think you are, and this competition should take place. After all, you two have a great deal in common." Chris picked up a chip and popped it in his mouth.

For the first time ever, he'd managed to leave Mary speechless. Not even his kiss had done that.

Lizzy steadied her mount. Thoreau was her choice for the night, but he was antsy and not at all his normal self.

"What's the matter, boy?" she asked, leaning over his neck. She gave him long strokes down either side, as she did whenever he was nervous, but tonight it did little good.

She wished Wes or Phillip were close by, but Phillip was busy with the Roman team, and Wes had been called away to adjust a shoe on Alice's horse.

"You're on next, Lizzy," Ella said, coming to stand beside her. She looked up with a frown. "Are you all right?"

"I'm fine, but Thoreau is a bit out of sorts. I suppose he'll be fine once we get out there." Lizzy straightened in the saddle. "Goodness, but I'll be glad when we get back to America. I don't know about you, but I'm ready to be done with the show. I haven't told Wes yet, but I've made up my mind to resign after this season."

"But Jason said he hoped you'd go another year . . . you know, just to give me extra time," Ella countered.

"You don't need extra time. You're already as good as I am, and I've been doing this most of my life. You have a natural talent, and I know you'll surpass me by leaps and bounds."

Out in the arena, Jason was announcing the next act.

"Looks like I'm up." Lizzy gathered the reins and adjusted

her feet in the stirrups. "Thoreau seems calmer now. I'm sure it was nothing."

Ella nodded, and Lizzy maneuvered the beautiful dappled buckskin toward the arena entrance.

"And now, ladies and gentlemen, boys and girls, I present to you the world famous Elizabeth Brookstone," Jason said through his megaphone. The small orchestra they'd arranged began to play, and that was Lizzy's cue to make her entrance.

For the first half of her act, things went along without a miss. Lizzy began to relax, seeing that Thoreau had finally fallen into his normal paces. They went through a series of tricks with Lizzy vaulting on and off the horse in between spins and drags. She knew that one day very soon this would all be behind her, but for now she had to admit she still loved it.

Jason began building the crowd's excitement by announcing that her next series of tricks were death-defying and required absolute silence. The orchestra stopped playing, and a hush fell over the audience. Of course, it wasn't really necessary for Lizzy or her horse, but it made things seem tenser, and that was a part of thrilling the spectators.

"Gentlemen, please keep an eye on your ladies, for this final series of tricks has been known to bring about fainting spells."

Lizzy smiled to herself. There *had* been fainting spells, usually by addlepated ninnies who wore their corsets too tight.

She made adjustments for the last run. Holding on to the front skirt corner of her saddle with her right hand, Lizzy twisted her left hand to hold the horn upside down. As she did this, she leaned forward. She reached the horse's neck, then pushed both feet up into the air and pointed her toes. From there she went forward into a sort of cartwheel, but something happened as she loosened her hold. She lost her grip, and before she realized it, she was headed for the ground. Somewhere along the way she hit her head. On what, she wasn't sure, but she saw stars and was disoriented enough that she nearly lost her grip altogether.

Thoreau instantly knew something was different. He was well trained, however, to go with the flow. Lizzy barely managed to swing herself back upright before guiding Thoreau out of sight of the audience. Once there, she brought Thoreau to a stop as her vision narrowed and she slid sideways from the saddle.

Then everything went black.

⋄⊱≕ NINETEEN ≓⊰⋄

But I'm fine, I assure you," Lizzy argued with the doctor.

"Nevertheless, you must have bed rest for the next few days."

"Don't worry," Wes said with a firm edge to his tone. "She won't get out of this bed even once during that time."

The doctor gathered his things. "I'm glad to hear it. She has a slight concussion, but if she takes it easy, I'm sure she'll recover without further complications."

"Thank you, Doctor," Jason said from the opposite side of the bed.

"Let me walk with you out, Edward," Henry Adler declared. The doctor gave a nod, and the two men left the room without another word.

Lizzy looked at Wes and smiled. "I'm really all right. You don't have to look so concerned."

"I want you to quit the show now."

"She can't do that," Jason said, moving toward the right side of the bed while Wesley took a closer position on the left. "People are counting on her."

"She's hurt," Wes countered, folding his arms across his

chest. "You only care about ticket sales, but I care about the well-being of my future wife."

"I care a great deal about Lizzy's well-being, as you certainly know." Jason crossed his arms, mirroring Wes's stance. "The doctor said she'll be just fine in a few days' time."

"It's too dangerous. I won't have her risking her life to line your pockets."

Lizzy found herself watching the argument volley from man to man. "I hope you realize I'm still in the room," she said, shaking her head. It did hurt, but she wasn't about to admit that to either of them.

"You're here only by the grace of God." Wes moved closer to the bed. "Lizzy, you scared the life out of me. I thought I'd lost you."

She smiled at the concern in his voice and reached out her hand. "Sit here. I'm perfectly fine."

Wes took a seat beside her and looked at Jason with a smirk.

"Jason, I promise I won't desert the show until the end of the season." She felt Wes stiffen and squeezed his hand. "And I promise you, Wesley, that I will follow the doctor's orders and take it easy for the next few days."

"It's ridiculous to continue risking your life when you've already decided to leave the show at the end of the year. There's no shame in leaving early. You said yourself that Ella is more than ready to take on the starring role, and there's only one show left anyway."

"But that isn't what people paid for," Jason protested. "Not only that, but you two promised to stage an engagement for us at the Expo. It's important that you go through with it, especially now that the president has died. Americans are in mourning and need something to cheer them up." He fixed Wesley with a look that suggested he had the upper hand.

It was the wrong thing to remind Wesley of, and Lizzy knew

he'd have no part in the production now that Jason was using it like a trump card.

"There isn't going to be a staged engagement. Oliver is ill, and now Lizzy is injured. I'm taking them both home."

"No!" Lizzy declared before Jason could respond. "Wes, that isn't called for. We gave our word."

"I can't believe you're defending this buffoon's desires. He cares only for the money and fame that can be had." Wes stood, and though Lizzy tried to keep hold of his hand, he pulled away. "I thought you'd understand, Lizzy. I thought you'd care more about seeing to Oliver's needs, even if you aren't worried about your own."

"That's hardly fair, Wes. You know I care about Uncle Oliver. I'm the one who insisted he stay in bed. I was the one who told him Jason and Henry could handle the show's announcements." It hurt her deeply that he thought her unfeeling.

"I heard your uncle talking about resuming his role at the Expo performance," Wes said, his anger growing by the minute. "I heard Jason tell him that would be wonderful—especially so that he could be part of our mock engagement."

"And it will be. Oliver will be much better by then, and his touch on the moment will be perfect," Jason said, as if it were all perfectly logical.

Lizzy frowned. This was the first she'd heard of Uncle Oliver planning to be part of the show when they returned to America. "I don't think it's good to encourage Uncle Oliver to perform. He needs a complete break from the show, and I intend to see that he goes home to rest."

"But just think how much he's looking forward to this," Jason argued. "He told me himself that the idea of being involved gave him a reason to get well."

"I'm betting it was your idea in the first place. You probably got him all stirred up with it," Wesley said and began to pace. "I think you've done enough to manipulate folks, don't you?"

"Is that what this is about?" Jason asked, his voice calm in contrast to Wesley's.

"You know very well that nothing has gone right with this trip to England, starting with that stunt you pulled in New York."

"I apologized for that," Jason said, looking unabashed. He pointed at Lizzy. "She's accepted my apology. Why can't you?"

"If you hadn't done what you did, then Oliver wouldn't have been drinking as much as he was and wouldn't have gotten ill. My brother wouldn't have been drinking and gotten himself thrown into jail, and while I appreciate whatever it was you did to get him out, none of this would have happened if you hadn't selfishly sent me back to Montana."

Jason's eyes widened. "I didn't realize you knew anything about that."

"Well, I do, and frankly it might have served Phillip better to let him sit in jail and face his consequences, but you seem to enjoy playing puppet master."

"Wes, it's hardly fair to blame Jason for choices Uncle Oliver and Phillip made." Lizzy's head was beginning to ache from the drama playing out around her. All she wanted to do was lean back against the pillow and close her eyes, but she didn't dare. She could tell Wesley was just a step away from making this a physical fight.

He looked at her, his brow furrowing. "Are you actually taking his side on this? You agreed with me before, as I recall."

Lizzy thought of all the problems it would cause if they ended the show. Uncle Oliver would lose everything. They would all lose out, and no one would be paid for their time abroad.

"It's not a matter of taking sides, Wes. It's just reasonable to expect that each man is responsible for his own actions. Uncle Oliver and Phillip could have gotten themselves in trouble drinking even if you were here. You can't hold yourself responsible for them. If they want to drink, they're going to drink."

"I want you to quit, Lizzy. I want you to stand with me on this."

She knew nothing she could say would make things right. She wanted to explain it all to Wes, but her promise to Uncle Oliver made it impossible. Maybe once she was able to speak to her uncle and explain that she needed to let Wesley in on things, then she could tell him, but for now she had to remain silent.

"I can't quit, Wes. I asked you to trust me on this, and I'm asking you again."

"No." His answer was absolute, and Lizzy felt heartsick.

"If you can't trust me, then maybe it's best if we don't stage our engagement. Maybe it's better to have no engagement at all." She couldn't believe she was saying this, but neither could she imagine a life where Wes had no trust in her.

He looked at her for a moment, his face void of emotion. Then he gave a nod. "If that's the way you want it. Maybe you and Adler can stage *your* engagement." He stalked from the room, leaving Lizzy in silent shock.

"I'm so sorry, Lizzy," Jason said. "It's better, though, that you know how he feels now rather than after you're married."

"Get out of here, Jason." She looked at him and shook her head. "He's right about one thing. Your actions completely complicated this, and while I forgive you . . . there are still consequences to bear."

"But, Lizzy, I—"

She held up her hand. "My head hurts and I want to rest. Please go."

Jason took a step toward the bed, then stopped. "I never wanted to cause you pain. I'm sorry." He bowed his head, then turned to go. He stopped at the door and gave her one more glance before leaving.

Lizzy felt hot tears come to her eyes. What had just happened? Was Wes really going to give up on their engagement? On their life together?

———◆—✕◆—◆———

"And then he said, 'If that's the way you want it,' and walked out of the room," Jason related to Mary and Chris the next day. His father had joined them and looked more than a little upset. "I don't know what we'll do for a finale now."

Chris looked at Mary. She nodded. "I have something in mind for that, and I think you'll both be pleased."

Jason and his father both looked at Chris, but it was Henry Adler who spoke. "What is it?"

"A shooting contest."

"We've had plenty of those and plan for one earlier in the day. That's nothing new," Jason said in disgust.

Chris smiled. "This one is. I took the liberty awhile back to write to a friend of mine and suggest a friendly competition at the Expo. I wasn't sure anything would come of it, but I've heard back, and my friend is willing."

"I don't see how this helps us," Henry Adler replied. "We've already had fliers printed up and posted at the Expo to declare we'll have a never-before-seen event."

"And so this will be." Chris put his arm around Mary. "Because my friend is Annie Oakley."

"Oakley has agreed to come to the Expo and shoot against Mary?" Henry asked. His expression bore both shock and joy. "Are you serious?"

"I am." Chris laughed. "Annie thought it sounded like fun. She and her husband will come by train and join us on the final day."

"You've saved us," Henry declared, slapping Chris on the back. "This is more marvelous than I could have imagined. Thank you,

Williams. I hope I can do something for you in the future." He turned to his son. "We need to make some plans. Williams, can you join us in my study? Say, in twenty minutes?"

Chris nodded. "Of course. I'd be happy to." He turned to Mary as the Adlers exited the room, deep in conversation.

"You've made them very happy," he told Mary.

"No, you did that. I'm just the one who will have to shoot against Annie Oakley."

He studied her for a moment. "You know, I think you look so lovely in your fashionable clothes, but you're every bit as pretty in your western clothes with your hair down or braided and your stylish red hat atop your head."

She gave him an odd look and shook her head. "What does that have to do with shooting against Annie Oakley?"

"Not a thing," he said, smiling. "Not a single thing. But . . ." He took her arms and pulled her closer. "I've heard that complimenting a beautiful woman before kissing her makes the kiss all the sweeter."

She cocked an eyebrow. "You heard that, did you?"

He put his hand beneath her chin and tipped her face up to meet his. "I did, and now I intend to see if it's true."

The kiss was longer than before, and Chris found Mary more than willing. He knew he was losing the battle to avoid an emotional entanglement. Perhaps he'd already lost it altogether, but for the moment he didn't care. All that mattered was Mary and the way she responded to his kiss.

<hr />

"I think I may have lost her this time," Wes told Oliver. He'd gone to check on the older man but found himself spilling the details of all that had happened. Oliver had already heard about Lizzy's fall from the doctor, so it hardly seemed to matter that Wes shared the rest of what had occurred.

"You'll never lose her, Wes. She's loved you for far too long. She's completely gone over you." Oliver smiled. His color was much improved, and he was itching, he told Wes, to be up and about his business.

Wes continued pacing. "You didn't hear the disappointment in her voice or see the way she looked at me. The show is so important to her, and she won't consider budging. It's only one show! But she's determined to stay, even if it kills her, and I don't understand why."

After a long silence, Oliver spoke up. "I know why."

Wes fixed him with a hard look. "Why?"

Oliver frowned and shook his head. "I made her promise me she wouldn't say anything. My pride once again getting the best of me, but also my desire to keep the others from worrying." He scratched his jaw. "It's all my doing, Wes."

"What are you talking about?"

"Lizzy won't quit because I told her that if anything happened to stop the show, we'd lose everything."

"I don't understand."

Oliver looked embarrassed. "I'm afraid the way I agreed to set things up for this trip to England tied all of the company's resources to the performances. We signed an agreement for twenty-two shows, and if we miss any of them, we will forfeit the contract and won't be paid for any of them. Lizzy isn't in this to please Adler or even herself. She knows that if we don't perform, everyone will lose their pay."

Wes was glad for the chair beside the bed and sank onto it. "Why didn't she just tell me?"

"Because I made her promise she wouldn't. When I fell ill, I felt I had to tell her. She wanted to close down the entire thing and go home."

"She did?"

"Yep. She was practically packed. I told her why we couldn't, and that's when the plan came together to have Jason make announcements in my place."

Wes put his face in his hands. "She asked me to trust her, and I refused." He'd never felt more ashamed. "I should have known better. It was just my anger that made me refuse to listen to reason."

"She loves you, Wes, but she cares deeply about her friends. She knows how much they're counting on this money. She's counting on it too—after all, she has a wedding to pay for."

"Maybe not. I said some awful things. I've tried to talk to her a couple times since then, but she won't see me."

Oliver shook his head. "She knows your heart."

"I demanded she leave the show." Wes heaved a sigh. "I all but accused her of not loving me. It's my fault."

"But it's not too late. In fact, I have an idea for how you can win her back. It'll require a little showmanship on your part though."

Wes leaned forward. "What do you have in mind?"

The final performance in London was met with another sold-out arena. The crowd was in high spirits as the performances played out through the evening. Mary's shooting competition once again ended with her triumph. Jason announced that she had bested every man in England, but it wasn't to England's shame at all. With one so beautiful to compete against, a man was certain to make mistakes. The audience applauded in agreement.

Alice finished the shooting portion of the show with her flaming arrows, and then the Roman riders took the arena and left the audience spellbound with their tricks. For the final act, the girls completed their new routine, which ended with Debbie standing on Jessie's shoulders and Ella standing atop Debbie's. Wes was surprised the girls could remain balanced atop a galloping horse, but they handled it with seeming ease. The new finish definitely met with the crowd's approval.

That just left the trick riding, which was always the highlight of the evening. Wes waited in the wings while Ella and Gertie performed the lion's share of the act. Lizzy was feeling much better but had agreed to perform fewer tricks at Uncle Oliver's request. Wes knew the request had come from his own concerns for Lizzy—but she didn't, and Wes aimed to keep it that way.

When it came time for Lizzy's final act, Wes was ready. She was riding Longfellow tonight, which left Thoreau free for Wes to use. Oliver had suggested he say nothing to Jason about his plan, and Wes was happy to comply. The less he had to deal with Adler, the better. Oliver assured him that despite the change in the routine, Adler would pick up on it quickly enough and figure out what to do.

Wes waited until Adler called for the music to end and absolute silence had fallen over the arena. He jumped into the saddle and nudged Thoreau to amble out into the open. He was dressed in a nice suit but wore his Stetson and boots. He looked like a cowboy come acourtin', which was exactly the look he wanted.

Lizzy sat atop Longfellow at the opposite end of the stadium. When she locked gazes with Wes, she froze. Adler started to say something about her trick, then caught sight of Wes. He fell silent as if some wonderful intervening angel had taken hold of his tongue.

Wes let Thoreau move slow and steady across the performance area until he stood just a few feet from Lizzy and Longfellow. Dropping the reins, Wes slid from the back of the horse and made his way to Lizzy.

"Elizabeth Brookstone, I've been a fool." He hoped he said it loud enough for his voice to be heard by one and all, but in truth, if only Lizzy heard—it was enough.

She smiled, and Wes took that as a good sign and dropped

to one knee. Gasps rang out across the stadium, and when he held up his hand, you could have heard a pin drop.

"Lizzy, I'm sorry for the way I acted, and I hope you'll forgive me." His voice was for her alone, and when she nodded, he grinned. He waited a moment for effect, then gave a shout. "Will you marry me?"

She nodded again and slid off her horse to join him on the ground as he stood. The audience erupted into such a cacophony that Wes feared they might well bring the place down. But he didn't care. Lizzy had wrapped her arms around his neck, and it seemed there was only one thing to do. He lowered his mouth to hers and kissed her. She was a remarkable woman— a woman of courage and devotion. A woman who put others first, even to her own detriment. A woman he planned to love for the rest of his life.

That night there was great celebrating at the Adler estate. Henry Adler had arranged for a party for the performers and crew of the Brookstone show to thank them for making the event more than anyone could have imagined.

"We've already had more requests for next year than we anticipated. Venues as far away as Germany and Switzerland have requested the Brookstone Wild West Extravaganza." He clapped and pointed at the various members of the troupe. "I want to thank you for your amazing performances, and I hope that each of you will be with the troupe next year."

Jason did his best not to look unhappy. He had been stunned when Wesley DeShazer made his way into the arena, but he'd known better than to take issue with it. The audience was enthralled by the cowboy romance playing out for all to see. He wasn't about to ruin the effect. His father would be thrilled, and it would ensure the show's success—at least for one more season. Afterward, Jason made sure to talk at great length with his father regarding Lizzy's performances with the show. He pointed out that she was too important to the success of the show to just allow her to walk away. They had to do something to entice her to stay.

"Are you saying this for the show's benefit or for your own?" his father had asked. It had made Jason want to hit the old man square in the mouth. How dare he?

Oliver Brookstone, who had convinced Lizzy to let him out of bed for the special occasion, stepped forward. "Based on tonight's success, I have taken the opportunity to have contracts written up so that each of you can read through them and see exactly what I am prepared to offer you for next year's show. After speaking with Henry and Jason and seeing the huge number of European requests, I'm almost certain we will spend most of the year abroad."

There were comments from around the room and a few questions posed as well.

"What about the staff? Will we increase again? It was a lot harder to perform *and* be responsible for our own gear *and* help with packing and unpacking."

"Of course," Oliver said, nodding. "We will need more performers and crew."

This was the first Jason had heard of the idea. Expanding the show might very well be a good course of action, but he hadn't suggested it. He resented that after helping make the show profitable, Oliver Brookstone would just reverse the changes without even asking Jason's opinion.

Glancing across the room, Jason saw Lizzy and Wesley standing by themselves. After a few more minutes, they slipped out the door and were gone. Jason seethed. How dare they leave? It wasn't proper for them to be alone. Lizzy was going to ruin her reputation if she wasn't careful.

"I also want to thank Jason," Oliver said, coming to where Jason stood. "He stepped up and served in my stead. Jason, you saved the show, and you have my undying gratitude."

Jason smiled, all the while thinking that he'd rather have Oliver's niece. He looked at his father. The older man wasn't smiling or beaming approval. Instead he looked at Jason with a stoic expression that suggested boredom.

One day I'll show you, Father. I'll show you exactly what I'm capable of, and you won't look at me like that ever again. I'll show you all.

⇥⇥ TWENTY ⇤⇤

The ship they took home to America was even grander than the one that brought them to England. There were no wardrobe surprises, but each of the suites had been lavishly appointed with flowers and the finest of furnishings. Two new girls were introduced as lady's maids for the cabin, and each was just as talented as Sarah and Miriam had been.

Mary was glad for the week they'd have at sea. She had already determined that one way or another, she and Chris were going to talk about his past and their future. She was in love, pure and simple. And unlike her relationship with Owen Douglas for all those years, this was the kind of love a girl dreamed of and fought for.

But on their first full day at sea, Mary saw very little of Chris. He was present at dinner, where everyone had come together to discuss their accommodations and any additional needs, but he disappeared shortly after and wasn't seen again until morning. Henry Adler and Jason kept him captive the entire time, planning the Expo show with Annie Oakley. Only once did they bother to ask Mary anything, and then it was a simple yes or no question, and none of the three men pressed for more information.

Mary was more than a little irritated as she made her way back to the cabin. Chris and the Adlers had left the dining saloon in a hurry, hoping to discuss some important matter with Oliver, who was remaining in his cabin to rest throughout the trip.

"It would be easier to find a unicorn onboard than get time alone with Christopher Williams," she said, slamming the cabin door behind her.

"What?"

Mary looked up to see Lizzy sitting in a plush chair. She wore her nightgown and robe and looked rather pale. "Are you all right, Lizzy?"

"I feel rather queasy. I didn't think I'd be seasick since I wasn't last time, but the water is rougher this time."

Mary put aside her outrage. "I'm so sorry. Can I get you anything?"

"No, but you can tell me what's wrong." Lizzy smiled. "Maybe it will help me keep my mind off my roiling stomach."

Mary took off her gloves and unfastened her jacket. She kicked off her slippers before curling up on the sofa nearest Lizzy's chair and making herself comfortable.

"I wanted to spend time with Chris, but the Adlers have him at their beck and call. All they want to do is discuss the Expo and Annie Oakley."

"And you want to discuss being in love?" Lizzy asked.

"Well, something like that. I didn't plan to fall in love, but now that I am, I want to know how Chris feels. I want to tell him that I know about his father and brothers."

"But you don't know for sure that you do. You've made an educated guess, nothing more." Lizzy reached out to take Mary's hand. "What if you're wrong?"

"What if I am? It will show him that even if the worst is true, it doesn't matter to me."

"But, Mary, it obviously matters to Chris. You must respect that. You surely know what it feels like to have something become public knowledge that you'd rather not. Just give him some time. Right now everyone, Chris included, wants to make sure they have the exhibition arranged to perfection. Surely you can understand that."

"I do, but . . ." Mary sighed and fell back against the thickly cushioned sofa. "I'm not a very patient person."

Lizzy laughed. "Neither am I, and I had to wait a long time to get Wes where I wanted him." The pitch of the ship shifted, and she grabbed her stomach. "Oooh. I do wish the seas would calm."

"Hopefully it won't last much after today. That's what they told us at breakfast."

"Until then, I think I'll head back to bed."

"Is that where Ella is?" Mary glanced toward the bedroom door.

"Yes. I'm glad she and I are rooming together this time. You don't have to witness our shame." Lizzy got to her feet and staggered toward the door. "Please know that I'll be praying for you."

Mary let out a long sigh. "Somebody needs to."

On the fourth day of rough seas and no time with Chris to herself, Mary decided to send him a note. She asked if he might call for her at precisely two o'clock—that she had something she wanted to discuss. To her relief, she received his response almost immediately. He'd be delighted to meet with her.

She dressed carefully in a burgundy skirt and white shirt-waist. Over this she wore a brocade vest in shades of gold, cream, and the same burgundy as the skirt. Over this came the coat that matched the skirt. She allowed the cabin maid to style her hair but wore it down instead of pinning it up in some fashionable coiffure. Chris had once commented on liking it down, so Mary had the young woman curl it with irons, then brush it back off her face and secure the sides with gold ribbons. Lastly, there was a large burgundy straw hat trimmed with gold edging and feathers.

"There's quite a breeze, miss," the girl told Mary as she arranged the hat. "I'm not sure the hat pins will hold if the wind catches the edge, so I'd stay inside, if I were you."

Mary nodded. "I plan to."

"At least the ocean is calmer," the girl said. "I think everybody is happier for that."

The maid finished, and Mary studied the result in the cheval mirror. She looked first one way and then another and finally shook her head. "I'm not going to wear the hat. It's too pretentious for what I have in mind, and that way if we do decide to take a walk on the deck, it won't be a hindrance."

The girl carefully pulled the hat pins and removed the hat from Mary's head. "Will that be all, miss?"

Mary took another look and smiled. "Yes. It's perfect." She knew fashion dictated that a proper lady wore a hat when going out, but life on the ship made things a little different. She was sure it wouldn't be too big of a disgrace.

The maid curtsied and returned the hat to its stand. Mary glanced at the mantel clock just as a knock sounded at the door. She didn't wait for the maid to get it but went herself. Opening the door, Mary smiled at the sight of Chris in his navy blue wool suit. He wore a dark burgundy striped tie, as if they had coordinated their colors.

"You are very prompt." Mary took his arm. "I like that about you."

"You are very beautiful." Chris pulled the cabin door closed as Mary stepped closer. "I like that about you."

She laughed. "Thank you for agreeing to meet me. I hope you didn't mind my sending a note. I just felt like I'd hardly seen you since we came aboard."

"Yes, I've been busy with my writing and with the details for the shooting competition between you and Annie. But you said this was important." He eyed her with a raised brow that betrayed his curiosity.

"And so it is."

"Where are we going?" he asked as Mary led him down the passageway.

"I thought we could go to the solarium and see all the flowers. I was told it's quite lovely, and since the ocean is calmer today, I felt it was perfect timing."

He looked at her with a sly smile. "Sounds romantic."

"It could be," she murmured.

They made their way up several decks and toward the stern of the ship, where the huge greenhouse awaited. Mary marveled at the warmth and humidity as they entered the solarium. All around them, carefully cultivated plants decorated the groomed pathways. Everyday, ordinary flowers mingled with more exotic tropical ones to create a riot of color.

"It's like another world." Mary found it fascinating.

"That it is," Chris replied. "They pipe in steam from special boilers, I'm told."

"I had no idea this was here until the cabin maid mentioned it. It's charming. Completely charming."

Chris glanced around. "But for all its charm, it doesn't seem there are very many people here."

"Maybe they're still recovering from the heavy seas. Ella and Lizzy are both still in bed."

"I heard they were ill. I hope they're back in the pink soon."

"Yes, they've spent most of the past three days in the green."

"But not you. You're made of sturdier stuff," Chris replied. "I'm glad you aren't sick."

Mary met his gaze. "So am I. I might not have had this opportunity otherwise. In fact, I'm rather glad the rest of the passengers have chosen to remain elsewhere. I hoped it would work out this way."

He looked at her with a grin. "Wanted me all to yourself, did you?"

Mary wanted to tease him, but at the same time she was losing her nerve. If she didn't tell him now what she'd come to say, she might never get it said. "A lack of audience makes this a little easier."

He sobered and led her from the entrance toward a stand of potted palms. "Sounds serious. What is it?"

Mary fingered the folded piece of newspaper she'd tucked into her glove. Should she show him the article, or just bring up the fact that she knew what he'd been trying to hide? For the briefest of moments, she heard Lizzy telling her to let Chris share the truth in his own timing, but she couldn't wait. She didn't want to return to America with this still standing between them.

"I want to talk about . . ." She stopped and shook her head. This was much harder than she'd thought it would be.

"About?" he questioned.

She met his blue-eyed gaze and felt encouraged by the amusement in his expression. "About us."

He smiled. "I see. And what about us would you like to discuss?"

"The future." She paused and drew a deep breath. "And the past."

She saw the doubt in his eyes and put her hand on his arm. "Chris, you know that I have feelings for you. In fact, I care very deeply." She paused in frustration. She was used to blurting out what she felt, but now it seemed the words were stuck in her throat. Then, without meaning to at all, she said the one thing she hadn't meant to say yet. "I know about your father and brothers."

His eyes narrowed. "What do you mean?"

Now that it was out, she had no choice but to continue. "Your father's name was Hiram, wasn't it?"

Chris gave a slow nod.

Mary countered with a more rapid one. "I've known for some time now but didn't know how to bring it up. I found this." She pulled the newspaper clipping from her glove. "I know all about them and what they did. I want you to know that I don't care."

He looked at the piece of paper in her hands as if it were a snake about to strike. "You should."

"Why? Because someone else might find out and comment on it? Because it's an embarrassment to have an executed father and brothers in your lineage?"

"But it *is* my lineage."

She shook her head and put the paper away. "Your name wasn't mentioned anywhere in that article. You weren't one of the offenders. You weren't one of the condemned, so why do you make it out like you are?"

He stared at her gloved hand for several long moments before finally answering. "The sins of the father."

"Are not the sins of the son," she countered. "Chris, you are a different man. Your father and brothers chose their way, and you took another path. I don't care what your father and brothers did. I only care about you. I love you."

Just then a group of passengers strolled by. One of the women in the party looked at Mary and held out her arm to stop the man at her side. "Wait! Aren't you Mary Reichert—the sharpshooter?"

Mary wanted to deny it. She'd just declared her love to Chris. She wanted to know what he thought of that and whether he felt the same, as she was almost certain he did.

She looked at him apologetically, then turned to the woman. "I am," she forced herself to answer.

"Oh, how exciting. I told my husband at dinner last night that I was certain you are the woman we saw shooting in London. How amazingly you master that rifle. I swear, when you shot at that man backward using that mirror, I nearly fainted. What if you had missed?"

"Then I suppose he would have been wounded," Mary replied, feeling a growing sense of frustration.

"Have you ever missed?"

"Of course."

The woman drew out a fan and began to wave it furiously. "While shooting at another person?"

"No. When I first began doing that trick, I used a straw dummy. I practiced it no fewer than five hundred times before introducing a real person into the act." Mary smiled. "Now, if you'll excuse me, my friend and I have business." She looked toward where Chris had stood only a moment ago, but he was gone. She frowned. "Or we did."

Where did he go? She looked down the path back to the door and then in the other direction. There was no sign of him anywhere.

Chris heard Mary's declaration of love echoing over and over in his head. Not only that, but he also heard her acknowledgment of knowing about his father and brothers. He didn't know which was a greater shock. He supposed the latter, because he'd already had an idea of the depth of her feelings for him.

He made his way to the promenade deck and walked for a time to clear his head. The seas were fairly calm, but the wind was chilly, so he made his way to the stern where he could watch the wake and consider what he should do. Had she told anyone else? Would she?

"You look deep in thought."

Chris turned to find Wesley DeShazer sitting in one of the deck chairs. "What are you doing out here alone?"

"Lizzy still feels a little seasick, so she decided to keep to her cabin. It hit her pretty hard. I guess it doesn't matter how nice the accommodations are or how exotic the food is when the boat is rocking like it has been."

"I'm sorry to hear that, but not sorry to have your company. How's your brother?"

"Sober, I think. He's been better since we left the Adler estate. I think the servants there made it their job to give him liquor. I think it was entertaining to them to make fools of the Americans."

"Maybe so. It sure put Oliver in a bad way."

"Yeah. I know Lizzy is terrified he won't make it home." Wes shook his head. "He hasn't been the same since he lost his brother. Brothers have a way of blessing our lives or leaving us feeling at a complete loss."

"Yes, that's something I know well enough, and I guess I'm wondering if you have time to help me with it."

"With your brothers?" Wes got to his feet and joined Chris at the railing. "I'm not sure I'll be much good, but I'll do what I can."

"Then take a walk with me and hear what I have to say." As they started toward the bow of the ship, Chris took a deep breath and began. "From my earliest memories I knew my father and brothers as cold, heartless men. My father was especially cruel. He ridiculed and harassed anyone who crossed his path. I never knew exactly what my father did for a living until years after going to live with my grandmother. When I was ten, I asked her about him, and she told me quite honestly that he was a vicious criminal who supported his wife and children by stealing. As the years went by, he became more and more violent in nature and encouraged my brothers to follow his example. I never wanted anyone to know about them because . . ."

"Because you figured you'd be judged by what they'd done."

"Yes. Because I have been. You have no idea." Chris saw a group of people walking their way. He frowned.

"Why don't we go below to my cabin?" Wesley suggested. "I'm sure Phillip is off playing cards or seeing to the horses."

Chris nodded and followed Wes down several decks. They made their way through the ship's passageways until they came to Wes's cabin.

He opened the door and motioned Chris inside. "We shouldn't be interrupted here."

The room wasn't overly large, but there was a small sitting area and a nice window that let light stream in onto the carpet of green and gold. A side door no doubt led to the bedroom.

"Thanks. I . . . well, you can understand why I don't want anyone else to overhear."

"Of course. Have a seat and go on."

Wes was so encouraging that Chris couldn't help but do exactly that. He felt a strange kinship with the cowboy.

"I went back to my hometown last year, and when people saw me, they knew who my father was. I look very much like him. They accused me of being there to cause trouble. Some of the people who were wronged by my family even went so far as to demand retribution. The sheriff paid me a visit and told me I wasn't welcome there." Chris gripped the arms of his chair. "I was six years old when my father and brothers went to jail. I was younger than that when they robbed their first bank, but these people acted as if I were part of the gang, the same as my older brothers."

"People can be cruel," Wes admitted. "Especially when they're afraid."

"I just don't know what to do. I want to be rid of this guilt I feel."

Chris turned to him. "Do you understand what I mean? I feel . . . weighed down . . . dirty. I feel guilty of all their wrongdoings."

"But you aren't. You're only guilty of your own sins, Chris. And you don't even have to bear those anymore. Remember what I told you before about Jesus going to the cross. Imagine what you're feeling, only a thousand—no, a million times worse. Jesus was weighed down with the sins of the world when He went to the cross. He bore the guilt and shame, the dirtiness of all the sins that had been committed and all those that would be committed. He did it so you wouldn't have to."

"How could He? Why would He?" Chris felt a lump in his throat, and tears came to his eyes. "Why would He die for me?"

Wes touched Chris's shoulder. "Because He loves you."

"I don't deserve His love. I'm the son of Hiram Williams, a killer."

"Forget about your earthly father and what he did. You are a sinner in your own right. You've made your own mistakes, and those will be counted against you . . . unless someone else pays the price for them. And, Chris, Jesus has already willingly done so. You don't have to keep carrying this."

Chris tried to fight the overwhelming hopelessness he felt. "I'll still be Hiram Williams's son. I'll still be thought of as a bad seed—a worthless man."

Wes shrugged. "You can't be unborn to Hiram Williams, but you can be reborn to Jesus Christ. The choice is yours, Chris. It has always been yours. No one else can answer for you."

Chris looked at Wes for a moment and realized that the words made sense somewhere deep within his soul. It was as if a small sliver of light had broken through a vast, deep blackness. "And if I ask for this . . ."

"Forgiveness?"

Chris nodded. "If I ask for forgiveness, God will give it . . . just like that?"

"Just like that," Wes said, nodding.

"And then what?"

Wes smiled. "Then you'll belong to God."

"And the pain will go away? The guilt will leave me?"

Again, Wes nodded. "It will. It might take time, as you grow to fully accept that God's gift of salvation is real, but it will come."

"I want to believe that. I need to believe."

"There will still be moments when the Devil tries to remind you of all the bad. He'll do his best to heap the pain back on you so that you doubt God's ability to take it. But if you keep your eyes on Jesus, if you keep taking it back to Him, He'll bear it all and then some. You'll never be alone again."

Chris felt a warmth spread through his heart and across his chest. He thought of all the pain and misery, all the years of guilt associated with his past. No matter the price, he wanted that peace—that freedom—that cleansing.

He looked at Wes. "Will you help me pray? Will you show me the way?"

Wes closed the door to his cabin after Chris left. He smiled at how God had put him in the right place at the right time, just when Chris needed someone to walk with him to the cross. Wes thought of all the times he had prayed and asked God to use him for whatever would bring Him glory. Most of the time Wes couldn't see that anything he did made much of a difference, but this was different. This time a man's entire life was changed, and Wes was privileged to have been a part of it. It was a wonder, to be sure.

"Do you really believe that stuff you told him?"

Wes whirled toward the bedroom door. Phillip stood there, looking at Wes as if trying to figure out the truth. "I didn't know you were here."

"I came down to take a nap. I woke up hearing you two talk."

"I hope you'll have the decency to keep what was said to yourself."

"You know I will. But that doesn't answer my question."

It was one of the rare times Wes had seen Phillip so serious. "And what was that?"

"Do you really believe that stuff you told Williams? That stuff about God?"

"I do. You should too. You were raised on it."

Phillip shrugged and sat on the arm of the overstuffed chair. "Seems like a lot of nonsense to me. Someone else dying for our sins. Someone else being willing to die in our stead. Makes no sense."

"It makes a lot of sense when you see it through the eyes of love. Maybe if you tried turning to God instead of whiskey, you'd see it too."

Wes could see the confusion in Phillip's expression. There was so much pain inside his brother, and yet Phillip wouldn't share it—wouldn't let anyone know the reason.

For the briefest of moments, Wes thought Phillip might want to discuss it further. And then the moment was gone.

Phillip got up and strolled across the room, the pain once again safely hidden by a mask of boyish charm. "Well, enough seriousness for today. I'm off to find some less sobering company. I heard there was a good game of cards to be had in the King's Lounge." He left without another word.

Wes knew all he could do was let him go, but his heart ached for his brother. "God, he needs You, and I don't know how to help him. Maybe You're gonna have to send someone else to show him the way. He doesn't seem able to receive it from me."

⊶⇌ TWENTY-ONE ⇌⊷

I can't believe I just blurted it out without warning him," Mary told Lizzy and Ella.

"How can you warn someone that you're going to tell them you're in love with them?" Ella asked with an impish grin.

"Besides, Chris isn't without sense," Lizzy countered. "You told me he kissed you twice. He knows you have feelings for him. I doubt his shock over that was as great as the shock over you knowing about his family."

"I feel so stupid. I know you suggested I wait and let him tell me, but I felt certain he would never do it. I worried that he would continue to carry that burden around and it would become an obstacle to our love."

Lizzy scooted up in the bed and patted the mattress beside her.

Mary sat down. "I'm sorry to bother you both with all this. I know you aren't feeling well."

"We were just mentioning that we felt much better. We're definitely well enough to discuss this matter with you."

"It's just that I haven't seen him since, and that was well over twenty-four hours ago. I even sent him a note, but I've had no response. I think I did more than shock him. I think I offended him."

Ella sat on the opposite side of the bed. "If he's offended by love, then you don't want anything more to do with him. If a person is either offended or defensive in regard to love, how can they possibly be the right mate for you?"

"I suppose you're right." Mary gave a long sigh. "It's just that I really do love him. I've never felt this way about anyone else. I mean, I loved Owen, but as a brother. I still love him. He's family. But I've never wanted to know everything about a man—and have him know everything about me—until now. Chris means the world to me, and if I've pushed him away . . ."

"You haven't," Lizzy interjected. "I think he probably just needs time to think and figure out how to proceed. He cares about you—at least to some degree. He doesn't strike me as the kind of man who would toy with your affections."

"He does seem sincere," Ella agreed.

"I've never known anyone to be more so," Mary admitted. "But you know how outspoken I am. Not everyone can accept or approve of that."

Lizzy took her hand. "Honesty is never wrong when given in love. Lies are Satan's tools, and they always complicate matters. You spoke the truth in love. You didn't go with the intention of using the truth to hurt him, as some with that knowledge might. I only suggested you wait until he felt comfortable saying something himself because I thought it would make it easier for you both."

"I know, and now I wish I had listened to you. What if he never speaks to me again?"

Lizzy shook her head. "That's not going to happen. I think he just needs time to consider all that has happened. You should just enjoy the voyage and rest. When we reach New York, you can seek him out."

"Maybe." Mary was unconvinced.

"Look, Wesley plans to visit me later. I'll ask if he's seen Chris and maybe encourage him to talk to him. Meanwhile, why don't you spend some time in prayer. Read the Bible. You can borrow mine." Lizzy reached toward her nightstand and handed Mary her well-worn Bible.

"I suppose it couldn't hurt." Mary accepted the book and gave her friend a smile. Lizzy had been such an encourager over the years, and she always believed that God was the answer to all of her problems.

"Mary, remember, these things often take a long time to resolve. Look at how long I've loved Wes. For most of that time, he didn't return my love, and even now we have difficult moments. I don't say that to be discouraging but rather to remind you that God's timing is everything and relationships take work. As far as I know from what you and Wes have told me, Chris isn't a believer, and if that's the case, then he would hardly make a good companion, much less a good husband. You believe in Jesus as your Savior, Mary. You don't want to be unequally yoked."

"No, I don't, and believe me when I say that though I love him, I'm hardly ready to walk down the aisle with him." Mary grew thoughtful. "I'm not nearly so worried about his feelings for me as I am concerned about how my knowing his past has upset him."

"Chris has carried this burden all his life. It's not going to be easy to change his perspective overnight. Give him time and pray that God will help him through it. God is the only one who can heal his brokenness, and Mary . . . you have your own brokenness to heal."

Lizzy was right, and Mary knew it. She thought of August and how much it still hurt to know he would never again be waiting for her after a show. Her brother's teasing and dry wit were forever lost to Mary, and only God had been able to get her through that pain.

"Sometimes when I first wake up and realize I'm back with the show, I expect to see August when I go to get my horse or check on my targets. He always loved to put little surprises in the crates just to tease me. Once he put a toy snake. It scared the daylights out of me, but I got him back."

"What did you do?" Ella asked.

"I put it in his bed. You could hear his yell all the way down the train." Mary smiled at the memory. "I miss him so much, but then he wasn't home that last year and I wasn't with the show. Maybe we went our separate ways in order to lessen the loss when he died, but if this is lessened, I can't imagine how awful it would have been if we'd been together the whole time."

"I always wanted brothers and sisters," Lizzy said, smiling sadly. "But I think that's why my folks let me perform. They knew I needed something else to focus on. It was lonely at the ranch without any other children."

"I'm the baby of the family, but I enjoyed my siblings," Ella admitted. "My sister Margaret is five years older than me, but we were still close. We loved to play with our dolls together, and then later, Mara used to play with me after Margaret thought herself too old for such things."

"Who's Mara?" Mary asked.

"She was my maid. Well, her mother was my wet nurse, and Mara and I grew up together as playmates. When I turned thirteen, Father declared she would be my maid, and she was until the day I left the farm. We were like sisters. I confided everything in her, and if not for her help, I would never have managed to get away from the farm."

"What happened to her after you left?"

"She's still there. Robert told me she's doing well, but I can't help wishing she were here with me."

"Maybe one day. Maybe we can work out some sort of arrangement. After all, Mara is free to go where she chooses."

"I told her one day I'd send for her." Ella picked up a brush and began to run it through her wavy blond hair. "I think she'd enjoy the wild west show. She knows how much I love to ride, and I think she'd applaud my doing what I love."

"I don't understand how you got involved with trick riding." Mary was glad to focus on something other than Chris for a while. She was too caught up in what had happened to think clearly, and focusing on Ella's life was helping her relax and clear away the fog.

"Robert and I used to go riding together. He's eight years my senior, and back then he was more than a little ornery. He used to challenge me to try dangerous stunts, and I loved to show him that I could do most anything. He told me once after seeing a circus that he thought I belonged there." She paused her strokes with the brush. "Now I don't know whether I can trust him or not. He has to do business with Father and Jefferson, and he has a family of his own. I don't know what he really believes regarding August and what happened, but it makes me sad that he just accepts that our father is involved in murder. And for what reasons, I can't even say, but I don't believe there's ever an acceptable reason to kill someone in cold blood."

"Nor do I." Mary shook her head. "It is so strange how God has put us together. I rejoined the show to find out what happened to August, but then I stayed on. I guess I keep hoping I can somehow get justice for him."

"And if you can't?" Lizzy asked.

"Then I'm still better for it. After all, if I hadn't come along, I would never have met Chris, nor gotten to know Ella." She smiled at her friend. "And I have really enjoyed our friendship, Ella. I hope you know that."

"I'm so glad, because I cherish it, and yet I would understand if you despised me. After all, I knew that Jefferson and my father had a hand in August's death long before I admitted it."

Mary shook her head. "I could never despise someone for responding in the same way I probably would have. Even if your father and Mr. Spiby never answer for what they did, I will be your friend and help you so that you never have to go back to that life. In fact, know this—if for some reason you can't stay with Lizzy on the ranch, you always can come stay with me in Kansas . . . or wherever I end up." She looked to Lizzy and held up the Bible. "Thank you for talking to me and loaning me your Bible. Thank you too for being willing to ask Wes about Chris. I'll feel better if I know that he's all right."

"I'm sure he is. Just give him time," Lizzy replied.

———————◆◈◆———————

"I'm glad you're feeling better, Lizzy," Oliver Brookstone said, patting the chair beside him. "Come sit by me and tell me all the news."

"It does my heart good to see you looking so much better, Uncle. As for news, I hardly know anything." Lizzy kissed the top of his head and then took her seat. "You probably know a lot more than I do, since you talk to Jason all the time and I've been sick in bed."

Jason sat across the table from her. He smiled, but he didn't feel it. Lizzy and Wes were closer than ever, and now Oliver wanted them to stage a mock wedding at the Expo. They already had the shooting contest with Annie Oakley scheduled and hardly needed to add to the show, but Oliver was insistent.

"Sorry I'm late," Wes declared, coming into the private saloon. "Oliver, it's nice to see you up. How are you feeling?"

"Well, this is about the full extent of my activity. But the doctor assures me my strength will come back a little at a time, so long as I keep on this course."

"Are you sure you're up to a meeting, Uncle?" Lizzy asked. "We could hold it in your cabin, and you could be more comfortable. You certainly wouldn't have to dress up."

"I'm fine," Oliver said, patting his niece's hand.

"In that case, what do you want to see Wes and I about?" Lizzy asked, gazing at Wes with such love that Jason had to look away.

Thankfully the steward chose that moment to bring their tea and refreshments. The conversation lagged until after the tea was poured and the food served. Jason was miserable watching how happy Wes and Lizzy were. If only she could understand that life with a cowboy would never be as good as the life he could give her. Why couldn't she put aside her childish emotions and think about the future? About how important he was going to be one day? Perhaps he'd even be prime minister, and then she could enjoy his power as well.

His father entered the cabin, smiling and greeting Oliver like a long-lost brother. Jason resented that his father had felt it necessary to join them on the trip back to America. With his father there, Jason's ability to manipulate the situation to his benefit was stifled. And while his father had said very little about the fact that Jason had put the show in the black, he had no difficulty commenting on his mistakes when they came to his attention.

Why can't he just leave this to me? Leave it all to me and let me deal with it as I desire? Then I could marry Lizzy and rid myself of her cowboy and anyone else who caused me trouble.

"So you see, while we have the shooting competition between Mary and Annie Oakley, we were hoping that for our final evening event we could stage a little wedding."

"Wes and I plan to marry back in Montana," Lizzy said, shaking her head.

"I know that," Oliver assured her. "This would just be for the show. It wouldn't be real, but imagine the thrill. Your public adores you, and how wonderful it would be for them to share in the wedding—even if it is pretend."

"Our marriage isn't the stuff of pretense," Wes said, frowning.

"Marriage is a very sacred thing, Uncle."

"Of course, of course. And I'm not trying to suggest otherwise."

Jason's father spoke up. "I think your uncle is saying that because you are so beloved, it's going to be difficult for people to understand that you're quitting. They're going to be upset to learn you're leaving. So we thought perhaps if we staged the wedding, given the engagement was such a hit, you and Wes could announce your retirement in order to seek a life of marriage and motherhood."

Lizzy blushed. "I suppose I never thought of it that way."

"We thought it would be a nice way to tell everyone with our final performance that you're leaving the show. Those who are able to be there to watch the wedding will be thrilled, and the blow will be softened," Oliver added.

Jason's father nodded enthusiastically, but Jason jumped in before anyone else could speak. "Exactly. Lizzy, I don't think you realize just how important you are to your fans. The letters we receive, either addressed to you or mentioning you, are fifty to one for anyone else."

"Goodness, I didn't have any idea."

"Sometimes those numbers are even higher," Jason hurried on. He'd had neither a hand in the mock wedding idea nor the event with Annie Oakley, and he was determined to regain at least a small amount of control.

"If the pretense bothers you, why not really get married?" Henry asked.

Lizzy shook her head. "Because I want to marry in Montana. I want my mother there, and since she wasn't able to come to England, I doubt she'll be able to come to New York. Especially with getting the calves to market."

"You could go ahead with your wedding in Montana," Henry replied. "In fact, I will pay for both weddings as a sign of good-will."

Lizzy looked to Wesley. "Maybe we could do something to make my final performance special." Again, there was that look of adoration in her eyes.

Why can't she look at me that way?

Jason picked up his tea and took a sip. He burned his tongue but didn't react. At least it took his mind away from how hopeless he felt. He didn't want to hear anything more about Lizzy marrying this buffoon, and he especially didn't want to hear his father talk about paying for it. Still, there was nothing he could do but listen and pretend all was well. The trouble was, he'd never admitted defeat easily.

They continued to discuss the matter, but Jason didn't care to pay attention. They would soon reach New York, and then he'd lose Lizzy forever. There had to be some way to convince her that he was the better man. And he was. He had fortune and social standing. He was both American and English, and they could easily live in both worlds. His father might want him to marry into nobility and bring more prestige to the Adler name, but he wasn't the one in charge. This was Jason's decision, and he wouldn't be put off just because Wesley DeShazer had some sort of hold over Lizzy.

". . . but I certainly don't need somebody else paying for our wedding," Wes was declaring.

Lizzy nodded. "Wes is right. We already have plans for our

wedding in Montana and have taken care of the expenses ourselves. What if you just present us to the audience? I can even
wear a white dress, if that's important. Wes and I could ride
out together and take a turn around the arena, and you could
announce that we're getting married and I'm leaving the show.
Maybe I could even perform a trick and end up in Wesley's
arms, and we could ride off on one horse. Wouldn't that be
romantic enough?"

"I think it might work well," Father said, nodding. "I like the
idea. We can have Mary and Miss Oakley perform together, and
then announce that we have one final thing to share and bring
out Lizzy and Wes."

Jason wondered what they'd do or say if he stormed the arena
during their little presentation and stole Lizzy away. He smiled.
It might be the kind of grandiose gesture Lizzy needed to realize
just how much he loved her. The idea continued to grow in his
thoughts. He could arrange a carriage waiting outside. He could
swoop in and steal Lizzy off her horse and race from the arena.
The crowds would love it, and if he planned it right, perhaps he
could hire some men to cover their retreat. The audience would
think it was just a fun performance, but Jason could make his
getaway with Lizzy.

But she'd never go willingly.

The thought tormented him. He'd never been the kind of
man to force himself upon a woman, but perhaps this time he
needed to be more drastic. It was the rest of his life he was
thinking about. Once he had Lizzy away from Wes, he would
need some way to hold her—to keep her until he could have
them legally wed. He would have to give this a great deal of
thought.

"Don't you think so, Jason?" his father asked.

"Ah . . . well . . ." His voice trailed off. "I'm afraid I wasn't
listening."

"I asked if you think that arrangement sounds romantic. Especially with an orchestra to play in the background."

Jason had no real idea what his father was planning, but he knew his own scheme. "I think it sounds marvelous." He looked at Lizzy and smiled as he raised his teacup. "To the wedding."

⊶═ TWENTY-TWO ═⊷

Are you upset with me?" Mary asked Chris at breakfast on their last full day at sea. She'd seen little of him, although Lizzy had relayed the news that he had accepted Christ as his Savior one evening while talking with Wes.

"Of course not. I'm sorry that I'm so occupied. I promise I want to continue our conversation, and I assure you that I'm not angry. I'm glad you told me what you did."

She wasn't sure if he meant the news about his father and brothers or the fact that she loved him, and she had no chance to ask.

"Chris, I managed to get that typing paper you needed," Henry Adler announced, taking his seat at the table. "It's been delivered to your cabin."

"Wonderful!" Chris gulped his tea and jumped to his feet. He looked down at Mary. "We will talk. Now, if you'll excuse me, I have been furiously working to put together the rest of the articles for my publisher. He will expect them when we dock in New York."

And with that, he was gone.

Mary frowned and picked at her breakfast until she lost all interest in it.

"Don't worry, Mary. He'll make it up to you," Lizzy whispered as she leaned close. "I know he will. It's easy to see that he adores you."

"I don't know about that. He did tell me he wasn't upset with me. In fact, he said he was glad that I said what I did, but for the life of me I don't know which part of the conversation he's referencing."

Lizzy smiled. "Maybe he was glad about the entire thing. Did you think of that?"

"I suppose I didn't." Mary touched her napkin to her lips and then placed it on the table beside her plate.

"He seemed quite at peace. Having Jesus in your heart will do that," Lizzy said, then sipped her tea.

"And I'm very glad about that. I'm so happy Wes could be there to help him through the shock of what I said and the burden he's been carrying all these years." Mary picked up her own china teacup and sampled the now tepid tea.

"You just need to be patient, Mary. Love is patient."

"Yes, but I never have been. Oma says I was born without patience and each time it was offered to me, I turned up my nose and walked away."

Lizzy chuckled. "If I'm honest, it's not a virtue well-known to me either. Still, I know that if it's right for you and Chris to be together, then God will bring it around . . . in His time. Maybe you could pray for patience."

Mary nodded. She knew it would have to be an act of God for her to endure the wait with any kind of patience. She liked to get what she'd come for and didn't hesitate to move when she knew what she wanted. But this time what she wanted involved another human being, and they had as much right to call the shots as she did.

"Why don't you come back to the cabin with Ella and me? We can figure out how we want to do things for our final show at the Expo. I'm quite excited to see the exhibits and what all they have going on there. Jason even mentioned taking a side trip to see Niagara Falls. Wouldn't that be wonderful? I've never seen it, but he says it's marvelous."

"Maybe we can convince Chris to come too," Mary said, getting to her feet.

"Maybe so. Everyone says it's such a romantic place. Who knows what kind of feelings it might bring out in him?" Lizzy winked.

Mary rolled her eyes, which only made Lizzy laugh.

Once they were back in New York, Mary decided the only thing she could do was keep busy. They would stay the night in the city to give Chris time to meet with his editor, and then the following evening they'd be off again to Buffalo on the routine they were all more comfortable and familiar with. England had been an amazing experience, and already there was talk about next year and expanding to a few other European venues, but for now everyone was glad to be back on American soil. The exception might be Jason Adler, who seemed moody at best and completely withdrawn at worst.

It was good to be back on the train. The Brookstone home away from home had been thoroughly cleaned, and to everyone's surprise, Agnes and her niece were back to help with costumes. Lizzy immediately told the older woman about the staged wedding presentation, and they got right to work figuring out how to alter one of her elaborate new gowns for the scene.

Meanwhile, Mary tried to keep busy during the day. She knew it was best not to think about Chris and how much she wanted to say. She had prayed a great deal and thought long and hard about what she hoped to have with him. His actions suggested he loved her. At least, she thought their kisses revealed that truth, but she could be wrong. She didn't have a lot of experience where romance was concerned.

"I knew I'd find you cleaning your guns," Lizzy stated as she entered the commons area from the costume room.

Mary looked up and smiled. "Did you get your wedding dress figured out?"

"Yes. Agnes is such a genius. She's taking that beautiful gown with the silver lace overlay and remaking it. She'll take off the lace because the underskirt is white satin. Then she'll retrim it with white lace and adjust the skirts in a way that will allow me to ride without having to use a sidesaddle. I think we'll make some satin bloomers to wear under it and split the skirt on either side."

"Sounds pretty."

"So long as it's maneuverable—that's all I care about." She plopped down on the chair across from Mary.

"Were you able to reach your mother?"

"Uncle Oliver had a message waiting for him at the station. She's not able to leave the ranch but is looking forward to us being home again."

"I'm sorry, Lizzy. I know you wanted her to come and be with Oliver."

"I suppose she's wise to stay put. There's so much work that has to be overseen. It's one of the busier times of the year. Besides, we'll be home in just a week and a half." Lizzy leaned back and stretched out her legs. "Have you decided what you're going to do?"

Mary frowned. "What do you mean?"

"About the winter and next year's show and where you'll live and Christopher. It is the end of October, after all, and decisions should be made."

"Oh, that." Mary laughed. "Just little things."

"Just the rest of your life," Lizzy said, laughing.

"Well, not exactly. I want to return to Montana to see you and Wes get married, but after that . . . I don't know. I want to see my family, so I suppose I'll go back to Kansas for a month or so. I've been thinking about the show and . . . well, it won't be as much fun without you, but I think I might stay another year."

"I know that would please Uncle Oliver to no end. Ella too. She's been worried she'd lose us both." Lizzy glanced toward the ceiling as she toyed with the end of her braid. "That just leaves Christopher."

"I have no answers for you regarding him."

"Uncle Oliver said he had meetings all day today. Mr. Adler was going along to a couple of them."

"The senior or the younger?"

Lizzy shrugged. "Both, I think. I'm not sure."

Mary fixed her with a knowing look. "You mean Jason stopped shadowing you?"

Lizzy rolled her eyes. "He wasn't shadowing me. He just wanted to make sure we had everything planned out in detail for the show's finale at the Expo. He's so excited about your shooting exhibition. He can hardly believe that Annie Oakley has agreed to do this for free."

"It isn't for free," Mary said, then quickly bowed her head to begin putting her rifle back together. "Pretend you didn't hear me say that."

"I can't," Lizzy declared, getting up from the sofa to come to the table. "What do you mean, it isn't for free?"

Mary drew a deep breath. "You can't say anything. Please promise me you won't."

Lizzy took the chair beside Mary's. "All right, I promise, but you have to tell me."

"Chris is paying her to come. He's paying her way and that of her husband and promised them a lovely hotel suite and all of their expenses."

"Why didn't he say so? I'm sure Jason would be more than happy to cover their travel and expenses. After all, he bought us a fancy wardrobe, and you know ready-made clothes aren't cheap."

"I think Chris just wanted to do this as a way of saying thank you for being included on the tour. But unless he says something about it, I won't say a word to Jason or anyone else. I told him I wouldn't, yet here I am."

"I made you tell me. It's not like you wanted to." Lizzy shook her head. "Christopher Williams is a fine young man. I like him very much, and I think you two will make a nice couple."

Alice and Carson appeared at the door of the commons car. "Oh, I thought we'd be the first ones here," Alice said, pulling off her wrap.

"First ones here for what?" Lizzy asked, getting up from the table.

"I thought you were here for the meeting," Alice said. "Mr. Adler called for an emergency meeting. I don't know what it's about, but he said it was serious."

Mary frowned and began to clean up her mess.

"Maybe the Expo closed early," Lizzy offered. "Since the president's death, I know some people pushed for that to happen."

"But he's been dead since last month," Alice countered. "If they were going to shut it down, don't you think they would have already done so?"

Lizzy nodded. "I would." She went to the sofa and took a seat. "But I've seen stranger things happen."

Wes and Phillip ambled in, followed by the rest of the performing team. Jessie, Debbie, and Ella sat together, squeezing onto the sofa with Lizzy. Gertie came in after that and took a seat at the table with Mary, who had finally managed to consolidate her cleaning supplies and firearms into a neat pile in front of her.

Jason and his father entered the car, looking grave. Mary

couldn't imagine what was wrong. She prayed it wasn't bad news related to one of the troupe. What if someone's loved one had died?

Finally, Chris and Oliver stepped in from the men's car. Oliver looked pale and just as upset as the Adlers. Chris exchanged the briefest gaze with Mary and offered her a sympathetic smile.

"What's going on?" she blurted.

"We've had some bad news," Henry Adler replied. "Apparently last night, Buffalo Bill's show was involved in a train accident in Virginia."

"North Carolina," Jason corrected. "They were headed to Virginia."

His father glanced at him, then nodded. "Yes. Thank you. They were heading to Virginia for their final show. Of course, Annie Oakley and her husband were also on that train."

"Oh no!" Lizzy gasped. "Was anyone killed?"

"No," Henry replied, shaking his head. "But Annie was badly hurt. They say she's paralyzed and will never be able to walk again."

Mary felt sick and bowed her head. What a horrible thing to happen. She whispered a prayer for all involved.

"What happened?" Ella murmured.

"Apparently another train hit them head on. Over one hundred horses were killed, along with other animals that they used in their shows. It's a complete loss for them, but no one was killed. At least not that we know of at this time. But things are quite grave." Henry Adler looked to Oliver.

"From what I've been able to learn, many of the actors and performers have been hospitalized with injuries. I know you probably know some of the folks involved, and of course I have long been friends with Bill. We sent our deepest condolences and have asked if there's anything we can do to help." Oliver shook his head. "We just never know when something like this might happen to us. I'm very grateful God has spared us such a disaster."

"Needless to say," Henry continued, "Annie won't be coming to perform with us tomorrow. However, I think it might be fitting if we dedicate our last performance to the Buffalo Bill's Wild West show."

"Absolutely!" Lizzy declared, and the others either nodded in agreement or voiced their approval.

"The audience had no knowledge Annie would be joining us for the competition, so we'll say nothing of it. Instead we will focus on Wes and Lizzy's matrimonial celebration."

Mary knew this wasn't what Wes and Lizzy wanted, but they would go along with it. Especially now. A twinge of guilt surfaced as Mary acknowledged that she was relieved not to have to perform against Annie Oakley. She had always admired Annie, and frankly, she didn't want to know who was better.

"We will do what we must and put this sadness from our minds lest it hinder us," Oliver said, bringing Mary's attention back to the meeting. "Above all, we must pray for those who were hurt, that God will restore them to health and prosperity."

Jason wasn't happy about the news regarding Annie Oakley. He had hoped the big competition would keep the show's personnel and audience so preoccupied that no one would have time to miss Lizzy until the very end. Now with her and Wes being the main surprise planned for the finale, she would be harder to separate from the others.

He had used what little time he had in New York to seek out some of the seedier members of his mother's extended family. They would do almost anything for money, including nabbing Lizzy. After discussing what he had in mind with the son of his mother's cousin, Jason was further inspired. The cousin had an uncle who was also interested in making extra money and happened to be a judge. Once in Buffalo, Jason was to take a letter of reference with him to see this man. The cousin felt certain that for a price, the judge would be happy to marry Jason and Lizzy, even if the bride was less than enthusiastic about the arrangement.

Getting Lizzy to agree to marry him had been the only real problem in his plan, and this development resolved that neatly. With the help of his newly hired team, he would have Lizzy chloroformed and taken to an agreed-upon place. He would then join her, leaving behind a letter that stated he and Lizzy were eloping. Once the marriage was performed—and consummated— Lizzy would have little choice but to endure the situation, and in time, he was sure she would be happy with it.

Jason smiled. He was certain he could make her happy . . . make her forget Wesley and all that she thought she loved. He was convinced that with his money and family's connections in England, he could make a wonderful life for them both. Even his father would have to see the brilliance in such a plan.

⊰⊱ TWENTY-THREE ⊰⊱

Chris stood watching in the wings as the Brookstone Wild West Extravaganza unfolded. A crowd of over twenty thousand was reported to be in attendance. The electric lighting that had been featured at the Pan-American Exposition was an enjoyable benefit for the audience and performers alike, but with strings of electric lights taking up space overhead, Mary and Alice had an additional obstacle to bear in mind. It was a good thing they were so precise with their shooting.

The evening was damp and cold, but no one really seemed to mind. They were there to be entertained by beautiful women who performed outrageous feats that served to stimulate and motivate an entirely new generation of potential performers. And unlike Jason Adler, Chris felt certain the wild west show would continue to appeal to audiences. After all, rodeos were now considered a novel entertainment for city folks. What had started as a way for ranch hands to relax and have fun after roundup was now watched with fascination and gained in popularity every year. No doubt it would be easy to combine the wild west show and rodeo into one big performance that would draw the attendance of many. Oliver Brookstone had even mentioned the possibility of adding rope tricks next year.

277

Watching as the Roman riders completed their performance, Chris marveled at the acrobatic abilities of these otherwise prim and proper young women. Ella had been raised as a Southern lady with all the respectability and manners of the finest social- ite, yet she was just as comfortable standing on the shoulders of another young woman, racing around the arena on horseback. He'd seen her performance many times now and had to admit that she was a natural. She had trained with Lizzy and picked up the tricks so easily that she seldom had to be shown more than once. Then, given her spirit and determination, she practiced those tricks until they were second nature. Her dedication to the art was certain to take her far.

Lizzy was convinced Ella would become famous, but what would that mean to her family and whatever secret they had buried at Fleming Farm? Something had happened there— something worth murdering a man over. Yet no one was willing to speak up about it. In fact, an entire town—even an entire *county*—was happy to remain silent on the matter. Chris's re- porter friend had tried to snoop around and discover what Au- gust might have seen. Fleming had confronted him, and when Chris's friend said it was just his way of doing a story, Spiby had told him he was no longer welcome. The reporter had thought it strange that this had come from Spiby and not Fleming, but nevertheless he was forced to leave.

This left Chris with a great sense of frustration. He wasn't even sure how to tell Mary the news. He was convinced there had to be a way to find out what was going on at the farm that had brought about the death of her brother. The reporter in him demanded answers and wanted more information. The man in love with Mary wanted only to keep her safe and as far from the threat that had taken her brother's life as possible.

Music signaled a change in the acts, and Chris watched as Phillip and Wes helped Mary and Alice with their props. Mary was dressed in her western costume. Deerskin, fringed skirt, and cream-colored cotton blouse trimmed with red silk fringe and black piping. She wore her customized red Stetson and tall black boots. She looked every bit the part of cowgirl. His cowgirl.

She had told him she loved him despite knowing what his family had done. He'd never replied to her declaration, because at the time he'd been too stunned. Then the demands of his job kept him busy, along with his newfound faith in God. He had spent a lot of time discussing matters with Wes, even receiving a personal invitation to return to the ranch for his wedding to Lizzy. Wes had teased that Mary would be coming back with them as well, and maybe that would give Chris the needed time and place to speak to her about his feelings. It seemed logical to Chris, so he'd accepted the invitation.

It wasn't long before the sharpshooting act began, and Chris found himself caught up in the performance. For nearly twenty minutes Mary and Alice alternated with their particular skills. Alice was quite the sharpshooter with the bow and arrow, and most of that she performed on horseback at a galloping rate. Chris doubted he'd be able to hit the target while standing still. When it was time for Alice's last act with flaming arrows, Mary hurried to the little dressing room where Ella and Lizzy waited to help her into her evening wear.

Henry Adler had taken over the job of announcing the act and was explaining some of the details related to riding and bow shooting.

"The American Indians were famous for their abilities on horseback. Skilled beyond the expectations of the pioneers, the natives were often able to drive back the thousands of whites who crowded in to take over their beloved prairies and mountain lands. But they weren't alone with their skills, for the art of mounted archery goes back centuries and is shared by people from all corners of the earth."

Chris thought Adler was a natural at the job, even if he had been raised to look down upon such a position. When Oliver fell ill, Chris had heard Jason Adler speak in disparaging terms about taking on such a demeaning task. Of course, he hadn't said that in front of Oliver or Lizzy.

Thoughts of the Adlers disappeared as Mary emerged again, dressed head to toe as a lady of refinement. Chris couldn't help but give her a smile as she passed him, pulling on her long white gloves. She was deep in thought, however, and didn't seem to notice him. Instead, she headed for the arena without so much as a glance. Chris would have liked to break her concentration and take her in his arms to kiss her with all the pent-up passion he felt. He sighed. "The show must go on," he muttered.

He made his way out to the audience so as to have a front-row seat. He loved to watch Mary perform, and tonight she had promised a surprise.

"How about another round of applause for the beautiful and talented Alice Hopkins!" Henry Adler called to the still cheering audience. They didn't disappoint. "And now for our final sharp-shooting act," Adler began. "We have something very special for you tonight. Our Miss Mary will shoot . . . blindfolded."

There were exclamations from the audience. Chris hadn't known her to do this before and was a little intrigued.

Alice appeared from behind the large heavy curtain used to stop or slow the bullets. She helped Mary finish setting up metal targets in the shape of animals. The targets were light-weight enough that they would snap down when hit. Once the targets were arranged, Mary went to stand in her usual place and picked up her pistol. Meanwhile, Alice came forward with the blindfold.

Henry Adler pointed at Chris. "You, sir. Would you come forward and witness that this blindfold prevents all possible vision?"

Chris stepped forward and received the blindfold. Alice wrapped it around his head, and blackness engulfed his vision. When she pulled it away, Chris nodded. "Complete darkness."

Henry further surprised Chris by pointing to a white-haired man in the audience about three rows up. "Would you come and witness this as well?"

The old man nodded and hurried forward. Once Alice had secured the blindfold, he shouted, "I can't see a thing!" The audience laughed.

He was returned to his seat, and Alice moved to Mary's side. Henry described what was about to take place. "Miss Mary is a precisionist. She knows exactly where to stand and how to position her firearm in order to hit each and every target, every time. I ask that you remain completely silent while she readies herself."

Chris had no doubt she'd handle this test as easily as she had everything else, but he couldn't help smiling. Her skills were impressive.

Alice secured the blindfold, and without warning, Mary went into her act. She hit seven targets in a row, much to the amazement of the audience. The roar of approval was deafening. Mary took off her blindfold and waved to her fans.

"And now we'll further challenge our Mary," Henry said, motioning to Chris once again. "You, sir, would you come forward again?"

Chris nodded and got to his feet. He joined Adler and waited to see what he might request of him this time.

"Mary Reichert will once again shoot blindfolded, but this time she will have a live target."

Live target? Chris glanced from Adler to Mary. She was grinning, thoroughly enjoying his sudden discomfort.

She came forward and reached for his arm. "Are you willing, sir?"

Chris nodded but wasn't sure that was the wisest thing to do. He followed her to the curtain and let her position him in front of the barrier. While he waited, she pulled down a paper shade as Henry announced that this would provide proof of each bullet's mark.

"You must stand perfectly still," she said in a whisper. "There isn't a real risk unless you move around."

"From now on I'm going to avoid sitting on the front row."

Mary grinned. "Would you like a blindfold too?"

Chris chuckled. "It might help. Next time you might warn me."

"Next time you might arrange to spend time with me."

He frowned. "Is this punishment?"

Mary gave a snort. "Hardly. Now buck up. You'll be fine, and remember, don't move."

She left him standing there and returned to her firing position. As she loaded her pistol, Henry made his announcement.

"Ladies and gentlemen, Miss Mary will now be blindfolded once again and fire all five shots from her Smith & Wesson .38 directly at our volunteer. Hopefully he won't move, because once Mary memorizes the position of her target, she is unable to recalculate."

Henry signaled the orchestra, and the drummer gave a loud drum roll to draw everyone's attention. The same drumming usually occurred prior to firing squads. Chris swallowed the lump in his throat and found his mouth had gone completely dry.

Alice secured the blindfold over Mary's eyes and then gave the master of ceremonies a nod. Henry Adler brought his arm down, and the drumroll stopped. Chris closed his eyes and heard five shots fire in rapid succession. He felt a whoosh of air rush past each ear and heard the paper tear to the right and left of his head. After that he could barely concentrate on remembering to breathe, much less worry about where Mary was firing.

The crash of cymbals was his first clue that the act was complete, and then the audience began to clap and cheer. Chris opened his eyes to find Mary had removed her blindfold and was waving to the crowd.

Henry beckoned Chris to join him. "Young man, give a wave and let everyone know you're all right."

Chris did as he was instructed, though he wasn't completely convinced he *was* all right. Mary drew him toward the audience. She raised his arm with hers in the air.

"Take a bow with me," she said as she began to bend forward.

Chris followed suit. Alice appeared with the paper shade. There were five bullet holes, as clear as could be. She handed Chris the paper and winked.

Chris took his seat, still a little dazed. One thing was certain: life with Mary would never be dull.

Jason waited in the wings until Lizzy had left the arena for her costume change. Gertie and Ella were performing a series of tricks for the audience in the meantime. Doing his best not to be seen, Jason made his way around the props to where Lizzy had left Longfellow tied to await her return.

He wiped his sweaty palms against his trouser legs. He'd never been more nervous in his life, but then, he'd never done anything quite so bold. He was convinced, however, that once Lizzy saw the extreme measures he'd taken to win her, she'd fall madly in love with him.

The thought made him smile. It would be quite a story to tell their children one day. He hoped there would be a half-dozen or more of them. He could just imagine Lizzy seated in the beautiful estate he would build for her, surrounded by their children. They would be so happy.

He checked his watch. His men were ready. Two waited outside with his carriage, and two were just inside the performance entrance to the pavilion. One final man waited just outside the dressing room. He had the chloroform and would render Lizzy unconscious when Jason stopped her from returning to the arena.

He positioned himself, and when Lizzy stepped out of the dressing room, he caught his breath. She was incredibly beautiful. Her brown hair was swept up into a waterfall of ringlets that spilled down from the crown of her head. She had changed to a beautiful white lacy gown—her wedding gown. For their wedding. She was perfect.

"Jason. What are you doing here?" She barely managed to ask before the man Jason only knew as Red stepped forward and slapped the drugged cloth over her face.

Lizzy's eyes went wide as she fought against his hold, and then her knees gave way as she succumbed to the fumes.

"Good job, Red," Jason said, his heart pounding. "We need to get her out of here unseen and into my carriage."

"No problem. You scout out the way, and I'll follow." Red easily lifted Lizzy and threw her over his shoulder.

"Be careful. Don't hurt her," Jason protested.

The big man gave a laugh. "She ain't hurtin'. Now lead the way."

Jason moved out of the shadows and started toward the exit. He didn't get but a few steps, however, before Phillip DeShazer appeared from where he'd been seeing to Longfellow. He smiled at Jason, but then Red appeared carrying Lizzy.

"What's going on? Is Miss Lizzy hurt?" Phillip asked.

Jason still hoped to leave without trouble. "She just needs some air. She fainted. The excitement was too much."

Phillip said nothing more, and Jason took that to mean he accepted the excuse. Jason and Red moved toward the exit, and the two men waiting there joined them.

"I think you'd better stay here," Phillip said, coming up behind them.

"She just needs a little air," Jason said. "Why don't you get your brother, if you're that worried? He can watch over her until she recovers."

"Wes is already in position on the other side of the arena, as you well know."

Lizzy started moving, and Red suddenly jerked and yelped in pain. "She bit me!"

"Help!" Lizzy cried.

"Let her go," Phillip demanded.

Red dropped her to the ground, then swung his fist toward Phillip's face. The younger man dodged at the last second and only received a glancing blow. He jumped at the bigger man, ramming into his gut headfirst. The two began to fight in earnest.

Meanwhile, Lizzy was getting to her feet.

"Take her," Jason instructed the other two men.

Lizzy looked at him, and her expression made Jason feel sick. She didn't understand. She thought he was some sort of monster.

"It's all right, Lizzy," he said gently. "I'm doing this for us."

She shook her head and began to scream as one of the men grabbed her. Red drew a gun from his pocket and pointed it at Phillip, but the wiry young man easily maneuvered out of the way and knocked the pistol from his hands. One of the men standing guard outside looked in to see what the fuss was about.

Jason motioned to him. "Help us! We have to get her out of here."

But the clumsy oaf managed to trip on his own feet as he started for Phillip and Red. Jason wished he'd thought to carry a gun of his own. He saw Red's gun on the ground and wondered if he could dodge the fighting men and get to it. He decided against it, however. Nothing else was going right, and that would probably just be an additional disaster. At least one of the men was dragging Lizzy toward the exit.

"What in the world is going on?"

Jason whirled around to find Mary Reichert gaping at the chaos. "It's nothing. Just go back to where you belong."

"I will not. Let her go, you brute," she demanded, heading for Lizzy.

"Get help, Mary!" Lizzy called. "They're trying to take me!"

Mary pulled out her pistol. "I have help. I said let her go."

The man froze for a moment, but then someone came up behind Mary and knocked the gun from her hand. The second man threw her across the floor, separating her from her weapon. Then, quick as a flash, he was at her side and trapping her within his arms.

Red finally managed to put his fist in the middle of Phillip's face. The boy slumped to the ground, mindless of anything else that was happening.

"Take them both," Jason said to the men. "We can't leave Mary here to sound the alarm. We'll turn her loose outside of town."

"Jason, this is madness," Lizzy declared. "You're insane. I don't know what you think you're doing, but you'll never get away with it."

He walked toward her. Her hair had come unpinned and flowed around her shoulders. Jason reached out to touch a curl. How often he had wanted to run his fingers through her hair.

Lizzy's eyes narrowed. "Don't touch me!" She kicked him hard.

Jason barely felt it. He was so lost in her beauty. "I'm your husband, Lizzy. At least I soon will be. You'll see. We're going to be so happy." He looked at the man who held her. "Come on. We have to go."

"You aren't going anywhere, Adler."

Jason turned to find Wesley still on horseback. His father wasn't far behind.

"Come on, Red. Let's get out of here," the man who held

Mary declared. He shoved her to the ground while Red did likewise with Lizzy. All of the hired men headed for the exit and were gone before anyone could figure out what to do.

Lizzy bent down to check on Phillip as he began to regain consciousness. Jason was perplexed. This hadn't gone the way he'd planned. What was he supposed to do now? He didn't have a plan. He needed a plan.

"What in the world have you done, Jason?" His father walked toward him.

Jason backed up a few steps. "Lizzy and I, we're going to be married. It's a surprise. But . . . now you know, so everyone can come." That was it. They didn't need to elope. They could just get married now with everyone watching and celebrating with them.

His father didn't look pleased. But surely he was. He liked Lizzy, and he had been after Jason to settle down and get married. No, he must just be shocked.

"I wanted to tell you, Father, but we had to keep it a surprise."

"Son, you aren't getting married," his father said.

Jason laughed. "Of course I am. You told me that I should take a wife, and Lizzy is a perfect choice. She's an American, just like Mother. You'll see. She's perfect."

His father shook his head and looked at Wesley, who was with Lizzy, checking on Phillip. They helped Phillip to his feet and turned their gazes on Jason. Everyone was looking at him like he'd lost his mind. Why couldn't they understand?

"I love you, Lizzy. I know you love me. We belong together," he pleaded.

Wes put his arm around Lizzy and pulled her close.

Jason frowned. "Stop it. She's not yours. She's mine."

His father took Jason's arm. "Come on, son. You need to go now."

"I can't go, not without Lizzy. We're going to get married.

Look, she's wearing her wedding dress." Jason tried to drink her in, but she had tucked her face against Wesley's chest. Beyond them, a crowd of people had begun to gather.

Jason pulled away from his father. "No. You can't do this. You can't ruin this. Not now!"

He ran for the exit and out to his carriage. He leapt up the side and into the driver's seat. He had to escape. He couldn't let them take him.

"I can't let them have us both. One of us has to escape to save the other." He urged the horses into a gallop. He heard yelling behind him and a commotion, but he didn't stop to see what was happening.

⊶⹀ TWENTY-FOUR ⹀⊶

The sorrow in Henry Adler's expression was palpable. "I'm so very sorry," he said to Lizzy for at least the tenth time that Mary had heard. She was glad for Chris's presence at her side, as she was still a little shaken up herself.

The show had ended, and the troupe was loading up at the railway station. No one had seen anything of Jason, although Henry had promised to hire men to find him so that he wouldn't be a further threat to anyone.

"I'll take him back to England and get our doctor's advice. Perhaps in time he'll recover his wits and be sorry for what he did."

"It wasn't your fault, Mr. Adler," Lizzy said graciously.

He gave her a sad smile, bowed his head, then left the station to search for his son.

"Our train is leaving shortly," Alice said, joining their small gathering. Alice and Carson were headed back to their Texas home but had already signed contracts to return for next year.

"I so enjoyed our part of the show, Alice." Mary gave her a hug. "I'm glad you'll be with us again next year."

"I don't know what else we'd do. A person in our position can scarcely make a lot of money working elsewhere."

"Carson, Mother is going to be disappointed you aren't helping with the ranch," Lizzy said. "I hope you won't forget us altogether."

"Hardly. I told Alice we'd be up there by the first of the year, and we will. No matter what jobs her mother finds for me to do in Fort Worth."

Alice looked heavenward. "Mama always thinks that if she can get Carson ample employment, he won't want to go back to Montana or the show. Little does she realize how much fun we have on the road." She hugged Lizzy. "I wish we could be there for the wedding, though. I'll want to hear all about it when we return."

Lizzy nodded and looked at Wesley, who was smiling. "I'm sure there will be stories enough for everyone." She turned back to Alice. "Did Uncle Oliver give you your pay and tickets?"

"He did. Not only that, but Mr. Adler gave each of us a very generous bonus. I think you'll be surprised—it'll make a very nice wedding present." Alice hugged Lizzy again, then looked up at Wes. "I wish you both the best. I hope your wedding is as beautiful as ours was."

Carson looked at Wes and shrugged. "All I remember of it was that she said *I do*."

Everyone laughed as the conductor called the final board of the Texas-bound train.

An hour later, Mary and the others were settled in the Brookstone commons car, waiting to depart. Mary was glad to be done with the season. There had been many more shows this year and far more focus on her, what with the shooting competitions. It would be wonderful to put it all behind her and have a few weeks of rest.

"I'm heading to bed," Wesley said.

"And you are too," Lizzy told her uncle. "In fact, I intend to tuck you in myself."

"I told you I'm feeling just fine."

"Yes, but I know how upset you are over the entire affair tonight. You should get some extra rest." Lizzy helped him to his feet. "Come along, or I'll be forced to have Wes and Phillip carry you." She stretched up and kissed his cheek.

Oliver grumbled but nevertheless gave her a smile and allowed her to lead him to the adjoining car.

"I'm going to bed as well," Ella declared. "I'm completely worn out." She looked at Mary and smiled. "Good night."

"Good night, Ella," Mary and Chris replied in unison.

"I'll be there as soon as I finish cleaning my rifle," Mary added. She looked down at the weapon and yawned. "In fact, I might just let it wait for morning."

Once everyone had gone their separate ways, Mary looked at Chris. "How about you? Are you as tired as the rest of us?"

"Not exactly. I only had to stand and face death, remember?"

She laughed, then pulled the blindfold from her pocket and handed it to him. "You weren't in any danger."

He held up the cloth and made a noise of surprise. It wasn't the same cloth Alice had tied around his eyes. In fact, she knew he could see every feature of her face through the thin material.

"Why, you little cheat. You switched out scarves."

"I did. If it's any consolation, I hit the metal targets using the other blindfold."

He smiled. "So were you unsure of yourself or of me?"

Mary laughed. "Neither. I was just getting tired and didn't want to take a chance."

"Well, he's not happy about my babying him," Lizzy said, coming back into the car, "but he'll just have to do as his stepmother used to say, and get glad in the same clothes he got mad in." She kept walking right past them. "I'll see you both in the morning. Good night." She didn't even wait for their reply but exited out the opposite side of the room to the women's car.

"She's amazing," Chris said, shaking his head. "To have gone through all she experienced tonight and still be in such great spirits."

"She is. I can't imagine going through all that."

"Well, as I recall, they had you too. You are just as amazing to sit here and laugh and joke as if you didn't nearly lose your life tonight."

Mary hadn't really considered the danger to herself. "God took care of us all—that much is evident. When I think of what Jason might have accomplished . . ." She shivered. "I'm so thankful that God spared us."

"Me too." Chris loosened his tie and pulled it from around his neck. "I hope you don't mind."

Mary smiled. "Not at all. Be comfortable."

He undid the top couple of shirt buttons. "All right, but just remember you gave your approval." He shrugged out of his outer coat and then began undoing the buttons on his vest. Mary just watched him.

When Chris shed his vest, he leaned back and gave an exaggerated sigh. "That's much better."

"You do look very comfortable." Mary felt a little awkward now that they were completely alone.

"I am." He ran a hand through his blond hair. "And I think it's time we talked."

"Oh, you finally think that, eh?" She crossed her arms. "I ought to go to bed and show you how infuriating it is to be ignored."

He gave her his lazy smile. "I don't think you're going anywhere."

She looked down at her cleaning supplies and rifle and then back at Chris. "Fine. I'm not going anywhere."

He laughed. "Mary, you always manage to surprise me, and when you cornered me on the ship and told me you knew all about my father and brothers . . . well, that was one thing. But then you told me you loved me, and that was something entirely different."

"It couldn't have been that much of a surprise. You'd already kissed me twice. You knew I was receptive."

"Receptive and in love are two different things."

"All right," she sighed. "You were surprised."

"I was in shock, and not because of my father, although that did set me back. I would never in a hundred years have expected you to latch on to that newspaper story. When you showed me, I knew God was telling me that I could no longer hide from the past. But He was also telling me that the past couldn't hurt me anymore. Not unless I let it."

"I'm glad, Chris, because it doesn't matter to me. You aren't your father. You aren't your brothers."

"No, I'm not. But that isn't all there is to it."

She put out her hand. "Then tell me everything."

Chris chose his words carefully. "For years I was convinced that their bad blood tainted us all. Then Wesley helped me see little by little that the blood of Jesus made everything right." He had longed to explain himself, and now seemed the right time. He covered Mary's hand with his. "Are you sure you want to hear this now? It isn't a short story, and you have had quite the evening."

Her brown eyes narrowed. "I'm just fine, Christopher Williams, and if you think for one second you're getting out of here without telling me everything, you're mistaken."

"Yes ma'am," he said, trying his best to sound like an obedient child. She smiled. "You see, I wasn't an anticipated addition to my family. My mother was very ill when she gave birth to my brother Raymond, and the doctor told her she'd never have another baby. Twelve years later I came along, and it set the entire family on its ear."

"How so?"

The train jerked into motion. He let go of Mary's hand and leaned back in his chair. "My birth weakened my mother's health, and she wasn't able to keep up with all the demands my father put on her. They were always fighting. Well . . . he was always fighting. My mother did her best to say nothing and tolerate whatever he said and did."

"How awful." Mary's dark eyes met his. "I'm so sorry."

He nodded. "It was a bleak time. Up until then, my mother had made most of the money for the family. She taught piano lessons and took in laundry. After my birth, she didn't have the energy to do much at all, so there was never money or food. My father liked to gamble and please himself. My brothers too. They womanized and caused problems for most everybody, usually just taking what they wanted. But my mother believed God would change their hearts and provide for us. She used to tell me that she prayed God would give me a better life. I didn't think much of God. He seemed just as scary and mean as my earthly father. When my mother was able to sneak us out to go to church, the preacher always talked about the wrath of God."

"But what about His love?" Mary interrupted. "I mean, my own faith was wrapped up with my grandparents' beliefs, but at least I knew God was good and wanted good things for us."

Chris nodded. "My mother said the same thing, but when all you live with is the example of anger and rage, it's hard to imagine that love." He shook his head. "Eventually I learned that my father and brothers robbed banks and anything else they thought profitable.

"When I was six, my father's rage seemed completely out of control. He often beat my mother and me, when he could catch me. My mama hid me if she knew he was coming. He'd tear into her something fierce, demanding she tell him where I was. She took so many beatings for me." He couldn't keep the sorrow from his voice. "I didn't understand how God could just stand by and let it happen. Even my brothers tried to make him stop, but that never boded well. My mother's health was further compromised by the beatings and a broken heart, and I think she just gave up on life. Before she died, she gave me a little case full of newspaper clippings and told me they were about my grandmother—my father's mother. She told me if anything ever happened to her, I should try to find my grandmother and she would take care of me. Not long after that, my mother died. She wasn't even cold in the ground when my father and brothers tried to rob the First National Bank in Baltimore and got caught.

"When the sheriff showed up and found me all alone, he told me I would have to go to the orphan's home, but I showed him my newspaper clippings, and he sent a message to my grand-mother."

"And she came?"

Chris nodded. "She did. She had no condemnation for the dirty, scrawny grandson she didn't even know existed until that letter from the sheriff. She was all smiles and joy. She took me in her arms and hugged me close, the way my mama did. I'll never forget what she said to me."

"What was it?" Mary was completely caught up in his story.

"'You will always have a home with me, and wherever you go, you will always be loved.'"

Mary met his gaze with a look of wonder. "What an amazing woman to say that to a child she didn't even know."

"Oh, she was amazing. She was everything I could have hoped for. I missed my mother something terrible, especially in that first year. I cried a lot, but Grandmother was never tempera-mental about it. She encouraged me to tell her the stories I remembered about Mama. She told me not to let go of the memories and even had me write down things Mama said to me and to journal what she looked like. There are no photographs of her. I suppose that's one of my biggest regrets."

Tears came to Mary's eyes. "We had a big photograph of my mother. She died giving birth to my younger sister, Kate. I was just four, and I don't remember her much."

"That's a hard thing for a child, isn't it?"

Mary nodded and wiped her eyes with the back of her sleeve. "It's the hardest of anything I know. Losing August was terrible, and the pain will be with me for a long time. But not having your mother leaves such a deep wound. Losing your father too. I was just nine when he passed on. My oma and opa were already raising us children because Papa was unable to deal with the pain of losing Mama. He'd gone off and joined Buffalo Bill's show, and we only saw him once in a while. Never enough."

The gentle rocking of the train left Chris feeling drowsy and worn, but there was still so much to tell Mary. They continued talking well into the night, with Chris explaining more about the life he'd known in London and then the news about his father and brothers facing death.

"I kept track of them from afar," he told Mary. "My grandmother wanted to know, and so I just kind of picked up where she left off. When I was old enough to take an interest, she just let me report to her what I found out. I was glad she died before she could learn they had killed someone. I know she was already heartbroken over their criminal records."

"Why didn't your father go to England with her when she remarried? Was he already a grown man?"

"By the time Grandmother and her husband left for England, my father was eighteen and married with a son, my brother Luke. The War Between the States had started, and he went to do his part—not because of any patriotism he felt, but for what he could get out of it. He was in trouble from the start for pilfering items off the dead."

"That must have been hard on your grandmother. Was he her only child?"

"Not exactly. There were three others, but they died young. So in a way, he was her only one. I remember her heartbreak when she talked about him. She had such hopes for him, but when his father died, he was only twelve, and it wounded him deeply. It's something I feel I can understand. I'm sure you can."

"Yes. And it affects each person differently. I had a friend who lost his father in an accident working for the railroad. He was never the same after that. He went the same way your father did."

"When my father was fifteen, my grandmother remarried. I remember her telling me that she hoped her new husband would be a comfort to my father, but it was the complete opposite of that. He wanted nothing to do with his stepfather and ran away. He wasn't heard from for well over a year, and by the time they knew where he'd gone, he was already in with bad company and had no interest in rejoining his family."

They fell silent. Chris felt drained from telling his story, but also lighter than he'd felt in years.

Mary got up and went to the sofa. She patted the cushion. "This is much more comfortable."

Chris joined her. "Are you planning to work your charms on me?"

Laughing, Mary slipped her hand in his. "Would I have to work very hard?"

He shook his head. "No. Not at all."

For several long moments all they did was stare into each other's eyes. Chris had never known the emotions he was experiencing. He had never allowed himself to feel this strongly for fear of where it might lead.

"I've never been in love before, Mary," he said. "I never wanted to risk it. I feared I would turn out like my father and brothers. After all, they were my blood kin, and even though my grandmother was too, my father was, well, closer in that line. I remember hearing sermons about the sins of the fathers revisited on the children, and I was certain that was God's punishment to me. I knew I could never put that burden on someone else, and I was determined not to give my heart to anyone."

"My situation was entirely different," Mary countered, "but up until now, I've never been in love either. I grew up with everyone expecting me to marry Owen Douglas."

"Your sister's husband?"

"Yes. Owen and I were close friends, and everyone assumed we'd fall in love and marry. I do love him, but only as a brother. We were supposed to marry last year around this time, but then August died, and it made everything so clear. I couldn't marry Owen. It wasn't fair to him. I could never love him as a wife. It was only after releasing him that I learned my sister was in love with him and had been for some time. Funny how we almost miss blessings because we're trying to force things to go our own way or the way someone else intended."

"Yes." He reached up and ran his finger down her cheek.

Mary simply held his gaze for a few moments, then pressed the conversation forward. "How did your grandmother die?"

"Old age. She once told me she hoped to outlive Queen Victoria. She didn't. She died in 1897, shortly after I graduated from Oxford. I think she was just waiting for me to finish my schooling. She knew I wanted to write and encouraged me to return to the States and learn how to be an American. So after I laid her to rest beside my step-grandfather, I did just that.

"When I came to America, I traveled around for a while and saw everything I could. I found so much of it fascinating and kept all sorts of journals about what I saw and who I spoke with. Then one day when I was in New York, I learned about a magazine that wanted to focus on unusual places and people in America. It was just getting organized, and I knew I wanted to be a part of it. I put together a portfolio of information and pictures from my travels and went to the owner-editor. I told him I wanted to write for his magazine. He asked me what experience I had, and I spread out that portfolio on his desk." Chris chuckled. "I think he was more than a little surprised."

"And did he hire you on the spot?" Mary asked, her eyes twinkling in delight.

"He did, and that portfolio became a good part of his first six editions."

"And what about your father and brothers? How did you find out they were sentenced to die?"

Chris frowned. "I had a detective agency sending me reports. When they escaped from prison and killed those guards, I knew that if they were ever caught, it would be the end of their lives. I suppose I reconciled myself to that truth because when I heard they had been recaptured, I concluded my dealings with the detective agency.

"You know," he continued, "I never wanted to see them again. I suppose a part of me was afraid of what I'd find. I didn't want revenge, though. I knew it wouldn't bring my mother back. I didn't even really want answers for why my father had taken that path in life. After all, it was his choice." He shook his head. "The truth was . . . I never wanted anything from him or my brothers, but I went to see them because I thought they might need something from me."

"Like what?"

"I don't know." Chris met her gaze. "Maybe forgiveness. Maybe understanding. Compassion."

"Could you have honestly given that to them?"

He shrugged. "I don't know. They never asked for it, so I never had to consider it. All they had to offer was hatred and bitterness, and I'd already had a gut full of that in my first six years."

"Did you . . . did you watch them die?"

He swallowed hard and pushed aside the memory that was forever etched in his brain. "I did. I don't want to talk about it. It wasn't pleasant, and—"

She put her hand in his. "You don't ever have to talk about it unless you want to. The past isn't really what I want to talk about anyway. I'm more interested in the future. You said you'd never fallen in love before. I want to know what you meant by that."

A deep sense of relief washed over him, and he gave her a smile. "I meant that before falling in love with you, I'd never fallen in love with anyone else. I do love you, Mary. I can admit that now, although it's still very new to me and I'm not sure where it will lead us."

She shrugged. "There's time to figure that out."

He put his arm around her to pull her close. "May I kiss you, Mary Reichert?"

"You've done so twice before and not once have you asked." She smiled. "Why now?"

He put his fingers under her chin. "It just seems the right thing to do. Maybe because now that I belong to God, I better understand the honor and respect I owe you."

She sobered and nodded. "Then yes. Yes, you may kiss me."

He pressed his lips to hers and savored the sweetness as she reached up to wrap her arms around his neck. Images of the past disappeared into a vapor. Gone was the burden it had put on his heart.

"You know," he whispered, pulling away, "if not for Wes helping me find my way to God, and God in turn giving me strength to face the past and consider the future . . . I think I would have run away like my father did."

Mary shook her head. "Then I would have just had to come

after you. You see, shooting isn't the only thing I'm good at. I'm a fairly decent tracker as well."

He saw the teasing gleam in her eye and laughed. "I'll keep that in mind."

"Just keep me in your heart, Christopher Williams. That will be good enough."

⇥⇒ TWENTY-FIVE ⇐⇤

ou may kiss your bride," the minister instructed Wesley.

He wasted no time taking Lizzy in his arms. Mary watched as he kissed her passionately despite the church setting. When they separated, Lizzy's face was flushed red, and Wes looked pleased with himself. Mary couldn't help but giggle.

The newly married couple signed their marriage certificate while their guests gathered out front to toss wheat kernels on them as they exited the church. The wedding attendants made certain everyone had a handful of grain to throw, then waited patiently in the cold November air for the couple to emerge. Mary shivered as she stood as close to Chris as propriety allowed. She had been delighted when he told her that Wes wanted him to be one of his attendants, since Lizzy was having Mary and Ella. Phillip was Wesley's best man, but as far as Mary was concerned, Chris was the better man.

For three weeks they'd been staying at the Brookstone ranch and getting to know each other better. Soon Chris would return to New York, and Mary would head back to Kansas to spend December and a bit of January with her grandparents. Her sister and Owen were due to have their first child shortly after the

New Year, and Mary wanted to be there for that special occasion. But after that, Mary could only wonder what the future would hold.

"Here they come," Phillip called from the open doorway. He jumped from the steps and took his place below with all of Lizzy and Wes's friends and family.

"Hip-hip-hooray!" they all cheered and threw their wheat to bless the union.

Wes and Lizzy laughed and made their way down the middle of the gathering. Wes held fast to Lizzy as if he were afraid someone would steal her away. And maybe he had good reason. Chris had mentioned earlier that Phillip was arranging some silliness with the ranch hands to kidnap Wes.

The wedding party made its way down Main Street to the hotel where a grand reception and wedding breakfast awaited them. Mary clung to Christopher's arm as they walked from the church. She shivered, finding her rose wool suit hardly sufficient against the early winter temperatures. Unfortunately, she and the others had left their cloaks and coats at the hotel.

Chris put his arm around her. "I'm sorry you're cold. It's just a short walk, though, and I will keep you as warm as possible."

"I've waited a long time for this wedding," Mary said, watching Wes and Lizzy laughing and teasing each other as they hurried toward the hotel. "Lizzy has loved Wes since she was just a girl. It's funny how people think children don't know their own mind, don't understand what's truly important, but Lizzy always knew she belonged with Wes. The trouble was that Wes didn't know he belonged with Lizzy."

"Sometimes we fellas are difficult to get through to." Chris smiled down at her. "I think your lips are actually turning blue. Maybe I should carry you the rest of the way."

She laughed. "You can try. But being back at the ranch and not nearly so busy, I think I've gained twenty pounds."

It was his turn to laugh. "Hardly. You are as trim and fit as ever."

They finally reached the hotel and hurried inside its warmth. Mary sighed in relief. The church ladies had arranged everything. A large room had been laid out with a breakfast buffet. Two old men with guitars and one younger man with a fiddle sat in the corner, softly playing music.

"Wasn't it a perfect wedding?" Rebecca Brookstone asked as she came forward to greet Mary.

"It was. Lizzy couldn't have looked any more beautiful. Or happy."

"Indeed. She's happier than I've ever known her." Mrs. Brookstone turned to Chris. "It's certainly been a pleasure having you here with us. I'm sorry you have to leave so soon after the wedding."

"Yes, well, my editor wants my article about this. He thinks the story of Brookstone's most famous performer finally marrying will be the perfect conclusion to our featured series."

"What are you going to do after that?" Mrs. Brookstone asked.

Chris shrugged. "I'm not entirely sure. I have the luxury of not having to work but the fortune of loving what I do. I think I'm going to write a book."

"On what topic?"

"Wild west shows." He looked at Mary and grinned. "Or at least their performers."

"I'm certain our ladies would be more than happy to tell their stories. Now, if you'll excuse me, I need to see if Oliver is comfortable."

"We were both so glad that he was able to walk Lizzy down the aisle," Mary said before Mrs. Brookstone could leave.

The older woman turned back and nodded. Her worry shone on her face. "He's far from healthy, but I think with plenty of rest and care, he'll recover."

"Does he still plan to return to the show in the spring?"

"Of course. But only time will tell if that's feasible. Oliver isn't as young as he thinks he is, and when you add in the other issues . . . well, I'd just as soon see him remain with us on the ranch."

She took her leave and made her way to Oliver, who was talking with a group of ranch hands.

Mary turned back to Chris and found him watching her. "Is something wrong? Has my hat gone askew?" She reached up to check that it was still secure.

"Nothing is wrong. I was just thinking how beautiful you are and how much I'm going to miss you while we're apart."

"And how long is that going to be?" They'd talked about a lot of things these past few weeks, but not that. She'd been afraid of the answer and so never posed the question.

"I don't know, Mary. I have my responsibilities, but I won't let them keep me from you forever. I'm looking forward to visiting your farm in Kansas."

"My opa's farm. I only own a tiny bit of acreage. Although I have saved up a goodly sum and have always thought about buying a bigger piece."

"In Kansas?"

She shrugged. "I always figured it would be there, since Opa and Oma are there and I was supposed to marry a Kansas farm boy." She grinned and crossed her arms. "But now I find myself rather distracted by a young man who is a strange mix of places. I have to admit, he fascinates me."

Chris's blue eyes narrowed. "And if he wanted you to follow him around the world, would you do that?"

Mary tried not to let herself be excited by the idea. "I suppose it would depend on the details of the proposition."

"Hey, you two, what are you discussing so seriously over here?" Lizzy asked, joining them. "This is my wedding day, after all, and serious business should be delayed until another time."

Mary admired her friend's beautiful ivory gown. "You look so lovely, Lizzy. This dress is perfect, almost as if it had been created just for you."

"Thank you." Lizzy gave a turn. "In a sense it was. I fell in love with something similar in a shop window in Washington, D.C. I didn't want to tell anyone about it, however, for fear Wesley might see it ahead of time. So I snuck over there, they took my measurements, and I told them about the changes I had in mind. I paid them a handsome deposit and gave them Mother's name and information to coordinate for future matters. Then I prayed nothing would go wrong and the dress would be safely shipped to Montana well before I needed it."

"So you bought it before Wesley had even proposed?" Mary asked.

Lizzy nodded and leaned closer. "But don't tell him. I don't want him to think I was taking advantage of him."

Chris laughed. "I think he would consider himself lucky to know you were so certain of his feelings."

"I'll remember you said that." Mary met his surprised expression with a raised brow.

"I believe we're ready to start the buffet, ma'am," an aproned young man came to tell Lizzy.

"Very well. I shall find my husband." She giggled. "I do love saying that."

Mary and Chris watched her weave in and out of the guests until she reached the head table, where Wesley already waited. She whispered in his ear, and Wesley called for everyone to quiet down.

"They tell me we're ready to start this meal, so I'd like to offer a prayer of thanks."

Everyone bowed their heads, and Chris surprised Mary by taking her hand.

"Lord, we give You thanks on this day for the blessings You've given. We thank You for joining Lizzy and I in holy matrimony and for the blessings that will fall upon us over the years. We ask for strength to face what will come our way and pray that You will always guide us. Bless this food now and the hands that prepared it. In Jesus' name, amen."

Amens rose up like a cheer. Mary and Chris went through the line together, mounding their plates with mashed potatoes and gravy, fried chicken, and a bevy of other delectable dishes. They sat with Phillip and Ella, as well as several other ranch hands, and were soon caught up telling stories of the past.

When the clock chimed noon, Mary knew it wouldn't be much longer until they had to head to the depot for Chris to catch his train. She felt a wave of melancholy spread over her. She didn't want him to go. Neither did she want to go to Kansas without him. What if they never saw each other again? What if one of them was in a horrible train wreck like Buffalo Bill's show had experienced? She sighed and did her best to keep a smile plastered on her face. This was Lizzy's big day, and she wasn't going to spoil it by being in a mood.

She went to retrieve her cloak. She would go with Chris to see him off and be of good cheer. The last thing she wanted was to be one of those silly females who cried buckets of tears.

"Are you all right?"

Mary turned to find Ella behind her. "I am. I was just collecting my cloak so I could walk with Chris to the train station."

"I figured that much. I knew he was leaving. He's telling everyone good-bye."

"Yes."

Ella touched her arm. "He won't tell you good-bye, Mary. He's far too much in love." She gave Mary a hug, then helped her pull the heavy black cloak around her shoulders. "This should keep you nice and warm."

Mary fought back the lump in her throat. "Thank you."

Only a moment later, Chris joined her. He put on his outer coat. "I should have had this at the church, then you could have worn it for the walk over here."

She waited while he buttoned the coat and then donned his hat. "Don't forget your luggage."

He nodded and retrieved the leather valise. They slipped from the hotel and headed down Main Street to Sixth and turned toward the depot. The wind had picked up, making conversation difficult, and neither of them said a word. Mary wondered if it was going to snow, as the skies were a gunmetal gray and clouds had moved in to hang low.

"We should have borrowed a wagon. You'll freeze on the walk back," Chris said apologetically.

"I'll be just fine," she assured him, trying her best not to cry.

Chris slowed his steps. "There's something I need to tell you. I've held off because I know it's not what you want to hear, but I promise I won't stop in my pursuit of the truth."

"What are you talking about?" She stopped and turned to meet his somber expression.

"My friend who went to Fleming Farm to investigate . . . he didn't have any luck. He said when he went looking for answers, he was caught by Fleming's staff and brought to Spiby. Spiby put an end to the interview and escorted him off the property."

"Oh." She was unable to say anything more.

"Mary, we will get answers. This just makes me all the more certain that something is going on there that they don't want anyone to know about."

"And that something got my brother killed."

She felt hopeless, but Chris fought to assure her. "Look, this isn't the end. We will keep striving to find the truth, to get justice for August. I promise."

"I know you'll do what you can . . . but maybe we'll never get to find the truth."

"Maybe. I suppose you have to ask yourself if you can live with that. What if God never gives you a clear answer on this? Will you still trust Him?"

She thought for a moment. "How could I not? What is there for me besides that?" She'd never really seen this before, and a sense of understanding this brought peace. "If I never know the truth, I will still trust in God."

He smiled. "That's my girl. Still, I have hope." He chucked her under the chin. "I know how to get the truth for my stories. Don't give up on me. I'll continue to look for an answer."

They heard the train whistle, and Chris put his arm around her shoulders as they continued toward the station.

The train was just arriving when they entered the depot. The passengers, what few there were, ambled toward the platform door. Everyone knew the train wouldn't be here long.

"Well, we timed that just right," Chris said, setting down his case. He searched his pockets for his ticket and finally located it in his top inside suit pocket. He held it up like he'd discovered gold.

Mary knew it wouldn't have mattered even if he hadn't found it. He was going away. Tears came despite her best efforts, and she looked away. This wasn't how she'd planned it. She was a strong woman, so why did she feel like wailing?

"Mary." He whispered her name, but she couldn't make herself turn to face him. "Mary." He took her arms and turned her around. "Mary, look at me."

She raised her face as tears trickled down her cheeks. She bit her lip to keep from saying something she'd regret.

Chris tenderly touched her cheek. "Don't cry, Mary." He smiled, still holding her gaze. "The time will pass quickly. You'll see."

She drew a deep breath and forced her voice to be steady. "I don't know why I'm being such a ninny."

"You aren't being a ninny. Your tears touch me, because I know you really care—that you're really sorry to see me go. No one's ever cried over me, Mary. Not since my mother."

"I am sorry to see you go. I—" The words caught in her throat.

"Will you wait for me?"

"Wait for you?"

He grinned. "Yes. Wait for me. Wait for me to come back to you. To marry you."

She sniffed. "Are you proposing to me?"

He looked around the empty waiting room. "There's no one else here, and certainly no one else I want to marry."

Her mouth quivered, and tears came anew as Chris got down on one knee.

"Mary, wherever I go, you'll be with me. And wherever you go, you can be assured that I'll be with you in spirit and heart. I want you to be my wife. Please say yes."

"Yes," Mary was barely able to whisper before she burst into sobs of joy.

Chris got back to his feet. "I love you, Mary. With all my heart." He kissed her soundly, then hugged her close.

The train whistle blew, and the conductor gave a holler. "All aboard!"

"I love you, Chris."

He kissed her once more, then grabbed his valise. Mary watched him make a mad dash for the train and followed him out onto the platform as the cars began to move forward. The scent of his cologne lingered in the air, making her smile.

He'd made her realize a sense of peace that hadn't been there before. The unspoken question of whether she could still trust God even if He didn't give her resolution regarding August had been shaking her faith in a way she hadn't known. It had been there all the time, underlying everything she said and did. Now she knew the answer. No matter what happened, she wouldn't walk away from God. He was her hope and would remain so.

The train whistle sounded as the locomotive moved out through the city. She waved even though Chris couldn't possibly see her now. "Wherever you go, my love," she whispered, "my heart goes too."

Tracie Peterson is the award-winning author of more than one hundred novels, both historical and contemporary. Her avid research resonates in her stories, as seen in her bestselling Heirs of Montana and Alaskan Quest series. Tracie and her family make their home in Montana. Visit Tracie's website at www .traciepeterson.com.

Sign Up for Tracie's Newsletter!

Keep up to date with Tracie's news on book releases and events by signing up for her email list at traciepeterson.com.

Also from Tracie Peterson

In 1900s Montana, Lizzy Brookstone's role as star of an all-female wild west show is rewarding but difficult. However, trials of the heart and a mystery to be solved prove more daunting. As Lizzy and her two friends, runaway Ella and sharpshooter Mary, try to discover how Mary's brother died, all three seek freedom in a world run by men.

When You Are Near by Tracie Peterson
BROOKSTONE BRIDES #1

You May Also Like . . .

Set during the atmospheric turn of the nineteenth century, three young women travel to San Francisco in search of answers that will drastically change their futures. Will these women be willing to risk their lives—as well as their hearts?

GOLDEN GATE SECRETS: *In Places Hidden, In Dreams Forgotten, In Times Gone By* by Tracie Peterson
traciepeterson.com

This blend of excitement, history, breathtaking scenery, and romance introduces three adventurous women who find refuge at the Curry Hotel, near the foot of Mount McKinley. Will they each have the courage to rely on their faith as they search for hope, healing, and forgiveness?

THE HEART OF ALASKA: *In the Shadow of Denali, Out of the Ashes, Under the Midnight Sun*
by Tracie Peterson and Kimberley Woodhouse
traciepeterson.com; kimberleywoodhouse.com

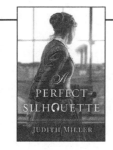

To help support her family and make use of her artistic skill, Mellie finds employment at a daguerreotype shop where she creates silhouette portraits. When romance begins to blossom with one of her charming customers, her life seems to have fallen perfectly into place—but when the unexpected happens, will she find happiness despite her hidden secrets?

A Perfect Silhouette by Judith Miller
judithmccoymiller.com

◆BETHANYHOUSE